BENEATH THE OPAL ARC

LEE COLGIN

ACKNOWLEDGMENTS

As always, to my critique partner, author Kat Silver, who never lets me settle for less than my best.

Thanks to Stephanie Briarton, Dale Drake, Sierra Charleston, and Barbara Leftih for reading this early and for all your help along the way.

To Dextre, thanks for doing my chores while I write.

Lastly, to my dogs, for making me get off my butt and go for a walk.

*S*tanding tall, arms reaching toward the stars, the witch left himself open to attack. Light sparked from his palms, illuminating the night sky. An enormous arc of energy formed from thin air, stretching over the forest's dense canopy and beyond the horizon.

Laurence stood twenty paces back, partially hidden by trees, enthralled by the stunning spectacle.

Werewolves sprinted past, headed away from the battle at the front line and deeper into pack territory. In their flight, they paid no mind to the lone witch, unguarded amongst enemies, vulnerable to claws and teeth.

What was he doing?

His posture didn't suggest an attack. He was focused, arms quaking with effort. Gaze directed toward his homeland, sweat glistening on his forehead, the witch ignored the racing wolves as he erected a massive barrier overhead. By the looks of it, he was trying to keep his own people out.

Laurence watched, captivated by the sight. He should flee with the wolves. Witches were gaining ground, and opponents caught in the fray would be slaughtered. Danger awaited those who remained, but someone had to witness…whatever this was.

Nothing so interesting had happened to Laurence in decades. A spell of this magnitude shouldn't be possible. He wouldn't miss its creation merely because staying left his life in peril. He'd lived long enough.

A colossal dome of iridescent ether formed above, not unlike a soap bubble, directed by the light erupting from the witch's shaking fingers. It stretched farther than Laurence could see, even with his enhanced vision, the outer reaches so distant as to be immeasurable.

And they said male witches weren't as powerful. This one clearly never read that missive. Energy vibrated the air around him, its waves raising the small hairs on the back of Laurence's neck. Soon they'd all be trapped within the arc. What would that mean?

The witch trembled and faltered, sinking to one knee.

Laurence took a step closer, then halted. A witch with such strength could kill him with a thought. Better to stay back, unseen.

A large werewolf raced forward. Horror spiked in Laurence as the predator's eyes narrowed in on his witch. This wolf didn't ignore the spellcaster like the others; he pivoted on his path and launched himself at the unguarded enemy.

"No!" Laurence harnessed every bit of his preternatural speed. He leapt at the oncoming wolf, slamming into him a moment too late. The impact threw the beast off course, but not before he swiped out with razored claws.

The blow knocked the witch to his haunches, but the spell remained unbroken. Hands still raised, he poured his magic into the domed barrier. Whirling air around him popped and crackled.

Laurence hurried to his feet and took a defensive stance between the witch and the wolf. "Go," he ordered.

The wolf snarled but obeyed, taking off in the direction of their safe house.

Laurence turned in time to see the spell finished, the protective arc of light now complete.

The witch looked smaller without the power of his magic coursing through his body. Fragile.

Laurence darted in and caught him as he sank backward, arms under his shoulders preventing his head from striking the earth. "Ho there, easy." He settled on the ground with the man crumpled half in his lap, body limp, but gaze intense.

Dazed, the witch peered at him through amber eyes still glowing with power and smiled. "I did it."

"I saw that." Laurence smelled blood. The scent was divine, but didn't bode well for the man in his arms. "What did you do, exactly?"

The witch sighed, his expression dreamy. "I stopped the war."

Laurence had been right. The magical barrier prevented other witches from attacking. "So you did."

Would he die for his trouble? Red oozed from his side, staining his muslin shirt and wool vest. Laurence nudged the fabric out of the way. Four deep gashes spanned the length of his abdomen on his right side. Not promising but likely not fatal —if Laurence could get him sewn up in time. The only healer close enough was a werewolf, and she would not want to help. "What's your name, witch?"

"Remy." He blinked. "Yours?"

"Laurence."

"Are you..." Inquisitive eyes widened as their ethereal glow faded. Long strands of honey-blond hair danced in the wind. "A vampire?"

Laurence nodded, surprised the witch knew. He looked human, after all, a man aged forty years, give or take.

"Hellfire." The color in Remy's cheeks faded. His labored

breaths ghosted over Laurence's wrist. "Are you going to kill me?"

"I'm not."

"Then can I see your fangs?"

Who was this creature? Stranded on enemy soil, wounded and exhausted, yet curious enough for such a question. "Later. You need stitches."

Remy's gaze flicked from Laurence to the injury. Upon seeing the blood, his expression twisted to pain. "I suppose I do."

"Come, I'll carry you." Laurence scooped the smaller man into his arms with ease. They must hurry, or the blood loss would be too great. He held the witch close against his chest and raced through the forest toward the safe house.

Remy clung tight to him, free arm thrown around his shoulder, face pressed into his neck, hiding his eyes. He whimpered, lips against Laurence's skin. The speed must be frightening. Perhaps Laurence should have warned him. Too late now.

They broke free of the dense copse of trees and passed into a clearing where the werewolves' manor stood, now Laurence's temporary daytime shelter. He glanced to the sky. The light forming Remy's dome had faded to an opalescent sheen. It stretched in every direction, magnificence unbroken, as far as he could see. An astounding piece of wizardry the likes of which Laurence had never dared to believe possible.

This witch must be protected.

The wolves would be furious.

With a sigh, Laurence pushed forward, holding Remy securely against his body as they approached the large stone house. The witch stirred when they slowed, lifting his head.

Dagna, the pack's alpha, kept watch from the front porch, an imposing figure guarding a more imposing dwelling. The gothic estate rose tall among a backdrop of ancient pines. Dark stones, rolling arches and towering spires gave the manor an ominous presence. As did the raven-haired woman sneering at them from the main entryway.

Laurence didn't care for Dagna, but then again, he didn't care for most werewolves. Living amongst them, even for a short time, was a bother he tolerated only to end the war. When vampires sided with wolves, they'd sent each pack an ambassador to aid in their defense. Laurence had been with Dagna's pack for a fortnight, and already he tired of their company.

Dagna crossed her arms over her chest and stared down at them warily.

"Let me pass." Laurence climbed the stairs, prepared to elbow her from his path if he must. "This man needs care."

"That is no man," said Dagna, blocking his way. "You'll not bring a witch through my door."

Remy tensed in his hold. Blunt fingertips dug into his shoulder.

Laurence clutched him tighter and glared at Dagna. "This witch saved us all. Surely you've noticed the barrier overhead? He made it." Laurence nodded to Remy. "I witnessed the creation firsthand."

"To what end?" she snarled. "Maybe he's trapped us here for an attack."

Remy shook his head. "No, I—"

"And if he has, we've a valuable hostage," Laurence interrupted. "Who'll be worth nothing if he's dead. Stand aside." He plowed forth. At the last moment, she cleared the way, and Laurence brought Remy in through the parlor toward the kitchens. "Fetch Adeline."

Dagna left with a cold scowl over her shoulder. Other wolves had heard the commotion and began to gather as Laurence set Remy on a table. He shifted to put a kettle over the stove, but the witch grasped his hand, eyes filled with terror. "Don't leave me."

Laurence allowed Remy to clutch his hand. With a glance to

a loitering wolf, he ordered, "You, set water to boil and find out what's keeping Adeline."

The wolf rankled, but did as he was told.

Adeline swept in before anyone had to search, her healer's kit in tow. "What's wrong?"

"The witch requires your attention," answered Laurence. "Stitches, I'm assuming, and something for the pain."

Remy's warm fingers squeezed his cold ones. Laurence squeezed back.

Adeline sniffed, her face a mask of disgust. "What he needs is a good axe in his neck, vampire. We don't save his kind. We kill them."

"You'll save this one." Laurence glared at her through narrowed eyes. "I demand it."

Adeline was small for a werewolf, with cinnamon-brown hair and eyes. She glared right back, undaunted.

Laurence continued. "A spellcaster this powerful is a rare gem, and I'll not have him bleed out on your table while we prattle on. I shall be his jailor. Now hurry, the color has gone from his cheeks."

Adeline pursed her lips and snorted. "Fine. Remove his tunic." She opened her kit and began laying instruments along the table.

The witch maintained an ironclad grip on his hand. So with the other he began to ruck up Remy's muslin tunic and the woolen vest along with it. Angry red slashes still seeping with blood lined his abdomen, the skin around them pink and irritated. If infection took root, Remy could die.

With no warning, Adeline splashed alcohol over the wounds.

Remy hissed and tried to curl in on himself, but was too weak.

Laurence leaned over him, close to his face. "I saw what you did out there. You can bear this. You must think of something else."

Remy's intense gaze focused on Laurence alone. His tawny brown eyes held volumes. Secrets unspoken. Pain and awe warred in his expression. He gave Laurence a small nod.

Adeline worked swiftly, cleaning the wounds with a hot cloth. Once the damage was laid bare, she began the task of stitching the gashes. Remy cried out softly, but managed to stay still while she worked.

Time dragged as Laurence watched the witch struggle with his pain, their hands still locked together. Steadfastly ignoring the inviting scent of blood, Laurence tucked stray locks of sweaty blond hair behind Remy's ears. "It's almost over."

Adeline set aside the needle and packed the wound with a poultice that smelled of lavender. Remy bore it in silence.

"Prop him up," she ordered. "Hold his clothes out of the way."

Laurence helped Remy to sit as Adeline wrapped strips of cloth around his torso to hold the poultice in place. The witch leaned on him heavily for support. She tied it off with a tight snap, and Remy let out a gasp.

Adeline, her part finished, stood back and eyed the results. "If he can keep it clean, the wound should heal."

"And for the pain?"

Her jaw clenched, but she dug in her satchel and retrieved a set of tin jars. She handed one to Laurence and measured powder from the other into an envelope. "Apply the salve when the bandages come off if he'll tolerate it. Again each night as long as he's sore. For the powder, take one dollop the size of your smallest fingertip in through the nose. Once a night. It'll sting."

Laurence nodded and placed them securely in the inner pocket of his cloak. "Thank you."

"If you want to thank me, monitor your charge well. It's on you to keep him from killing us."

"I will." Laurence bent to collect Remy in his arms. The

witch collapsed boneless against him, completely depleted. "I'll need food for when he wakes. And fresh water."

Adeline turned to the group of leery wolves who'd joined them. "Linota, gather a days' rations and leave them in the cellar with the vampire."

The woman nodded and began preparing a basket.

"Thank you." Laurence took Remy to his rooms below ground. The sun would soon rise, and he must take cover. Having a witch in his private chamber should probably unsettle him. A dangerous risk if his gambit proved foolhardy, but one he'd nonetheless committed to. He had a feeling about Remy and doubted the man would attack without provocation.

Down a flight of stone stairs and through a large wooden door so heavy a human couldn't budge it, Laurence carried his charge. Oil lamps lit their way. The rooms were cool, but thick wool blankets lay piled on the bed to counter the chill—not that Laurence could feel it, though he found the bedding comforting. A good thing, as Remy would need them.

He settled the injured witch on his bed and awaited the delivery from Linota. Remy caught his wrist before he could back away.

"Laurence?" His quiet voice came with a tremble Laurence found worrisome. Not for the first time, he wondered if the witch would die.

"Yes?"

"Stay," Remy whispered, eyes pleading. "Please."

"I won't leave, but I must collect the food and secure the door. Rest."

Remy released his wrist, but didn't close his eyes.

Linota met him halfway down the stairs and handed over the basket and a wineskin.

"My thanks."

She bent her head and left.

Before returning to Remy, Laurence closed and locked the

door, barring it with a large plank. The witch watched through watery eyes, his face pale. So fragile a breeze could break him. Best not forget underneath the delicate surface, a powerful magic churned.

Laurence set the food on his desk. "For you. If you wake hungry during the day."

"Thank you."

"I must ask you to remain in these rooms until sundown. It isn't safe for you alone in a house of wolves."

"Of course."

He brought the wineskin to the bed. "Drink."

With some effort, Remy managed to sit and down a few swallows, enough to appease Laurence, then sank back into the mattress. Silently, Laurence removed Remy's shoes and helped arrange him beneath the covers for warmth. The witch let his body be moved like a doll, but his eyes remained active, scanning their surroundings with a curiosity that refused to be dampened by something so small as circumstance.

What must his lair look like to an outsider?

Sparse. Dark.

He hadn't been here long and didn't intend to stay after the war ended. Traveling with only essentials, the trappings of this cellar were nearly all borrowed. The bed, a couch, a table, a wardrobe, a desk. Nothing to indicate a life beyond these walls.

At least Laurence had insisted on carpeting, pillows and blankets, which Dagna grudgingly provided in return for the added security a vampire on the premises brought to her pack. Fabric and texture turned the damp cave into...well it wasn't luxurious, but it felt less like a gaol cell. The air smelled of wet stone and soil. Not an unpleasant scent, but likely not what Remy was used to either.

Laurence collected a spare blanket to bed down on the couch for the day.

"I need you," came the weak voice of his wounded guest. Remy's bright golden-brown eyes shone even in the dim light.

"What do you need?" He didn't think Remy would be hungry, but he could bring the basket to the bed. Or perhaps he needed a bucket. It had been almost a century since Laurence had dealt with chamber pots.

"You," Remy answered.

Approaching with caution, Laurence tilted his head, distrustful of the vague entreaty. He sensed no deception from Remy, but trust did not come easily. "Explain yourself."

"I'm drained. I've never been so empty." Remy took in a breath. Held it. "Your energy could replenish me, if you'll allow it. But I must touch you." He let the breath out slowly, his face a picture of vulnerability.

Reluctance flared even though Laurence's instincts told him to help. Loath as he was to share his essence with a potential enemy, the plea was tempting. Remy had shown no hostility. At present, the witch would be hard pressed to squash a bug.

Remy continued, "You won't notice; you have an abundance. It flows from you freely, but I'm too weak to harness it from any distance."

Lips pressed into a thin line, Laurence considered the petition. He'd come this far for the stranger. Forced his hand with the wolves. Why leave it half done? The witch would be an easy target for harm in this state.

On the other hand, at full strength he could prove a massive threat. It made no sense that Remy would protect this territory just to turn around and attack it, but Laurence had to consider the possibility. What if there was something he wasn't seeing? The fate of many rested with his decision.

"Please?" said the witch, pink lips quivering.

Laurence approached. "What shall I do?"

"Nothing, only sleep next to me. Let me touch you, and when we've rested, I'll be strong again."

Sleep next to him.

It had not occurred to Laurence that whatever Remy needed would take more than a moment. Hesitation must have shown on his face.

"I'm sorry to have to ask." Remy cast his eyes down, lashes fanning across ghostly white cheeks.

Resolved, Laurence discarded his boots and cloak with a sigh. He peeled back the covers and carefully climbed in, settling on his back. Staring at the ceiling, Laurence counted the timbers, waiting for whatever Remy would do, but the witch remained still as stone.

Ordinarily Laurence would be happy to sleep with someone like Remy. Petite and handsome with lovely, expressive features. Sultry, sweet voice pleading for help like honey dripping off the comb. Laurence could think of better uses for the bed than rest were it not for Remy's youth. Perhaps only twenty, certainly no older than twenty-five. His every word indicated inexperience. He'd probably been coddled. A young prodigy. And he was in no condition to be a playful bedmate. Any one of these traits would put Laurence off; together they made the thought unsavory.

Remy turned to face him. "May I touch you?"

Laurence kept his gaze aloft. "Very well."

A hand crept over Laurence's arm to his stomach. Tentatively, Remy slid his fingers beneath the leathers and under Laurence's shirt to rest against his ribs. So the witch needed skin. His palm felt warm against the coolness of Laurence's flesh, but if energy was leaving him for the witch, he couldn't tell.

"Is that enough?" asked Laurence.

"It should be," Remy whispered. "You're very powerful."

Silence stretched so long between them, Laurence thought his companion asleep until he said in a tentative voice, "Have I made you angry?"

Did he seem angry? He hadn't meant to. "You have not."

"But you're not sleeping."

"Neither are you," Laurence pointed out.

"You're very tense."

"Is my relaxation required for your magic?"

"It isn't."

No further explanation forthcoming, Laurence pressed, "How would you prefer me?"

A pause as Remy deliberated his answer. "I'd have you comfortable with my touch. I'd have you touch me in return."

Laurence took a deep breath in through his nose and out through his mouth. He pulled his arm from where it rested between them and circled it about Remy's slight shoulders. "Just so?"

"Just so." The witch curled into the embrace and worked his hand farther up Laurence's torso to lie on his chest. "Thank you."

"Will you sleep now?"

"I shall try."

Laurence was beginning to realize he'd plunged into waters quite beyond his depth with this witch. Not one for regrets, he let the worry go.

Leaning in, he caught the scent of Remy's flaxen hair. It had been perfumed to smell of roses. Coddled, surely, though the sweet fragrance was lovely. Underneath, something more earthen and natural. And deeper still, blood—copper and delectable. But Laurence would never drink from a witch.

Too dangerous.

In his sleep Remy hitched a leg over Laurence's thigh. If he wasn't trapped before, he was now. As dawn claimed him, Laurence's last thought was that it would be a long wait until sundown to uncover what sort of entanglement he'd gotten himself into this time.

2

Remy came awake by degrees in a warm cocoon of his magic, curled tight against another body. Relieved to feel his usual power vibrating pleasantly below the surface of his skin, he flexed his fingers over the soft, curly hairs beneath them.

Cool flesh.

No heartbeat.

Last night's events rushed back with biting fury: his aching side where claws had slashed deep; his risky, desperate attempt to prevent the genocide of an entire species. That his barrier held brought solace, though it would be short lived. Whispered voices drew Remy's attention. Above their tranquil bed, discord churned like a whirlpool.

The wolves had gathered upstairs and not to welcome him. His sensitive hearing picked up the argument though he had to strain to decipher their words. Using his magic, he amplified the voices.

"He cannot stay. We must send him back to his own kind."

"But how? You've seen the barrier. It's impenetrable."

"I say we kill him."

"And risk the vampire's wrath?"

"I don't fear Laurence."

Remy recognized the last speaker. Dagna. The pack's leader. If she wanted Remy dead, the others would back her.

With a sigh, Remy ignored them and focused instead on the magnificent vampire he clung to like a barnacle. Laurence slept on, ignorant of the werewolves plotting murder one floor up, his perfect stillness a dazzling new discovery for Remy. Previous bedmates had kept him awake with their restlessness, but not Laurence. He slept like the dead.

Or undead.

Remy stifled a laugh and let his gaze wander the vampire's handsome features. Hair black as ink cropped short on the sides and longer on top, tousled from the previous night's adventures and gleaming even in the dim light of the cellar. The urge to run fingers through it tempted him, but the urge to continue staring unnoticed won out. Long ebony lashes fanned over pale cheeks with bone structure that could cut glass. His nose was crooked on his otherwise symmetrical face—broken before he'd turned, probably. Somehow, it only added to the allure. Blush garnet lips, dark as wine, almost as if he wore paint, but surely he didn't. The whole picture was easy on the eyes, and Remy took his time, drinking the vampire in like strawberry mead, sweet on the tongue.

The solid bulk of him felt divine against Remy's smaller frame. The swell of his chest between broad shoulders made for an inviting pillow. A tall man with a husky build, Laurence was just Remy's type. How lucky, then, to still be alive and to have— against all odds—ended up safe in his bed.

Well, relatively safe. If you didn't count the pack of werewolves planning to kill him.

Remy could handle the wolves. The question was, would Laurence side with him...or them? The thought of losing the vampire's favor soured his empty stomach. He hoped Laurence would remain his champion. Remy had never had one.

As much as he wanted to stay cuddled under the blankets plastered to the vampire's side, it was time to wake him. Sunset approached, and the wolves would expect them to rise. Better to plan ahead.

Careful not to jostle Laurence, Remy rose to his elbow. Hovering over him, lips to his ear, he whispered, "Laurence, you must wake."

The vampire stirred. His lids fluttered open to reveal questioning gray eyes darting about the cellar then honing in on Remy.

Remy stilled him with a hand pressed firmly against his chest. "Shh, listen." Voice little more than a breath, he worried the werewolves might hear them. As to which species had better hearing, vampires or werewolves, Remy didn't know, but speaking at all was a risk if they wanted the element of surprise.

Laurence's face took on the faraway expression of a person whose attention roamed elsewhere. Remy followed suit, listening to the progression of the pack's squabble over his fate.

"I still think we should attempt to restrain him first."

"You saw how powerful he is. What holds something like that back?"

"But he's injured."

"All the more reason to do it now, while he's weak."

"Right."

"So it's settled?"

"You kill the witch. Erik and I will handle Laurence." Dagna pronounced their fate with confident finality.

Laurence growled low in his throat. Remy felt the vibration in the places where they touched. Perhaps the vampire would side with him after all. Laurence opened his mouth to speak, but Remy stopped him with a finger to his lips.

"They'll hear," he mouthed. "I can get past the wolves. Will you come?"

Laurence raised his eyebrows. Remy realized he was waiting for permission and lifted fingers from his mouth with a little smile of apology.

"How?" asked the vampire, expression full of doubt.

"Magic." Remy's smile broadened to a grin. "I'm better, thanks to you."

Laurence narrowed his gaze, unconvinced. "We're going to take on an entire pack of werewolves?"

Remy shook his head. "We're not. I am."

"By yourself? But I can help."

Remy's heart beat faster. "Thank you. I won't need help to get us out. I won't even need to hurt them."

"What should I do?"

"Follow my lead. Don't resist the magic when it calls."

"What do you mean *calls*? How will I know?"

Remy winked and clambered out of bed. "You'll know."

Laurence grabbed his wrist. "Your injury?"

Deflating a bit, Remy insisted, "It's not bad," but he wasn't so certain. It pulsed with every beat of his heart. Tight, hot, and a little itchy, the wounds were still tender. Nothing to be done for it. They had to get out of there.

They collected Laurence's things, a spare blanket, medicines, and the food meant for Remy. He'd slept straight through the day without eating, and his stomach rumbled in protest. Food would have to wait until they were safely away from Dagna's pack. He glanced longingly at the bread and cheese as Laurence stuffed it into a satchel then slung it over his back.

Silently, Remy laced up his boots and straightened his clothes. He pressed a hand to his side, assessing the tenderness. The wound hurt to touch. Not for the first time, he wished for healing magic, like his grandmother's, but only time would mend the flesh now that he'd isolated himself from everything he'd ever known.

Laurence watched, concern evident in his gaze.

Remy dropped his hand and steeled himself against the pain. It wouldn't matter one whit for what he had to do next. Energy danced along every nerve ending, welling in his chest, alive and ready for him to command.

Remy raised his eyebrows and mouthed, "Ready?"

Laurence still looked skeptical but nodded. "I'll get the door."

"No need." Remy proceeded up the stairs, eyeing the massive plank barring the exit. He raised his right hand, and the beam slid to the unlocked position. On the other side of the heavy door, wolves startled into motion. Laurence stood behind him, close enough Remy's back would bump into his chest if he leaned only a smidgen. With the same hand, he pushed forward, and the door burst open.

Dozens of eyes met Remy's curious glare. Some of the pack had shifted to their animal forms. Hackles raised. Fangs bared. Others remained human, though their retinas glowed crimson. These wolves meant him harm, but Remy would spare their lives. His wish was to end violence, not spark it.

A low growl rumbled from deep in Dagna's throat.

Magic sizzled in Remy's chest, burning a path to his fingers. With both hands raised, he sent a flash of energy raging forth.

Wolves yelped as they stumbled and fell. Howls of alarm pierced the quiet of the early evening.

"Get him," Dagna roared.

Snarling, they charged, though none could penetrate the barrier.

Remy's spell wavered under their onslaught, but he'd designed it to be flexible, to give and take instead of remaining rigid and vulnerable. Calmly, he stepped forward. One hand kept them back, and the other made a come-hither motion to Laurence.

"Come, vampire." Remy felt guilty for entangling Laurence in the dangerous web he'd woven. The least he could do was give the impression he'd left the man no choice.

Without a backward glance, Remy knew Laurence followed. He could sense the vampire behind him, a lingering result of the energy they'd shared. They pressed ahead.

Wolves growled and huffed on all sides as Remy parted the crowd to create a path to the exit. Veins stood raised in their necks, muscles flexed with useless tension. They bit at the air, jaws clacking.

Remy ignored them and opened the front door. Fresh air beckoned, along with the scent of soil and dew. Only when they reached the relative safety of the tree line did he turn back. One last glance revealed the frustrated wolves, imprisoned behind his barrier, all ready to pour out and attack.

Remy used his magic to slam the door, breaking the original spell even as he cast another.

Slinging an invisible web around Laurence to keep them together, he swept them up in a wave of energy and thrust them into the forest. They went uphill through the trees farther from his homeland and into the great unknown. Traveling faster than the wind, Remy urged them onward—out of harm's way—creating a lead between them and the pack of angry werewolves.

They tried, though, racing out of the house and charging after them. The pack stampeded through their territory along well-worn trails, pounding the dirt as they fought to catch up.

Thankfully, Laurence offered no resistance. The vampire allowed himself to be moved as Remy wished. If the magic made him uncomfortable, he bore it in silence.

The effort drained Remy's power. Most of what he'd regained overnight was spent in their escape. Energy that had filled his chest returned to the ether, leaving him hollow. His muscles grew soft and weak. He needed to rest and eat.

When he'd taken them as far as he could without completely exhausting himself, Remy slowed their breakneck pace and brought them to a stumbling halt. He released Laurence from the spell that kept them together and cast his sprawling net of awareness backward, searching for the wolves.

Had he taken them far enough away?

The answer left much to be desired. Dagna's pack raced doggedly behind them, chasing their scent, and would catch up within the hour. How far would they give chase? The border of their own territory? Farther? Remy would have to rally in order to widen the gap.

But first, food.

He turned to Laurence.

The vampire had a look on his face Remy couldn't quite interpret. Maybe awe. Maybe annoyance at having his life uprooted. Could be either.

"They follow," said Remy, exhaustion already creeping into his tone.

"I know." Laurence swung the satchel from his shoulder and rummaged inside. "We have time."

"Only a little." Remy took the opportunity to sit on a fallen tree. Cool, pine-scented air ruffled his hair in the breeze. Dampness signaled coming rains. He connected to the earth and began to draw the energy he'd need to continue.

Laurence handed him the canteen. Suddenly Remy was very thirsty. He drank in careless gulps, the water leaking down his chin until he had to slow down or risk choking.

"Careful." Laurence sat next to him—not too close—taking food from its cloth wrapping and handing it over.

Remy bit into the hunk of cheese like a starved wildcat. Then the bread. He guzzled more water. As he ate, the depth of his predicament began to sink in.

On the run in the middle of enemy territory, pursued by a pack of angry werewolves, and likely wanted by his own kind for treason. With a creature who lived on the blood of others as his only companion. His side throbbed, a reminder of his injury. Ill-equipped for surviving in the wilderness, he longed for his room in the Elder Village, his own bed with sunny yellow sheets and the scent of the honeysuckle vines that grew outside his window. He might never see home again. Chest tight, tears forming, Remy wished his grandmother were there. She'd know what to do.

Laurence chose that moment to speak. "I can take over from here."

Remy snapped out of his wool-gathering. "What do you mean?"

"You're tired, but we need to keep going to throw the wolves off our trail. I can outrun them."

Remy's shoulders caved forward. "I can't. Not without magic."

"Rest while I carry you," Laurence rumbled, his deep voice calming Remy with its easy confidence.

"Why would you do that?" Remy glanced at him, catching his slate-gray eyes and locking on to them hopefully. He'd always wanted to meet a vampire, though the prospect had been frightening. Vampires were supposed to be wicked. Greedy. But Laurence had been kind though Remy was a perfect stranger—an enemy at that. Laurence could have killed him yet chose to save him instead. Had he been lied to growing up?

"Because we can't stay here." Laurence packed away the last of the food and stood. "Come."

"That's not an answer, but all right." Remy reached for the pack, and Laurence handed it to him. "If you're going to carry me, let me ride on your back this time. I'm strong enough to hold on now."

Laurence gave a nod and knelt, presenting his broad back. Remy grasped the vampire's shoulders and hitched one leg over his hip, then the other. Laurence rose, clutching Remy's thighs. "Ready?"

"Yes." Though Remy was more prepared for Laurence's preternatural speed this time, the rush of wind through his hair as the vampire took off still startled him. He clung to Laurence, chest against his back, thighs squeezed around his waist, and watched the trees fly by in a blur of green and brown.

Laurence was faster than Remy. He hadn't known vampires could attain speeds of this magnitude. They'd outpace the wolves in no time.

The terrain became rocky as they crested a hill then traveled downward at a steep angle. Remy pushed back panic as their velocity increased. He must trust Laurence. The vampire was all he had. Dismissing fear, he embraced the exhilaration of the breeze whipping his hair back, the gurgle of water as they neared a creek bed, the sounds of a forest slumbering as night set in.

Nothing so exciting as this had ever happened to Remy. His life until now had been full of books, practice, and endless studies, trying in vain to please the elders. They'd never told him vampires could fly.

Though Laurence wasn't really flying, just running so fast he may as well be. As they neared the bottom of the hill, he slowed. The blur of trees untangled, and Remy could pick out one from the next. They stopped at the creek.

Laurence spoke over the sound of water rushing past rock and root. "I'll use the creek to throw them off our scent." He knelt, and Remy clambered off his back. "Top off the wineskin while I lay a false trail."

A spike of anxiety welled in Remy's chest and bubbled up his throat. He didn't want Laurence to leave. "Wait!"

Laurence leaned in but didn't touch him. "What is it? Are you all right?"

Remy felt foolish for his fear. Why would Laurence abandon

him now? The vampire wouldn't save his life and help him get this far only to leave him, and yet Remy couldn't shake the flutter of unease. "I don't want you to go."

"I'll only be a moment." Their gazes locked. Whatever Laurence saw in Remy's expression was enough to change his mind. "All right. Drink and refill the wineskin. I'll wait, then take you with me."

Grateful, Remy released the breath he'd been holding. His emotions were scattered like wildflower seeds. Being frazzled wasn't unusual for him, but normally he would hide it. With Laurence, he chose to be open. When he finished, Laurence knelt wordlessly, and Remy climbed onto his back.

"Thank you," Remy said against Laurence's ear as the vampire stood.

"I'll head east until the ridge, then double back. We'll follow the creek out of their territory, and that should keep us safe for tonight. Unless you desire otherwise?"

Remy shook his head. "As you say, please."

With that, Laurence took off again.

Remy tightened his grip. Laurence felt powerful between his thighs, and Remy's thoughts wandered. How would Laurence be as a lover? Heat rose to his cheeks, making Remy glad the vampire couldn't see his face. He forced himself to stay in the present. It would be better to memorize the landscape in case he ever needed to come back. With dogged tenacity, he focused on that instead of the shifting muscles of Laurence's back and shoulders.

They tore through wilderness. At the ridgeline, Laurence brought them to a stop. "I thought you'd want to see."

Stunned to silence, Remy's head spun at the view. The moon was near to full, lighting the night sky under its silver rays. Rolling hills tumbled into the distance before giving way to snow-covered mountain peaks. The crisp air cooled his cheeks and filled his lungs with every breath.

Above them, the opalescent sheen of his barrier sparkled in the moonlight, holding strong, at least for now.

Remy had never felt so alive.

He took a deep breath and gave Laurence an affectionate squeeze. He pressed a quick kiss to his temple then cast his gaze over the breathtaking horizon in the distance. "Thank you. I've never seen anything so magnificent."

Laurence was focused singularly on Remy's glittering great arc.

"Neither have I."

---

3

*L*aurence carried Remy back the way they'd come, then followed the creek until he thought Dagna's wolves would lose their trail. Remy's injury worried him. The witch had remained stoic, but his pain was obvious. They needed to rest and formulate a plan.

And Laurence had questions.

When they came to a clearing, he stopped for a break, letting Remy down from his back. A narrow valley stretched between hills, too small for human settlement but perfect for deer and rabbit. Lush with vegetation in varying shades of green and surrounded on all sides by tree cover, the valley was an oasis for plant eaters of all kinds. Laurence would build a fire and catch something for the witch to eat. Then he would need to rest as well. So much running had tired him out.

"Have we gone far enough?" Remy took in their surroundings, one arm hovering protectively over his side even as awe overtook his features.

"For now." Laurence opened the satchel and pulled out the wool blanket. He handed it to Remy. "Take this. Sit down. Your wound needs attention."

Remy didn't argue. Spreading the blanket over the grass, the witch moved slowly, favoring his injured side. "Thank you for getting us here. Where are we?"

Brown eyes flashed up to Laurence, gratitude etched in his expression. Remy was easy to read. He hid nothing of what he felt from his face. Something about the petite witch suggested both innocence and suspicion at once. An interesting combination Laurence hadn't found in one person for a long time.

"Near Dagna's southern border. We should cross it before sunup." He dug in the satchel for the ointment and powder Adeline had provided. "Take off your shirt."

Remy complied, his movements an awkward shuffle in an obvious effort to avoid pain. Being jostled around on Laurence's back for miles probably hadn't helped. He struggled out of his vest and shirt, revealing pink skin on either side of the bandages. Laurence frowned. That could be infection setting in. After everything he'd done to keep this witch alive, infection was a cruel opponent to contend with.

"The bandages too," said Laurence.

Remy searched for the end to unwrap himself, twisting as he reached to his back, and let out a whimper.

"Here, let me do that."

Remy's shoulders slumped. "Sorry."

"Don't be." Laurence settled next to him. "Lift your arms."

Remy raised them, and Laurence gently unwound the cloth from his torso. Though the skin was flushed and irritated, the pinkness did not darken to red as he'd feared. The stitches held, but the wound seeped in places. The smell carried no telltale scent of rot or dying flesh. Better than he'd expected, given the signs of discomfort.

"Is it bad?" Remy's voice held fear.

"I don't think so. The ointment should help. Lie back."

Remy lay on his good side, arms pillowed under his head, knees tucked up.

Laurence sat at his back and removed the lid. The sweet-smelling balm hinted of sage and lavender. He dipped two fingers into the salve.

"Ready?"

Remy nodded. "It's going to hurt, isn't it?"

"Some. Think of something else."

He spread the ointment gently but thoroughly along each line of stitches, being sure to work the medicine into the flesh. Remy squeezed his eyes shut and bore it in silence. Laurence worked quickly, cursing the wolf who'd caused this much damage.

"All done."

Remy breathed a sigh of relief. "It wasn't so bad."

"I'm glad." Laurence replaced the cap and sat back.

"If I were home, a healer would have seen to this. It would be gone by now."

Laurence knew there were healers among the witches, but he hadn't known their powers were as profound as that. As quick to heal as a vampire? Fascinating.

"You can't heal it yourself?" asked Laurence. Obviously Remy couldn't, or he would have, but Laurence wanted to keep him talking.

Remy flinched as he sat up. The wound would be even more tender for having been prodded. Hopefully it would feel better as the medication had time to set in.

"I cannot. My magic has never worked that way, though my grandmother is a healer. She'd have had this mended with little more than a thought and a kiss."

Laurence picked up the cloth bandage and gestured for Remy to lift his arms again. "And your magic? What does it do?"

As Laurence redressed the wound, Remy answered, "Many things, but at the heart of it I move particles with energy."

That was only the beginning of the explanation Laurence wanted. "Back at the house, how did you stop the wolves from attacking us? I didn't see anything move." Laurence knotted off the bandage and leaned back.

Remy put his shirt on, covering up freckled shoulders and a slender torso. Laurence would have looked away, an offering of privacy when really there was none to be had, but he was too interested in the answer.

"Ah, it was the same. I used my magic on the dust that floats in the air, particles so small we cannot see them." Remy threw his vest over his head and tied up the lacings. "I made them impenetrable and pushed them against the wolves to hold them back."

Particles so small they couldn't be seen. Laurence would never have guessed. "And larger things? Are they harder to move?"

Remy reached toward the satchel with an outstretched hand. The bag jerked and flew from Laurence's side into the witch's lap. "Depends how large. That wasn't any harder."

"Show me." The second it left Laurence's mouth he regretted the words. He hadn't meant for them to sound like a demand, and besides that, Remy was tired.

Before he could take it back, the witch rose. He lifted both hands skyward to the pines they'd emerged from, and as one, the treetops swayed and bent his way. With a flick of his wrist, he released them, and they stood straight once more.

Remy flopped back down with a huff, grinning. "Now," the grin spread wider, covering half his face, "I want to see your fangs. It's only fair."

The request startled a chuckle from Laurence, who could hardly say no. "All right." He opened his mouth, curled his lips from his teeth, and let his fangs drop, watching as Remy admired them. When the witch reached forward with a pointed finger, he snapped his mouth shut. "No touching, they're sharp."

"They look it." Remy's hand dropped back into his lap. "How long have you been a vampire?"

"A while." This conversation was sliding off track. Though wary of revealing his own personal details, Laurence needed to know more about Remy's.

"Are you hungry?" Remy tilted his head to the side, still eyeing Laurence's mouth. "You must be. I'm starving. Do you need blood?"

"I'm fine. You eat. Finish off the bread and cheese while I hunt a rabbit. Can you start a fire?"

"I can, but—"

"Do that." Laurence rose from their blanket. "And take some of the powder for the pain. I'll be back."

Remy jumped to his feet. "Can't I come with you?"

"No. You'll scare the prey. I won't be long," Laurence assured him, but Remy didn't look convinced. He stood on the balls of his feet, ready to follow, his large brown eyes wide and pleading. Laurence studied him. "What's wrong? Surely you can take care of yourself until I return."

Remy glanced down, then looked up through his lashes. "Promise you'll return?"

Ah, so that was it. The witch was afraid to be abandoned. But he'd bravely entered enemy territory all by himself, though he hadn't been injured then. Laurence held his gaze. "I promise."

Remy hesitated before nodding. "All right. I'll start the fire."

"Thank you. And take a dose of the powder."

"Yes."

Laurence left, continuing along the creek deeper into the valley. Grass stood tall as his thighs in some places. He resisted the urge to glance back and check on Remy. The witch would be fine without him.

Remy presented a compelling puzzle. The bold curiosity that drove him to reach out and touch a predator's fangs combined with the fragile fear of being alone didn't wed. Laurence had seen him both bursting with power and completely depleted. Now he was somewhere in between.

Once the witch had eaten, Laurence would ask after his plan. What was he helping this dangerous creature to accomplish, and how long would his barrier hold? Laurence raised his gaze to the heavens and observed once more the iridescent arc hanging in the sky. Remy had done that. To stop the war, he'd said. But why put his own life on the line to do it? Could he not have made the arc within his own territory and stayed safe among his own kind?

Laurence put the questions aside and focused. Listening carefully to every movement beneath the ground, he tiptoed through the meadow in search of sleeping rabbits in their warren. Tiny heartbeats pulsed a sleepy rhythm from where they nestled in their tunnels. Laurence crept closer, silent as snowfall. When he was certain he'd pinpointed the exact location, he struck.

Punching into the earth with such force the tunnel collapsed, he wrapped his fingers around a warm body of fluff and pulled the squealing rabbit from its den. With a quick shake of his wrist, he broke the creature's neck. He didn't want the animal to suffer.

Gripping his catch by the hind legs, he returned to find Remy nestled next to a small fire. Spruce smoke drifted pleasantly along the night air. The bread and cheese had been demolished, and the envelope of powder lay next to the wineskin. Good. The witch looked happy to see him, a small smile tugging the corners of his lips.

Remy motioned to the carcass. "How did you catch a rabbit in the dark?"

Laurence sat across from the fire and explained the process as he skinned the animal. He fashioned a spit from a stick. Though he hadn't cooked in decades, the skill came back easily enough. When dinner was set to roast over the flames, he turned to Remy.

"Are you feeling better?"

"Much." Remy held both hands in his lap, one stroking the other.

"Tell me, what is your plan?"

Remy's eyebrows rose. "My plan?"

"Yes."

"I've no plan beyond that." Remy gestured to the mighty barrier overhead, then returned his hands to his lap.

Laurence found that hard to believe. "None? No plan at all?"

Remy shook his head and gave a small shrug. "Sorry to disappoint. I hadn't expected to live this long, to be honest. I didn't anticipate a handsome vampire coming to my rescue."

Laurence leaned in and turned the rabbit, eyebrows raised. "Why'd you do it?"

"I told you. To stop the war." Remy's intense gaze made his answer seem genuine, but Laurence couldn't be sure.

"Why stop the war when you could have won it? With powers such as yours."

"I don't know that I could have won it on my own, only that the elders would have forced me to try."

"And why not try?"

Staring at the ground, Remy mumbled, "You don't understand."

That much Laurence could agree with. "Then explain it to me."

When he glanced up, Remy's eyes had grown watery. "They were going to make me kill everyone in the area. All of them. Werewolves, humans, animals. Maybe vampires too, I don't know." He shook his head vigorously, as if trying to rid himself of the very idea. "But I could never..."

"How?"

Remy stilled. When he spoke, his voice was low. Tentative. "You asked how my magic works. I only told you part of it. I channel energy to move things, but it's more than that. I'm not limited by distance like other witches. If I can cast a spell, it will reach as far as I direct it."

The implications began to set in, but Remy was holding something back. "Go on."

"If another witch casts a spell...even a sort of witch with gifts I don't have, say, a witch with an aptitude for poison...I can spread her spell, though I didn't create it."

"So your elders, they can use you to boost a spell's reach? A spell from anyone?"

"You've got the right of it."

"And they were going to make you do this? With some sort of killing spell?"

"Yes." Remy pulled his knees to his chest and held them. "There's a witch who can poison the air. Helewise. With my help, she could decimate entire populations."

Poison the air?

The appalling possibilities began to set in. Terrible ramifications. Hundreds dead. No, thousands. Tens of thousands. How big of an area could they target?

Werewolves, people, livestock...utter destruction.

Another potential conclusion arose unbidden. The witches were losing this war. If Remy were killed, their last hope would be dashed. Wolves and vampires would almost certainly be victorious.

"You cannot tell people this," Laurence said firmly.

Remy's eyes shot up, offended. "But you asked!"

"Tell no one else. They could simply kill you, and the war would be won."

Remy's mouth dropped open to form a perfect O.

Laurence wished he hadn't said it, though it needed to be said.

"I hadn't thought of that."

"Don't dwell on it. Only, be more careful what you share."

Remy nodded, silent. The breeze blew a lock of blond hair

across his eyes. Laurence fought the urge to reach out and tuck it behind his ear. He didn't like to see Remy vulnerable. The image of the lone witch standing tall and casting the most powerful spell Laurence had ever seen formed in his mind. Strong and fearless, risking his life to avoid killing others. Glancing at Remy now, curled in on himself, lost and at risk, struck a chord low in Laurence's gut.

"Remy."

The witch looked up, amber eyes solemn. "Yes?"

How can I keep you safe? What should I do? "The rabbit is done."

"It's for me?"

"Of course it's for you." Laurence took the spit from the flames and passed it over. "Who else?"

Remy took the rabbit, exchanging his serious expression for curiosity. "I thought it yours. Or that we might share."

"I'm a vampire. Had you forgotten?"

"Only blood then? I wasn't sure. Do you need mine?" Remy's offer stunned Laurence with its casual air.

"No!" The word came out sharper than he'd meant. "I mean, yes, only blood, but no, I don't need yours." Vampires did not drink from witches. Some witches could control you after. Did Remy know this?

Remy shrugged, unbothered. He blew on the rabbit. "Let me know if you change your mind. You're doing everything for me; I'd like to be useful for you."

"Finish eating. We should clear out of Dagna's territory." Laurence packed their things away into the satchel. "And then we need a plan."

4

"Where are we going?" Remy asked as he followed along next to Laurence. They'd packed from their break and continued south. At least Remy thought they were heading south. He'd never had to pay much attention to direction before, and certainly not without the sun to guide him. The farthest he'd traveled was to his grandmother's cottage and back each summer, and that journey could be made in a few hours. Otherwise he lived at the Elder Village, honing his skills at their instruction.

"Out of pack lands and to a place to rest during daylight. Beyond that, we'll need to decide."

They had enough of a lead that neither had to whisk the other away for miles on end. Which was fortunate, since both were too drained to continue at that pace unless it were life or death. So they walked, the night sky black beyond the shine of Remy's barrier.

"Have you any suggestions?" Remy asked. "I can't go back."

"The spell," Laurence guessed correctly. "They'll know it was you?"

Remy nodded. "Yes. Most magic is traceable. I've no skill at masking mine. When they've devised a way to shatter the arc, they'll come after me." He eyed Laurence. The next words were difficult to say, but he meant them with all his heart. "Then you should run. Save yourself."

Laurence's brows knitted together. "Your *magic* is traceable. Are you?"

"What do you mean?"

"If you stop doing magic, could they still find you?"

"No, but—"

"Then you must stop," said Laurence with his usual confidence, as if it were a simple thing.

"I can't stop my magic!" The thought of it alone was jarring. "It's part of me."

"We don't need your spells now, we're far enough ahead. Leave no path, and they won't know where to search."

Remy considered it. Could he stop using magic? Maybe. He'd never tried. With Laurence's help, it might be possible. "Can you teach me to start the campfire with no magic?"

"Yes."

A thick patch of brush made walking side by side impossible. Single file, they trudged along, Remy deep in thought.

If only there were some way to prevent Helewise from casting her poison. If she couldn't perform the spell, they wouldn't need Remy to spread it. But it was too late for such hopes. They'd never accept him back after what he'd done. He'd be captured and forced to comply until he was no longer useful. Then he'd be killed. He couldn't let that happen. That outcome would break his grandmother's heart. Better to die free than live as the elders' weapon.

And there was Laurence, who'd appeared out of nowhere to save him and was now ensnared in the mess Remy had made of his life. Guilt sat heavy on his chest. He couldn't live with himself if they killed Laurence to get to him.

Remy had to know. "Why did you do it?"

Laurence glanced over his shoulder. "Do what?"

"Save me when you could have eaten me."

Laurence shrugged. "I wasn't hungry."

Remy grinned. "You speak in jest, right?"

"Right."

Remy let the laugh bubble over. "I didn't know vampires were funny."

"I'm not, usually."

"Will you answer? Because I don't understand why you're helping me."

Laurence whacked overgrown brush out of their way with a stick he'd picked up and a knife he'd taken from the sack, carving an easy trail for Remy. He swung and chopped long enough Remy thought he wouldn't answer. When he did talk, he picked his words slowly.

"You are...*interesting* in a world I've found dull for a very long time."

Remy wanted to ask for more but stopped himself. So Laurence found him interesting, which had kept him alive until now. A shiver took hold of his spine. Remy forced it back.

After several hours of slow going, the thicket cleared and mature old-growth forest thrived around them. Tree trunks wide as houses towered into the heavens. Pinecones cracked and snapped under their feet.

As Remy wondered how much longer they'd need to travel, Laurence announced, "We've cleared Dagna's territory. I don't think she'll give chase beyond her border."

Relief fluttered and stretched in Remy's chest. "Does that mean we can stop soon?"

"A little farther on a human village lies tucked in the hillside. I know a safe place there. Can you make it?"

"Yes," Remy said and found it to be true. Though he was tired, hope of a safe place nearby spurred him on. And he found humans fascinating. He'd always liked them, but the elders had discouraged his mingling, then banned the interaction all together. It had been years since he'd kept company with humans.

"Are they friends of yours?" Remy asked hopefully.

Laurence shook his head. "I don't know them."

That left Remy curious, but Laurence trekked forward without offering explanation, and Remy didn't want to pester him further. He followed at a short distance, tossing thoughts round his head in an effort to ignore his aching feet and sore stitches.

Before long, they approached a massive graveyard grown over with lush vegetation. Laurence picked his way through as Remy scanned the grounds. There didn't seem to be a living population in these parts large enough to support a dead one of this magnitude, unless the village Laurence spoke of was really a city. But if that were true, he'd sense it.

Remy peered at the ancient gravestones, the dates so faded he could barely read them. He made out 1036, nearly four hundred years prior. A population must have lived and died here long ago.

Remy paused over another stone. "I had something else in mind when you said 'humans tucked into the hillside.'"

Laurence rumbled a laugh and smiled. "There is a living human village through there." He pointed to where the two hills narrowed into a valley in the distance. "I can go and collect the supplies you'll need. Then we can sleep here for the day."

"Here?" Remy looked around. They were going to sleep amongst the dead? Where? In the open? He wouldn't mind overly much except the rain that had threatened all night had finally begun to fall. And surely Laurence must escape the sun.

"There." Laurence gestured to a crumbling mausoleum. Old stones had darkened and rounded with age. The above-ground portion appeared to be barely standing. What shape must the portion below ground be in? Remy sighed. He would not be picky. Besides, he was so tired he could probably sleep through a horse auction at this point.

Laurence led the way to the leaning stone structure, its frame bent sideways enough that the blackened door was jammed. The vampire gave it a rough shove with his shoulder, and the door creaked open.

A wave of musty air hit the back of Remy's throat. He coughed.

Laurence looked over his shoulder. "I don't remember it being this bad."

"You've stayed here often?"

"Not often." Laurence plowed ahead. "Come. You can escape the rain, and I'll run for supplies."

"I don't want to stay here alone," said Remy, on his heels.

"I have to. You'll be safe."

They descended below ground on steps worn uneven over time. The chill in the air drowned away the musty scent. Remy wasn't sure which was worse—the stale smell or the bitter cold.

"I'll leave the door open so you can see out." Laurence set the satchel upon a dusty marble stand where stood a sconce that made Remy wish for oil. "I'll hurry back, but I must leave."

"Why?" Embarrassed at the panic in his voice, Remy covered it with another cough.

"You'll need some things for our journey," Laurence explained, "and I do need to feed."

"Are you going to kill someone?" Remy blurted without thinking.

Laurence blinked, his stunned expression turning cooler than even this deathtrap. "Of course not. Why would you suggest such?"

"I'm sorry. I shouldn't have," Remy stammered. "I know very little of your kind."

The vampire's face softened. "I don't kill people, Remy, though I fear I will have to steal from them just a little."

Remy's heart sank. "Blood?"

"*Supplies*, not blood."

"Don't steal on my behalf, please."

"I'll be careful not to take what they can't make do without."

"I'll make do. I don't need anything, really," Remy insisted.

"You'll need a better blanket to stay warm."

"I can use my magic for that."

"You mustn't. Think. We cannot leave a trail for your people to find you by."

"But stealing is—"

"Necessary," Laurence insisted before Remy could say *wrong*. "I don't have time to argue." Laurence turned his back and hurried up the stairs. "Wait for me here, I won't be long."

He did not look back.

Remy refused to panic. He could wait there, amongst the dead, for Laurence to return without using his magic. But oh how he wished it wasn't raining and he could wait outside instead.

He glanced around the small tomb while pretending to be braver than he felt. As his eyes adjusted to the darkness, he noticed coffins stacked on either side of the narrow chamber. The stone caskets remained intact, but the wooden ones had begun to rot away. Remy could picture the bones of the inhabitants within.

How would their spirits feel about hosting guests in their final resting place? A witch and a vampire, no less.

Were it not for Laurence, Remy might have his own crypt already. He should not have accused the vampire of killing people to feed. The more time he spent with Laurence, the more he questioned the things he'd been taught. Even now the man was gathering supplies for Remy's benefit.

Well, stealing them, but no one was perfect.

Collecting the satchel, Remy pulled out the blanket and spread it over the craggy floor of ancient stonework. It would not be the most comfortable of beds, but he'd pass out once Laurence returned, of that he was sure. Next he dug for the powder and took another dose the size of his smallest finger. The bitter medicine stung his nostril, but the relief would be worth the temporary discomfort. He drank a swallow of water and sat upon the blanket to wait.

When Laurence had said *feed*, what had he meant? He wasn't going to kill a person, but would he ask permission first? How did the process go? And why had he refused Remy's offer with such vehemence? Questions with no answers were becoming too common.

The longer he waited, the more the chill set in. He longed for his magic. A simple warming spell would be such a comfort, but Laurence was right. Any spell at all could be tracked, and it would take days for the magic to dissipate. If he quit altogether, the elders would never be able to find him.

His thoughts drifted back to Laurence like a magnet to its pole. Remy had never felt such a pull. It made previous dalliances feel shallow in comparison. More than simple desire, there was something about the vampire that enchanted him. Sadly, he didn't get the impression Laurence felt the same way.

Footsteps thumped from outside, bringing Remy to full alert. They sounded like Laurence's gait, but he wouldn't relax until he saw the vampire with his own eyes. He dashed up the stairs.

The sky had lightened a fraction. Soon the sun would rise. Though the sun's warmth would be a welcomed comfort on his shoulders, Remy could only think of sleep.

His chest relaxed at the sight of Laurence dodging weeds and vines as he made his way closer. The vampire carried a second satchel, and it was full to bursting at the seams.

His color had changed, Remy noticed, narrowing his gaze.

Laurence's cheeks were ruddier, as if he were flushed. It suited him, but so did everything.

"I'm glad you're back." Remy made way for him to enter.

Laurence handed over the new pack—worn leather, the strap dangling off the side, nearly broken. "I brought you a thicker blanket. It smells of horse. As you disapprove of thievery, I tried to only take things people weren't using. These folks had a dozen such horse blankets for only seven horses."

"Thank you." Remy pressed the bag against his chest. "And you, are you well?"

Eyebrows raised, Laurence forced the door shut tight. His handsome features dissolved to darkness. "Am I well? I've not been gone a half hour."

"I meant, did you, uh…get enough to eat?" Remy wished he could decipher Laurence's expression. Had the vampire forgiven him for misspeaking earlier?

"Oh that. Yes, and without killing." The answer came out gruff.

Remy hesitated, a question dancing on the tip of his tongue.

"Go on," said Laurence, voice softening. "Ask it."

"What did you eat?"

"A cow tonight, but sometimes I feed on humans. Will that bother you?"

Remy wasn't certain. His instinct said yes. People weren't meant to be food. But it wasn't Laurence's fault he was a vampire and needed blood. And who was Remy to say how he should get it?

A trifling nugget rose in the back of his mind—Remy wanted Laurence to feed from him, not someone else, *him.* The desire came as a surprise, something to be sorted later.

"No, I suppose it won't." It might, but Remy dropped the subject and took the blanket from the bag. He sat on the other while spreading the new one over his legs. "Will you come to bed?"

Laurence shook off his cloak and added it to Remy's makeshift nest.

Remy held open the covers for him. "Please? Can I touch you again?"

"All right." Laurence crawled in and lay upon his back, holding an arm out for Remy to settle next to his side.

He cuddled in gladly. Exhaustion clung to his very soul. Tucking his hand under the vampire's shirt, he felt his skin. "You're warm! How are you doing that?"

"The cow," said Laurence. "I can produce my own heat if I've fed well enough. I thought you would need it tonight, since you can't use your magic."

"You fed...for me?"

"In part." Laurence wrapped his arm over Remy's shoulder and closed his eyes. "Go to sleep."

Remy continued to stare. He couldn't make out details in the dark, but he could see the line where Laurence's black hair swept back from his forehead. He could make out his garnet lips. And he wanted to taste them, even knowing what Laurence had eaten for his supper.

"Laurence?"

"Mm?"

"Do you sleep with men?"

Laurence cracked open one eye. "Evidently."

"No, I meant—"

"I know what you meant."

"So," Remy pushed. "Do you?"

The vampire sighed. Remy's hand rose and fell in time with his chest.

"On occasion," said Laurence, his tone exasperated. "Now, go to sleep."

So Laurence slept with men, just not with Remy. His hopes deflated within the span of a heartbeat. Saddened, he laid his head on Laurence's strong shoulder and shut his eyes. The vampire's disinterest couldn't have been more apparent if he'd laughed in Remy's face.

Which Laurence would never do.

Because he was kind.

Which only made Remy pine for him all the more.

5

Day gave way to night, and Laurence woke with Remy still pressed to his side. The hard stone floor beneath him was a far cry from his plush bedding at Dagna's, but he was glad to be out of the wolves' den. He hadn't relished his time there, finding the pack brash when he preferred calm. Remy made a far better companion, even if all Laurence had to show for it was a puddle of drool on his chest.

Laurence stroked his hand down the witch's spine, then brought it up to rest on the back of his head. Soft, flaxen hair tickled his palm.

Do you sleep with men?

In truth Laurence preferred men, though he slept with whomever tempted him in the moment. He'd realized Remy's interest, but had hoped the witch wouldn't pursue him. It wasn't lack of attraction on his part—Remy was beautiful—it was his youth. His bright-eyed innocence. Laurence had no desire for the sort of clingy relationship Remy would undoubtedly crave.

No attachments, no strong feelings, no strings. Those were Laurence's rules. He wouldn't forsake them for a witch struck with puppy love, no matter how pretty. And he wouldn't risk leading Remy on. Better to feign apathy.

Stretching under the woolen cover, the length of Remy's body warm against his, Laurence sighed. Pity they couldn't fuck, but he wouldn't have this youth falling in love and getting his heart broken. He scooted out from beneath him, cradling his head so it wouldn't fall against the stones.

Remy stirred and reached out, but Laurence evaded. He shoved opened the crypt's door. Fresh air rushed into their dank, morbid dwelling, bringing the welcome scent of forest after a heavy rain. The skies had cleared and stars shone over the gravestones. An owl's call echoed through the treetops.

When he turned, Remy had sat up, mouth open mid-yawn, arms stretched overhead, hair in tangles over his slim shoulders. Laurence couldn't help staring.

Remy's eyes blinked open. "Everything all right?"

Laurence looked away. "Yes, fine. You should eat. There are apples and nuts in the bag. I'll return shortly."

"Where are you going?"

"Not far. Be ready to go when I get back." He left before Remy could question him further.

Really, there was no need to leave, but he was accustomed to spending time alone. So he walked amongst the towering evergreens, passing time restlessly as the witch readied for the night's journey. Listening with ears so sensitive they could pick out bugs laboring in their underground tunnels, Laurence found another clutch of rabbits. He caught one for Remy's lunch and tied its hind legs with a length of vine. He'd latch it to the outside of the satchel later.

He returned to find Remy packed and waiting. The witch sat upon one of the larger monuments, cross-legged, finishing an apple. His face lacked the shining smile Laurence had grown accustomed to, instead his features were drawn, contemplative. Perhaps a little sad.

"Shall we?" said Laurence.

Remy hopped off the stone and slung a pack over his shoulder. He held the other out to Laurence. "Let's."

The smile made an appearance, as if Remy couldn't help himself. Smaller, but present. Laurence smiled back and took the pack. "Thank you."

They left the cemetery behind, crossed a creek, and continued uphill, heading east.

"Where are we going?" asked Remy.

"Ah, yes. I suppose we must discuss that."

"Now is as good a time as any."

"Have you a preference?"

Remy's shoulders drooped forward, making him appear smaller. "I don't even have any ideas. Wolves would kill me. I assume vampires that aren't you would kill me. My only hope might be a human settlement, but what would I do?"

"The world is full of dangers, but you are strong. Do not doubt you'll find your place." Laurence spoke with more confidence than he felt. The world was at war, and Remy would be hated on all sides. Except maybe one. "I've an idea, but you may not like it."

"I'm listening."

"I want to get you out of werewolf territories and north to the land controlled by my kind. I believe our ruling class will listen to reason, and when they realize you're the witch who created the arc, they'll offer protection."

"North? Haven't we been traveling south?"

"Yes. This route was quickest to escape Dagna's pack. We'll need to head east, well outside of her border, then north over Keeper's Pass."

"And you think vampires won't kill me upon first sight?"

Actually, Laurence did worry about that. Though if they stopped at Livia's on the way, she could send messengers in advance of their arrival. "I'll be with you."

Remy's eyes sparkled with gratitude. Laurence got caught in his gaze. Twin amber jewels, full of trust.

"All right." Remy shrugged. "It's better than my plan."

"I thought you didn't have a plan."

"I thought of one as we talked. Traveling bard. I'll need a lute."

"You play the lute?"

"Not yet." Laughter threaded through Remy's voice.

Laurence nodded, hiding a grin. "I see. Well, then yes, my plan is better."

"I concede to your judgment."

Some hours later, they took a footpath leading to the road that split the heart of werewolf lands in two. Wide enough for carriages, it made for easy going. The wolf packs who shared the road allowed free passage. Most of the travelers would be human anyway, peddlers moving from one village to the next, traders carrying goods from farmers and blacksmiths alike. Humans would be unable to see Remy's arc, and most were unaware other species existed.

Laurence and Remy would stay on the roadway until they'd crossed the Sutiri River. Once past its wide waters, Laurence would guide them off-trail where they'd be less likely to run into trouble. As long as they kept a lookout for stray wolves and dodged perimeter guards, all would be fine. It helped they'd only be traveling at night.

Laurence noticed Remy holding his side. With a wave of regret, he realized he hadn't applied the ointment. In his rush to escape the intimacy of waking up together, he'd forgotten.

"Should we stop for a rest?" Laurence suggested. "You must be hungry."

Remy had been silent for much of the journey, but he turned to Laurence with a pleasant expression and nodded. "I was just beginning to fantasize about that rabbit hanging from your pack."

"Then you shall have it." Laurence slung the satchel from his shoulder as Remy led them to a flat spot. He untied the rabbit. "Do you know how to skin it?"

Remy shook his head. "Not without my magic."

"Sit, I'll show you."

Laurence taught him how to build a fire as well. Remy listened intently, eyes focused on each task as he committed them to memory. Life skills he'd probably never needed because spellwork had made things easy until now. Laurence had learned these simple chores when he'd been a young man on hunting trips with his father. Long ago he'd looked forward to teaching his own children, but those days were stolen. He'd never had the chance to father children. Though he'd no need for these skills in a century, they came back with little effort, and reminded him of times gone by.

As the rabbit cooked, Laurence's mood grew melancholy. He glanced to Remy, busily munching on nuts while they waited. "How do you feel?"

"I'm all right."

"I'm sorry I forgot the salve. Shall I apply it?"

"It can wait, but thank you."

"Remy, I've been wondering something. How long do I have to get you to safety?"

"You mean, how long will the arc hold?"

"Aye."

Remy's eyes cast skyward to the ever present opal sheen of his barrier. "I don't know. A few weeks, maybe less? I didn't even know it would work until I tried. I've never attempted a spell designed to last on its own like this. There has never been a reason before."

"If it falters, can you rebuild it?"

The witch's gaze shifted from the sky to his feet. "I don't think so. If the arc fails—or I should say when, because surely it will fail—it will be because another witch broke my spell. After they've broken it once, they could do so again." Remy sighed. Opened his mouth. Closed it. Finally said, "I'm sorry. I've no more tricks up my sleeve."

Laurence got the impression Remy held something back but didn't want to push. He already felt bad for having forgotten the salve. Instead he took the rabbit off the flames and passed it over.

"Eat up then. The sooner we make it to my home the better."

"You're taking me home?" Their eyes met. Remy tipped his head. "I didn't realize. I should have. Will you tell me about it then? Your home."

As Remy ate, Laurence told him of Bran Vigny, the castle where the ruling class of vampires lived and governed, where the rolling hills became mountain peaks tickling the clouds, and of the human towns they'd pass along their way. He'd expected young Remy to be daunted, but the witch only looked more excited.

"I've never been to a castle!"

"You'll get to see two on this journey."

"What an adventure." Awe filled Remy's eyes, tempered by a seriousness that turned his pretty features handsome. "If only it were due to better circumstance."

"If only," Laurence agreed.

After the rabbit was reduced to bones, they set back out on the road toward the Sutiri. This night proved warmer than the last, a humid breeze rustling the leaves in the darkness. They bypassed a small village as they continued east, traversing open farmlands for several miles before rejoining the road.

Smoke wafted from somewhere nearby. Campfires most likely, but as far as he remembered, there was no settlement by the river crossing. Why people were stopped, he didn't know. As long as they were human and not werewolf, it shouldn't be a problem.

"There are people up ahead," said Remy.

"Yes," Laurence agreed, "but how do you know? Are you using your magic?"

"I'm not. I can sense them. It happens with hardly any effort on my part. I couldn't stop gathering the information if I tried. My natural senses aren't traceable in the way that casting a spell would be."

"Tell me, can you determine if they're human or werewolf?"

"Human," Remy answered with no hesitation. That was more than Laurence could decipher at this distance. Impressive. And useful.

"Do you know why they've stopped?"

"I don't. I can't hear them this far away, and I can't read minds."

"Are you always so forthcoming with information?"

"You'd rather I weren't?"

"I'm glad you tell me things, but your honesty and trust won't always serve your best interests. I'd caution you to keep the extent of your powers to yourself. There are those who would use you."

Remy's face darkened. "I know."

Laurence dropped the subject. They pressed closer to the river and the group gathered there. He could smell them now, regular people, not wolves. The sound of rushing water grew louder as they approached with caution.

Humans camping in the middle of the road when there were villages at regular intervals was strange, though even stranger were two men traveling instead of sleeping at this hour. Better to avoid difficult questions altogether than to explain their nocturnal schedule. Except avoiding them might prove impossible, as they gathered next to the bridge crossing.

Or they gathered next to where the crossing used to be.

Laurence stopped in his tracks. With the bridge gone, the narrowest section of the Sutiri was still too deep to ford. Could Remy swim? Would that be wise with his stitches?

Scanning the area made it obvious why so many men camped here. Cartloads of straight tree trunks trimmed of their branches lay piled beside the riverbank. They were going to rebuild the bridge.

Remy gaped at the workers' tents and wagons with curiosity ablaze in his eyes. No doubt come morning he could befriend this group and hustle his way across the river with their help, but Laurence was reluctant to leave him, even for one day.

"What do we do?" Remy whispered.

Laurence put a finger to his lips and mouthed, "Shh, don't wake them."

Snoring thundered from one of the wagons—it was a wonder the others could sleep through the racket. A closer inspection of the camp revealed a log raft, but the current would sweep it downriver if they tried to use it to cross without help.

Someone shuffled in their tent. Laurence took Remy by the shoulder and pulled him close as a man climbed out through the flap. They backed away, but he happened to glance right at them.

"Ho there," he greeted, friendly but with eyebrows raised. He kept his tone low, and for that Laurence was grateful. He didn't want to wake the entire crew. "Bridge's down."

Laurence resisted the urge to roll his eyes. "I see that."

"Hello," said Remy from where Laurence had shoved him behind his back.

"What's yer business? Didn't the villagers warn ye about the bridge?"

"Aye. Thought maybe we could swim."

The worker chuckled and drew close. An older man, past his prime but built like an ox. "Not with the rains we've had, no. It's not safe." He thrust out an arm, and Laurence took hold of his wrist and shook. "Name's Ulric."

"Leif." He gestured to Remy before the witch could answer

for himself. "And this is Renald. I'm escorting him to Wyckshire to purchase a lute."

Remy grinned and held out his hand. "Pleasure to meet you, Ulric."

"Likewise," Ulric said with a nod. "I'm out for a piss, but go on and settle in. We'll get ye across the river come sunup."

"Many thanks," said Remy as Ulric tottered off to make water. He glanced to Laurence, eyes questioning.

"Over there." Laurence pointed to an empty spot where the riverbank leveled off and grass covered the ground. They took off their packs and spread out the blankets. Until Ulric went back to sleep, they had to make a show of setting up camp.

Remy took a handful of nuts from the pack and popped one into his mouth, gaze darting from the tents to the river. "I could cast one last spell."

Laurence shook his head. "It's not worth the risk."

Ulric shuffled back to his tent and collapsed inside.

"Well then, we could swim." Remy shrugged. "The current's not that bad. I can make it if you can."

Laurence narrowed his gaze warily. "Your stitches."

"I'll be all right."

"No. I'll swim. You'll sit on that raft, and I'll push you across."

Remy's eyes grew wide. "We can't take their raft!"

Laurence gestured to the abundant stacks of tree trunks. "They can build another."

"No," said Remy, his tone firm.

"Do you have a better idea?"

Remy cocked his head to the side, squinted at the shoreline, and nodded. "I suppose…we could borrow it."

"How?"

"They've plenty of rope." Remy pointed. "And that tree is well situated. If we tie one end to the raft, wrap it about the tree and hold onto the other end, once we're across, we could pull the raft back. It would be ready for them when they need it."

Clever witch. It was a good idea and would likely keep any of the men here from complaining to other passersby about them. "All right. Let's get to it."

While Remy set about rigging the rope, Laurence packed their things. He shucked off his boots and clothes, all but his braies, and stuffed them into the satchel. With any luck Remy would be able to keep them dry from his place on the raft.

As Laurence approached the riverbank, Remy turned and froze. His mouth fell open. He stared a moment before coming to his senses, then color flushed his cheeks and he cast his eyes away.

Laurence wanted to tell him not to worry, he could look his fill. He wanted to invite Remy to touch, as the witch so obviously desired, but it couldn't be. He wouldn't take advantage of Remy's youth and have them both come to regret it later.

Making his way down the riverbank, Laurence stepped into the water and tried not to cringe. Freezing. Of course it would be, with the summer melt pouring down from the mountains. The cold wouldn't hurt him, but that didn't mean he liked it.

Remy sidled up next to him, being careful to keep his eyes north of Laurence's bare chest. He reached out for their bags. "Ready?"

"Yes, let's get this over with." Laurence clenched his jaw, resigned.

"I'm sorry it has to be you."

"Don't be. Come." Laurence offered his hand and helped Remy onto the raft. The witch tucked their things in his lap and gathered the loose end of the rope. "Here we go."

Pushing the raft forward, Laurence strode into the river. Swift but manageable, the chilled water lapped at his shoulders and soaked the ends of his hair. He swam against the current, keeping their line across the river near to straight, hands gripping the raft tightly. He glanced up to find Remy watching, amused. Mirth danced in his eyes.

"And now that you've gotten your bath, what shall I do?"

Laurence laughed despite himself. "Careful. I can dunk that pretty head of yours without getting the stitches too wet."

The flush returned to Remy's cheeks. He clutched their things tighter to his body. "You wouldn't, vampire."

Laurence splashed him, the arc of water spritzing soundly across his face. "Don't test me, witch."

They were still grinning when they reached the opposite bank. Remy disembarked the raft, and Laurence took the rope from him and began to tug. When he'd successfully pulled the raft to the other side, he tied off the rope so it would stay there until the workmen cut it free.

Laurence headed up the bank to find Remy half-naked. It was his turn to stare. Shucking off all but his smallclothes, Remy was lithe and freckled beneath his clothes. He carried more muscle on his frame than Laurence would have guessed, particularly his thighs which were well defined and flexed as he kicked off one sock and then the other. Perhaps not quite so young as Laurence thought then.

"What are you doing?" Laurence forced his mouth to a thin line to avoid gawking.

"You've had a rinse. I need one too."

"The water is frigid."

"I'll warm up after. I assume we've nothing but more walking ahead of us?" Remy raised his brows, found confirmation in Laurence's lack of response, and shuffled down the bank.

Laurence couldn't stop his gaze from lingering as Remy stood hip deep in the water. He splashed his face and arms, worked his hands along his scalp and mostly avoided the wound on his side. Though the skin around the stitches still flared pink and irritated, it appeared no worse for their days spent trudging through the forest. Remy washed it last, only a light rinse. He climbed from the water and shook like a dog.

Eyes sparkling, Remy said, "You weren't joking. That water's cold as ice."

Laurence shrugged with a laugh. "I did try to spare you."

"Yes, well, now I don't stink. You should thank me."

They dressed in a rush, Laurence eager to put some distance between them and the Sutiri before sunrise, Remy probably because he was frozen. If they made decent time, they could reach Livia within a week. With her help, Laurence was sure he could find Remy safe harbor among the vampire elite.

His eyes settled on Remy's slender form, shivering despite the humid air. He stepped in until they were face to face, and instead of putting his cloak back on, he wrapped it round the little witch. Remy leaned forward, and Laurence took his shoulders in both hands and rubbed vigorously to warm him up.

"How did you stay in that water so long without freezing?" Remy asked, voice muffled because his face lay buried in Laurence's chest.

"It doesn't affect me as it does you."

"I miss my magic," Remy said between chills.

Laurence tousled his hair. "You're doing fine without it."

Remy glanced up, wide amber eyes locked on Laurence's mouth. "Only because I have you."

If Laurence leaned down a fraction, they'd be kissing. Remy wanted it. Laurence wanted it. The moment pulsed between them, expanding and contracting with their breath.

Laurence turned aside.

"Come, you'll warm up faster when we're moving. We've only a few hours until sunrise." Leaving his arm about Remy's shoulders, he led the witch to the road and back on their way.

6

When Remy was a child daydreaming about what it would be like to meet a vampire, he hadn't counted on waking up in so many graveyards.

At least he had Laurence to curl up with. He no longer needed the extra energy—his wound was healing well, and he drew magic naturally from his surroundings without even trying—but he hadn't admitted as much to Laurence. Waking up against his side, snuggled under his arm, was too much of a pleasure to give up, even if the vampire didn't return his interest. So he continued to sleep with his hand on Laurence's chest, as if it were more important than a simple comfort, all the while feeling a bit guilty for not confessing to the ruse.

The latest of the mausoleums was newer and not so dank as the last few. He woke well-rested, and they made good time. Around midnight they'd gone far enough east to begin heading north. The terrain grew steep in places, but Remy didn't mind; he liked the exertion, the feeling of his heart pumping and his lungs expanding to capacity.

The climbs had little effect on Laurence. His breath remained slow and steady even as Remy huffed and puffed.

"Tell me about your friend," Remy asked to distract himself from the burn in the backs of his legs. "The lady we're going to see."

"Livia? She's lovely. Protective of those in her circle, but if you cross her, beware. She's much stronger than she looks."

"Aren't you all?" That was *the* thing about vampires, as far as Remy knew. Superhuman strength for the lot of them. "How'd you meet her?"

"It's a long story."

"Let me check my schedule..." Remy looked around. Path behind him. Path before him. Trees on all sides. "Oh look, I'm free."

Laurence laughed even as he shook his head. "A long story I don't want to relive right now. Don't fret, you'll like her."

Remy had learned not to pry further. Laurence always dodged questions about his past, and when pushed, became grumpy and silent. Remy would have to change the subject or continue their hike without the benefit of conversation. "Will she like me?"

Laurence stopped and caught Remy's eye. "Of course she will. Are you worried about that?"

He hadn't been, not really; he just wanted to keep Laurence talking. Remy loved the sound of that deep baritone rumble. "Not everyone likes a male witch."

Laurence continued uphill. "Why is a male inheriting magic so rare? Do you know?"

Remy shook his head, following behind him. "Not for sure. Magic runs strongest through the female lineage. From mother to granddaughter, often skipping a generation. Most families have only one, maybe two powerful witches at a time, with the other family members wielding simpler magic. Rarely do the men have magic at all. Rarer still that the family's strongest witch would be a son, not a daughter. But it does happen."

Laurence cast him a glance over his shoulder. "Of that, you are the proof."

"My grandmother, Evanora, is a strong witch. My mother has only mid-range powers, and my sisters have almost none. I think they hate me for being born with what they believe should have been theirs."

"That isn't fair. To hate you for something beyond your control." Laurence leapt up a rock face nearly as tall as himself, turned, and reached down. Remy clasped his hand, and Laurence hauled him up.

"Since when is life fair?" Remy muttered.

Laurence's gray eyes darkened to slate. He held on to Remy's hand longer than was strictly necessary before dropping it to continue on their way. Whatever he was thinking, Remy knew he wouldn't share it.

"My grandmother loves me," he continued. "When it was discovered I'd inherited her strength with magic, my mother sent me to be raised by the elders. I think she and my sisters were glad to be rid of me. But summers I spent with my grandmother in the countryside. All my favorite memories are from those trips."

"You don't like the elders?"

Remy shivered. His youth had not been full of kindness. "No. Most of them...no."

"Why couldn't you stay with your grandmother instead?"

"It's tradition to send witches with abilities like mine to be trained in the Elder Village. It was difficult enough to obtain permission to leave for summers. They never let me out of their sight for long."

Remy thought of Emmeline, the witch who'd always tried to control him through fear. The one who'd convinced the others Remy should be used to amplify Helewise's air poisoning spell.

Used to kill entire species.

Emmeline had obtained far too much influence among the

elders. He repressed a tremble and began to understand perhaps why Laurence didn't like talking about his past. Apparently Remy didn't either.

"Were they cruel to you?" Laurence asked, his voice soft.

"Not all of them and not often. It was more a constant low-level disapproval. Never right. Never enough. Cast from one to another so I was never one witch's problem for too long."

"I'm glad you left them."

"I'd very little choice. I won't be a tool for slaughter." Remy stared at Laurence's broad back as the trail led upward. The twittering of nightjars sounded from treetops below. "And what of you? How did you end up at Dagna's fighting alongside werewolves?"

Laurence took a deep breath and let it out through his nose. "When our rulers, The Dozen, chose a side in the conflict, they wanted a swift end to the war. Sending a vampire to each wolf pack would help ensure that victory. We're stronger and not as susceptible to spellwork."

"Why you? And why the frontline?"

"I've spent many years serving as a messenger between the species. That's why I know these routes so well. My service is not yet complete. They can send me where they wish. I don't know why Dagna's pack, but I also didn't care. One wolf pack is just as irritating as another."

Remy chuckled. "You don't care for werewolves?"

Laurence glanced at him from over his shoulder. "Not particularly, no. I can't imagine you do either after your experience." Laurence motioned to Remy's side.

"I won't hold that against them. Our species are at war. I expected to be attacked. What I hadn't counted on was being rescued."

Laurence had no reply, so Remy continued, "And what of your service, what does that entail?"

"Enough questions for now, please. We're almost to the summit. You will like the view, and it's time you should eat."

Remy's stomach rumbled on cue. Though he was dying to know more about vampire culture and whatever Laurence meant by "his service," he'd been surprised to get as many answers as he did. Perhaps he could bring it up again another time. For now, he was ready for a break and to eat the quail Laurence had caught for him earlier that evening.

The vampire hadn't lied about the view. As Remy crested the last of the rocky steps to a massive granite slab, shrubs gave way to scattered clouds and miles of rolling hillside under the starlight. The staggering scale drew a gasp from Remy, followed by an indulgent smile from Laurence.

"I knew you'd like it," the vampire crooned, grinning wide enough Remy could see the sharp points of his fangs.

Remy wasn't sure which he preferred, the stunning view, or the rare glimpse of carefree happiness from Laurence. He stopped to admire the vampire's wide smile, the crinkles that formed at the corners of his eyes, the shining gray of his irises.

Upon reflection, Laurence definitely outshined the view.

Supper on the summit of a mountain held a certain majesty a regular meal did not. Especially after climbing the damn thing. Remy gobbled down the quail and guzzled enough water he'd need multiple breaks before sunrise, but he couldn't be bothered. The moment was too splendid for worry. What must this mountaintop look like in the light of day if it was such a sight in the moonlight?

"Laurence." He glanced to the vampire seated next to him, who'd been content to stargaze as Remy ate. "Do you ever miss the sunshine?"

Laurence's eyes remained forward, focused on something out in the distance. "I hardly remember it."

"How old are you?" Remy had asked this once before, and Laurence had dodged, but the mood was different now.

Laurence caught his eyes, narrowing his own.

"You don't have to tell me," Remy backtracked under the intensity of his gaze.

"I'm aware I don't, but thank you for letting me know." The words were blunt, but Laurence's tone remained light. Teasing.

"It's impossible not to be curious."

"You're curious about a lot of things."

"Is that bad?"

"It could get you into trouble."

"Not with you mother-henning me as you do."

"Mother-henning?" Laurence asked, incredulous.

Remy chuckled. "Have you eaten enough? Is your side all right? You need a rest. Let me help you with the salve. You should eat something," he teased. "You're worse than my grandmother."

"I'm older than your grandmother."

Remy thought about that. He really hadn't been able to guess at Laurence's age. He appeared in his prime, a man of perhaps forty years, but appearance meant nothing in a vampire.

"One hundred and thirty come October," said Laurence into the silence that yawned between them. "If I've counted correctly."

Delighted to have gotten a straight answer, Remy grinned. "You *are* older than my grandmother!"

Laurence smiled back. "Old enough to have been her grandfather I should say, though not so old for one of my kind." He stood. "Come, you've finished. Let's continue to Livia's. It should only be a few more hours."

Remy rose, packed, and settled in his familiar position trailing behind Laurence as the mountain sloped downward. He stared at the vampire's broad back until he tripped over loose rock and nearly tumbled. After that, he concentrated on his footing until the steep grade lessened and the ground flattened out. They hiked in companionable silence for miles, Remy lost in thought.

"We're nearly there," said Laurence, breaking Remy from his reverie.

They'd just passed through a charming human village and its surrounding farms. The pungent scent of livestock lingered in the breeze. Livia lived startlingly close to it in a charming cottage built into a hillside.

Remy had gone from feeling quite tired to unnaturally awake. His nerves tingled as they approached. He sensed several vampires inside. Laurence had only mentioned Livia. He drew closer to Laurence, both wary and excited to meet others.

The front door opened before they'd reached the yellow wooden fence surrounding the property. Laurence let them through the gate, seemingly unconcerned by a male vampire headed their way. The man was shorter, like Remy, but more broadly built with carrot-orange tresses and an icy blue glare.

"Who are you, and what is your business?" asked the man.

Laurence took a breath to answer as a woman emerged from the cottage and beat him to it.

"Laurence, dear!" she said, her voice warm and sweet like melted chocolate. At her greeting, the redhead stood aside and let Laurence approach but still held a glower for Remy.

"Liv," said Laurence, opening his arms.

Remy stayed where he was and watched.

Livia wore a simple dress of green velvet belted around a slim waistline and open at her ample bosom, revealing a line of cleavage just shy of indecent. Flowing chestnut waves gathered and tied over one shoulder hung to her ribcage. Her almond eyes lit up for Laurence, gazing up at him with a fondness that suggested more than friendship as she fell into his open arms.

When Livia tilted her head to be kissed, Laurence met her halfway. Remy's heart sank as their lips met. Laurence hadn't said anything about Livia being his lover. Of course, why should he have to? He owed Remy nothing, but even a hint of a warning would have been appreciated. Remy wanted to look away, but he couldn't tear his eyes from their reunion, even as his throat constricted and his breath shallowed.

Laurence stepped out of their embrace. Smiling, he turned to Remy and gestured for him to approach. "Liv, I've someone I'd like you to meet."

Her gaze fell on Remy like a hammer striking a nail—heavy and all at once. Fighting not to cower under the weight of her full attention, he walked by the redhead to stand before her.

Old.

No… Ancient.

Though unsure how he knew, Remy was certain nonetheless.

"Stregone," she whispered, but the word rang out loud and clear. The wind caught her curls and ruffled them in the breeze.

Laurence held his arm out for Remy to move closer, but he was frozen where he stood, awaiting her judgment.

"Remy, come," Laurence beckoned. "Livia, this is Remy, a friend. He is the witch who cast the arc and is under my protection."

Her eyes flitted back to Laurence before returning to Remy and softening somewhat. She held out both hands, palms up. "Vieni qui."

As if pulled by an invisible force, Remy stepped in and laid his hands in hers. More than ever, he wished for his magic, but he wouldn't call on the energy unless he had to. Her hands were cool under his as he slowly raised his gaze to meet her golden-brown eyes.

"Tell me, do you mean me harm?" asked Livia.

Remy studied her mouth as it formed the words, petite pink lips over teeth he knew could easily rip through an artery. Laurence had kissed her—she was his type. Feminine and beautiful with soft curves to hold and caress. He'd never compare.

But he did not wish her harm.

Laurence answered before Remy could find the words. "Of course not. I would never bring harm to your doorstep. Remy has risked his life to stop the killing on both sides. He needs protection."

Without letting go of Remy's hands, she spoke to Laurence. "I thought he had yours." Her lips curled into the slightest of smiles. Nothing like the expression she'd greeted him with, but more inviting than the look she'd cast on Remy.

"He does, but—"

"He needs mine," Livia finished with confidence, her gaze falling back to Remy as her smile broadened.

Remy found his courage. "I mean harm to no one."

"You don't," she said simply. Letting go of his hands, she took his shoulders gently and pulled him in. "Welcome, young one. I'm sorry to have frightened you."

Relief swelled in his chest, and tense muscles relaxed a fraction. He returned the embrace. He was a hair taller, but only just. Her waist felt fragile in his hands, but it was an illusion. This woman was carved from stone.

Livia released him, took his hand and tucked it into her elbow. "Come inside, we've much to discuss."

Laurence and the redhead followed behind them.

Inside, the cottage glowed under the light of oil sconces hung about the walls. Warm and inviting, her home smelled of magnolia blossoms. Livia led them to a sitting room with lush furniture arranged in a wide oval. Colorful quilts and afghans lay over the backs of chairs and settees, reminding Remy that despite the false burst of energy, he was tired. Suddenly he longed to curl up under a pile of them and sleep the day away.

Livia guided him to sit next to her on a lounge, and Laurence took the chair across.

"Conor, take Bertrand with you and leave us for the day

please," she ordered casually, her voice back to the sweet honeyed tone she'd used for Laurence.

"Yes, Liv," said Conor, the redhead, as he went deeper into the house, presumably to fetch Bertrand. A moment later he left with another man in tow, and the three of them were alone in her den.

"I'm taking Remy to Bran Vigny," said Laurence. "Can I count on you to help persuade The Dozen to see to his protection?"

Livia tipped her head in the barest of nods. "I'll be there."

"Thank you." Laurence's shoulders dropped a fraction with this news.

Remy was unsure what all of this meant, but he lacked options, and Livia's affection for Laurence had been genuine. He no longer sensed any hostility from her. They sat close, nearly touching. He felt he could lean into her space and she'd hold him, though he didn't know why.

"Laurence, dear, you haven't fed enough." As Livia spoke, she took Remy's hand and held it in her lap. "Go see to it, and let me get to know Remy for myself, please."

Though phrased politely, Remy understood it for what it was. An order. Laurence looked to him as if for permission. Remy mustered up a smile because Laurence seemed to like it when he smiled. He nodded his assent. He'd either be fine with Livia, or he wouldn't. He got the impression there was nothing Laurence could do if Livia decided to harm him, so they may as well be alone.

"Of course," said Laurence. "And thank you for the hospitality. I shall return soon."

With Laurence gone, Livia turned sideways on the lounge to face him. She toed off each shoe and tucked her feet beneath herself. "Please, Remy, make yourself comfortable. You are welcome here."

Remy followed her lead and removed his shoes so he could

face her as well. Though his nerves hadn't entirely settled, she now exuded a calming presence. So with effort, he slowed his breathing and relaxed his posture. Her silence left Remy to open the conversation.

"Have you and Laurence known each other long?"

Her eyes crinkled at the edges when she smiled. It only enhanced her beauty. "I suppose he would say so."

"And you wouldn't?"

Livia chuckled, low and sultry. "I wouldn't. I'm much older than Laurence, but you already knew that, didn't you?"

"I did. You're ten times older. At least." He couldn't help his curiosity. "Why do I know that?"

"Give me back your hand."

Remy did so. Livia flipped it over and studied his palm. This time he let the silence swell until she filled it.

"You are a special sort of stregone. You've yet to reach your full potential." Her gaze flicked from their hands to his eyes with cool intensity. Brown with golden flecks, enchanting. "You are the stuff of legends. Without even trying, you've guessed my age and know my power though I've taken precautions to mask it. Draw from me now, I'm offering."

Oh.

That's why she wanted them to touch, so he could glean the energy that radiated from her in waves. Remy opened the channel. Power flooded his system. Had he been standing, he'd have staggered. In his current position he only sank further into the soft cushions beneath him. His blood felt warmer in his veins, and his heart thumped wildly in his chest. A pleasant tingle vibrated along his skin.

"See?" Livia murmured, stroking the back of his hand.

"Yes," Remy sighed, so full he could build a second arc. He closed the channel and glanced up at her through dazed eyes. "Can you teach me to hide my magic? So that other witches cannot find me?"

Her elegant mouth dipped into a frown. "I cannot. I'm no magician myself. I'm sorry."

Remy shrugged one shoulder, pleasantly drunk off her power. "It was worth a try."

"Yes, it would fix your biggest problem, wouldn't it?"

"Not quite, but it would help."

"What can I do for you, young Remy, stuff of legends?"

Warm from the energy swirling in his system, Remy's inhibitions melted away. "I don't suppose Laurence has a brother that favors men you can introduce me to?"

Her laughter rang out like silver bells, tinkling in the air before dying away. "Oh dear, not you too? They all fall for Laurence."

Though Remy was jealous of Laurence's affection for this woman, he found he liked her anyway. "How long have you been together?"

"Laurence and I? Oh, darling, we're not together. You've misunderstood. Laurence has many lovers; he isn't one to stay around long."

That really wasn't any better. Many lovers, but not Remy.

"Don't look so sad. He fancies you too."

"He really doesn't though." Remy's eyelids began to droop.

"Before you fall asleep, what did you think of Conor? I could call him back to see to your needs. He'd be eager to play your bedfellow."

It was Remy's turn to laugh. "I'm afraid of him. Did you see the death stare he leveled at me when we arrived? My balls are hiding at the thought of it!"

"I tried." She gave him a playful wink. "Keep working on Laurence. Wear him down. He isn't as noble as he pretends."

"He wants you."

"And you," she insisted, but Remy couldn't believe it. Laurence had all the chances he needed and hadn't taken any of them. No, he would not stand between Laurence and this beautiful woman he so obviously favored.

"You are fading. Here, go to sleep. I'll fix you something to eat when you wake."

What was it with vampires and their constant need to feed him? Did they miss food that much? Remy lay back against the cushions, unable to do anything else.

Livia tucked him in with the blankets he'd been admiring. "May I kiss you goodnight?"

Remy grinned. "Someone should."

She leaned in and planted a tender kiss on his mouth. Her lips were even softer than he'd imagined. No amount of pretending it was Laurence would work, so he didn't. He kissed Livia back and shut his eyes.

"Thank you."

"Sweet dreams, stregone."

$\mathcal{U}$pon his return, Laurence found Remy sleeping soundly on the soft red cushions of Livia's settee. Nestled on his back amongst a throng of fluffy blankets, he looked at peace. Long delicate lashes fanned over freckled cheeks. Laurence crept closer on quiet feet, careful not to wake him, and swept a stray blond lock from across his forehead to behind his ear. When the little witch didn't stir, he bent down to press a kiss to his temple.

"Sweet dreams," Laurence whispered, reluctant to tear his eyes away.

He turned to find Livia watching with a warm smile across her ageless face. She leaned against the doorframe, arms crossed below her breast, and gave a small nod. "He's precious, that one."

Laurence could not agree more. "Thank you for looking out for him. He'll need all the friends he can get."

"Aye. If the world finds out what he can do, everyone will want a piece."

Laurence fought back a scowl. "His own elders have already tried."

"Pity." Livia pushed off the wall. "Come, we'll retire to the back of the house, and you can tell me the story."

Laurence hesitated. He glanced back to the pretty picture Remy made, asleep with his hands curled under his chin. "He's used to sleeping with me."

"Funny, that's not the impression I got," she said with a hint of a smirk.

"What do you mean?"

"Nothing at all," she cooed. "Only that he's exhausted. It would be a crime to wake him. Let him rest while we escape the sun."

Leaving the sleeping witch proved difficult, but Livia was right. Remy needed rest, and if he woke he could seek Laurence out then.

Livia beckoned. He followed her down the steps to the part of the house buried in the hillside, tucked safely away from the sun's harmful rays. The in-ground lair was a sprawling hallway of rooms. Livia enjoyed company and rarely had the house to herself. She could easily host a dozen vampires in these rooms, though when Laurence stayed here, he'd always slept in hers. Would she be offended if he didn't? Did he really want his own room when he could have the comforts she offered?

Livia made the decision for him, pushing open the door across from her own. "You may take the yellow room in case our dear Remy should wake and search for you."

Relieved, Laurence nodded his thanks.

"But for now, come to mine." She swept open her own door and stepped inside. "I'd like the tale of how you came to be protector of a young male witch, Laurence, and I shall need you to start from the beginning." Livia twirled, presenting him with her back, and lifted her hair from her neck.

Laurence fell into the habit of unlacing her gown without much thought. Pulling the ribbons through the eyelets, he revealed the elegant curve of her spine. He'd known Livia nearly a century. She'd been there for him when he'd had a violent falling out with his own maker and through times of trouble thereafter.

"Thank you, dear. Please, make yourself comfortable and do get started. We don't have all night."

There was no avoiding it, he'd have to give her the details if he expected her help. While he didn't mind sharing the story with her, Livia's keen perception was second to none. If she hadn't sussed his inappropriate feelings for the youth already, she surely would after the telling. He didn't want her to think less of him as a result.

Laurence took off his boots and hung his outer clothes on a hook behind the door. Livia traded her dress for a lace sleeping gown. She climbed into her feather bed and threw back the cover for Laurence. He settled next to her, arm around her shoulders as she lay against his chest. Her familiar sweet scent of magnolia flowers soothed his nerves.

"I'm waiting," Livia reminded him, a hint of impatience in her low tone.

With a deep breath, Laurence relayed the tale. He left nothing out, from the impossibly daring creation of the arc, to the wolf who'd attacked Remy and their desperate race through the forest to get to the healer in time. He told her of Remy's magic, how he could siphon energy and move invisible particles with enough force to hold back a pack of angry wolves.

As the story unfolded, she melted against him, a familiar weight. The curve of her back felt lovely under his palm.

Laurence spoke uninterrupted until his tale ended with their arrival on her doorstep. "Remy will need you as an advocate if The Dozen are to be persuaded to protect him."

"Have you thought this through?" she asked, her voice laced with caution.

"Repeatedly, but what do you mean?"

"If they understand even an inkling of his power, they will seek to use it to their own ends."

"I know, but how can it be avoided?" Laurence had tossed this dilemma over in his mind ad nauseam. "With The Dozen, at least he will have choices. If his elders capture him, he'll fare far worse."

She ran a fingertip down his sternum. "Let me think on it."

"Please do." Arching into the touch, Laurence tightened his hold on her waist. He knew Livia to be a playful and generous lover. After nights of tension spent resisting Remy's charms, he found her near to irresistible. And that wasn't fair to her.

"Liv…" he began, but nothing followed. Torn between desire to bed her, and restraint as Remy lay sleeping upstairs, he let out a frustrated huff.

"You've got it bad for him?" Livia murmured against his ear.

"I don't," he lied, even knowing the attempt at deception was useless.

She leaned back and looked him directly in the eyes. "He adores you, you know."

"He doesn't." Laurence forced himself to meet her assessing stare. "It's youthful infatuation, nothing more."

"It could be more." Her knowing gaze never faltered. "If you let it."

"You know me better than that." He blinked, offended. "I won't take advantage of him."

She drew her brows together. "How could you? You cannot *take* what he offers freely. Eagerly, if we're being honest."

Though she may have a point, Laurence wasn't ready to concede. "He's too young."

"By that logic, you're too young for me," Livia pointed out. When Laurence made to interrupt, she stopped him with a finger on his lips. "Remy is a man full grown who's taken his life into his own hands and risked it to save others. Don't sell him short. You can trust him to know his own heart."

Laurence shook his head. She removed her finger. "I won't be responsible for breaking it."

"Then don't."

"Liv—"

The finger returned. "You've fooled yourself into underestimating him, but I can see you won't be swayed easily. Perhaps me then, if you won't allow yourself to have him." She trailed her fingertip from his lips, down his throat, and under his shirt to stroke a nipple to attention.

The touch sizzled a line of heat to his groin. Laurence let his head fall back to the sheets. Was he really underestimating Remy? He thought so highly of the witch, it seemed doubtful, but Livia often had the right of things. He knew Remy wanted him, but surely he'd want too much. Grow too attached. And when Laurence felt the inevitable itch to move on, it would be Remy who'd end up hurt.

That, he couldn't risk. Better to resist and spare Remy's feelings.

As he reflected on his situation with the witch, Livia's hand crept lower, over his abdomen and to the growing bulge in his trousers. She wrapped her fingers around his shaft over his smallclothes and tugged gently.

Laurence moaned.

Livia could tease out the most incredible sensations with those talented fingers. With her mouth. His breath quickened at the memories, but his mind stubbornly fixed on Remy, asleep in the other room.

She gave a little twist of her wrist and massaged the sensitive glans.

Moaning, he bit his cheek to cut off the sound.

"Shh," she whispered with a warm chuckle, but he couldn't keep the groans from his throat.

"It's been a while," he murmured, hips rising to her touch.

"I'll quiet that mouth of yours." Her kiss was a cool burn of promise, a seductive beginning to what Laurence knew could be an explosion of passion.

He kissed her back. His body ached for this, but his heart wasn't in it.

With a giggle, Livia nipped his bottom lip sharply, drawing a round bead of blood and a yelp from Laurence. The coppery aroma filled the air.

She licked it away and sat back, removing her hand from his cock to give his knee a knowing pat. Laurence loved her for it. She always read him clearly.

"I'm sorry," he sighed. "I just can't."

"I know. It's all right." Livia's mouth curved into a full beguiling smile. "Perhaps you've learned something tonight, then?"

"Perhaps I have." He leaned in and dropped a kiss on her forehead before getting up to go to his own room.

If Remy woke, he wanted to be available to hold him. He'd grown accustomed to the little witch warming his side, and though he loved Livia, it was Remy he craved.

8

Though Remy's heartbeat pounded loudly in his chest, the noise wasn't enough to drown out the moaning coming from somewhere farther in the house. The unmistakable sound of people kissing followed, then Laurence gave a cry of pleasure. Remy's heart was a tight, heavy thing threatening to sink from his chest to his gut if he heard any more.

Intellectually, it was one thing to know that Laurence had a lover.

Realistically, it was another to listen as he fucked her.

Remy grabbed his shoes and satchel before sneaking out of the house on socked feet. Once outside the gate, he laced up his boots, shouldered the pack, and took off as if the cottage were on fire. In a burst of reckless energy, he ran toward the rising sun, putting as much distance as he could between himself and Laurence without using his magic. He'd come back later, when he was sure enough time had passed they'd be done.

When his lungs threatened to burst, Remy collapsed amidst a copse of evergreens, huffing and puffing to catch his breath. The scent of pine needles wafted in the breeze. Leaning against the trunk of a behemoth, he watched the sun's rays creep along the forest floor. He'd missed daylight. As the air warmed, he told himself to calm down. He'd known Laurence wasn't interested in him. That he was interested in Livia shouldn't have been so shocking. The woman was gorgeous; even Remy could see that, though his attraction had never veered toward women. He would not begrudge them their time together no matter how much it hurt.

With a deep breath, he scanned his surroundings and willed himself to regain control. His stomach rumbled. This was the perfect opportunity to put Laurence's lessons to use. If he could hunt and cook his own meal without magic, he'd be one step closer to independence.

Remy pursed his lips, closed his eyes in concentration, and listened. A gentle breeze ruffled the leaves in the trees, birds called their morning songs, insects crawled amongst the scattered pine needles...and rabbits stirred in their warrens. Remy grinned. He'd pinpointed their location just as Laurence did when he hunted. But Remy couldn't punch his fist through the earth like the vampire, so he'd have to be clever to get them to come out on their own.

Making a little camp for himself, he spread the blanket and cleared a spot for a fire. Once a small blaze burned, he lit the bundle of twigs he'd fastened together and brought it to one end of the burrow. He blew out the flames and tucked the smoking sticks inside, then with his pack he fanned the smoke farther into their tunnel.

On tiptoe he crept to the other side and waited, poised to strike. Listening carefully, he heard their little hearts beating faster as the smoke incited panic.

When the first rabbit to flee the warren emerged from the burrow, Remy snatched it up with a howl of victory. With the struggling bunny flailing in his grip, he dreaded the next part. Steeling himself for the kill, Remy shut his eyes tight and flinched as he thrashed the rabbit to break its neck. Laurence had made this part sound easy but following through proved difficult.

At last, the bunny hung limp in his grip. Somewhere between sadness and triumph, Remy returned to the fire to cook his meal. Killing for food with his magic was far less personal than killing with his bare hands, but the need to feed himself trumped any squeamishness in the end.

After eating, Remy put out the fire, shouldered his pack and continued his walk. Trekking with the sunshine warm on his shoulders made for a welcome change. Thoughts of Laurence came and went as he wandered from the towering pines into hardwoods. He hadn't asked Laurence what would happen after he'd escorted Remy to the ruling class of vampires. If they offered sanctuary, what would come next? Would Laurence leave him? Surely he wouldn't be sent back to Dagna's pack after what had happened. Was it even up to Laurence? If Remy knew more about what "service" entailed, he may have a better idea of the possible outcomes, but Laurence dodged his questions.

Would there be a place for Remy amongst vampires? He'd spent a lifetime with plaguing curiosity about the species, but now that he was about to be immersed in their culture, found himself hesitant.

Worry niggled at the back of his mind as the day progressed. The more tired he became, the stronger his anxiety grew until he was nothing more than a heap of raw nerves eager for the escape of sleep. Finding a shady spot beneath the canopy of a massive white oak, he fluffed the dense layer of old leaves and settled into them for a rest. He'd return to Livia's before nightfall. He swept the leaves over him, covering himself as protection from the afternoon sun. He'd little more than closed his eyes when sleep stole him away.

Arriving at his grandmother's home for the summer made Remy's heart swell. His eyes roamed the gray stone cottage with gardens spilling from the front steps and out in both directions. Flowering plants thrived under Evanora's care, as did Remy. He treasured his time with her more than anything.

With a warm smile across her face and a faded purple apron tucked neatly round her waist, Evanora appeared at the doorway to welcome him home.

"Remigius, doll baby, don't just stand there, come and give me a hug!" Her voice rang out clear and joyful, putting a grin on Remy's face. He ran to her and held tight.

"It's so good to see you, Gran." He savored a deep breath of her comforting scent. She smelled of baking today, cinnamon and sugar, but underneath, always of roses. She used the flower to make soaps, and thus her clothes and skin smelled pleasantly of flower petals. Roses would always remind him of Evanora.

"It's good to see you too." She held him at arms-length and studied his face. Remy gazed into eyes so like his own, caramel brown and full of curiosity. Her lovely silver hair curled close to her head, the short length framing her round face. "How have you been?"

"Well, thank you, and now I'm even better. Have you made cinnamon rolls?"

"Of course I have, they're your favorite. Shall we have them for dinner?

Cinnamon rolls for dinner? His grandmother was sweet as an angel, but such decadence turned her place into an actual paradise. He couldn't agree fast enough.

After he'd carried his things to his room and had a wash, they sat down to an early dinner complete with blackberry tea. All of Remy's worries and stress from his lessons with the elders melted like the frosting as it hit his tongue with its familiar burst of sweetness. Muscles unclenched, his shoulders relaxed, and the permanent smile he wore every summer at Evanora's settled in.

Remy polished off three rolls with ease and reached for another.

Evanora laughed. "Don't the elders feed you kids anymore? Why do you always come to me starving each year? Twelve-year-old boys need to eat."

Her words were in jest, and yet Remy did feel starved. Not for food, of course, they provided that, but for the love and attention only his grandmother seemed to spare for him.

"I wish I could live here."

"That would be lovely," she agreed. "I enjoy our time together tremendously, but your lessons are too important. You must learn as witches have before you, and as your children will after."

A pang flared in Remy's gut at her words. "Would you be very disappointed if I didn't have children?"

Evanora sat her tea down, giving him a serious look. Remy tensed a bit as he awaited her answer. She studied him carefully. "I'm proud of you, doll baby."

The sound of her nickname for him along with her kind words soothed Remy, though he didn't miss that she hadn't answered yet.

"Nothing you do could disappoint me, but you're very young to have decided not to have children. Are you sure?"

Remy nodded. "Quite."

Evanora tilted her chin, her gaze gentle but assessing. Then she raised her tea glass as if to toast. "A life free from crying babes and soiled diapers. I always knew you were the smart one in the family."

Remy sighed in relief. He hadn't told anyone of his preference for boys, but he would tell his grandmother if she pressed. Though he was glad she didn't. He hadn't known long himself and wanted to live with the idea a while before sharing it.

Sunny summer days and warm summer nights flew by when they were together. Remy spent his time learning to tend the garden, pulling weeds and harvesting plants by hand instead of magic because Evanora insisted the labor was good for them. Remy thought so too. Watching her cook dinner from the fresh chard and peppers they'd picked that morning had its own kind of magic. And the meals they shared tasted better than anything the kitchen witches fixed for them at the Elder Village.

Time passed as fast as lily blossoms could bloom and wilt, and before long, Remy began to dread leaving. He kept it from Evanora as much as he could, but she knew. Late one evening as the moon bugs lit yellow sparks across the yard, Remy and Evanora sat side by side on her patio. He practiced his more difficult spells as she guided him.

"Yes, good. Look there, you've moved it!" she praised while Remy concentrated on shifting a boulder at the edge of her acreage.

With his hand extended, he gave a push and the big rock tumbled backward. He let out a yip of triumph.

Evanora breathed a warm laugh. "Excellent. Now, move it back."

Remy's brows knitted together in concentration. He tugged with his outstretched hand and with his mind.

Nothing happened.

"Easy," Evanora said gently, "it's not a test of your will or strength. It's a question of your harmony with the Earth's energy."

Relaxing the muscles in his face, Remy took a breath and tried again. Instead of focusing on pulling, he simply directed the energy around the boulder to lift it and bring it forward. Like manipulating the current in a pool of water, once in motion the movement felt effortless. The boulder drifted, heavy and weightless at once, until it hovered before them.

"You're quite the overachiever, Remigius. Shall we put it back together?"

"I've got it." Remy directed the boulder back to its resting place and set it down with hardly a thump. A sly glance to Evanora confirmed her delight with his efforts. His chest warmed...until he remembered once more that summer was fading, and he'd have to leave soon. He deflated at the thought.

Before he could say as much, Evanora stiffened beside him. Remy startled and reached for her to help but didn't know what he should do. Her body had gone rigid. She sat straight and tense, frozen in place, her unblinking eyes wide with second sight.

A vision?

Remy knew she'd had them, but he'd never known what it looked like. His hands rested on her shoulder and forearm, ready to support her if needed, but he had the sense the only thing to do was wait.

Evanora shook gently. A slight tremor rose from her core and vibrated to her extremities. Her chin tipped back as if she sought to stare at the sky, but her eyes remained dreadfully unseeing. Remy slid his arm behind her back, bracing her for...what? He didn't know.

As fear threatened to overwhelm him, a shocked sound escaped her lips. Her eyes fluttered closed.

"Gran?" Remy leaned in, unsure how to help.

She took his hand in hers. "Give me a moment."

Remy gazed at their entwined fingers. Her soft flesh wrinkled with age while his remained firm and smooth.

She took deep breaths, rolled her shoulders, and opened her eyes. Her gaze met Remy's. She lifted her hand to his cheek.

"Are you all right?" asked Remy.

"Perfectly fine, you brave, strong witch." Her grin broadened to a smile. She gave his cheek a fond pat then let him go.

Remy did not feel brave. He'd been terrified. "What did you see?"

Her jaw tightened. "Visions are hardly foolproof and should only be shared with the utmost of caution. These details, I think I should keep to myself. But Remy dear, if there comes a time in your life when you must risk everything for what you believe is right, know that you're not alone. When you need me, I'll stand with you."

"Gran—"

"That's all I have to say on the matter. Now, for something truly important..."

Remy sat on the edge of his seat. "What?"

With a twinkle in her eyes, Evanora said, "Shall we eat the last of the honeyed almonds before bed?"

9

Throat clenched in panic, Laurence couldn't form words. Remy was gone. His things were missing. His scent had vanished to almost nothing. It must have been hours since he'd left, and Laurence had slept the day away as if all were well.

"We'll find him," said Livia with a hand to his shoulder.

Laurence shook her off and grabbed his boots. "*I'll* find him. You stay here in case he comes back."

"All right, but please, don't worry—"

"Don't tell me not to worry!" He tugged on his shoes and laced them hurriedly. "He's all alone. And for some godforsaken reason, you chose to live near the Marshland Pack's territory."

"They give me a wide berth, and Remy couldn't have gone far."

That first part may have been true, but the second part wasn't. If Remy wanted to, he could be hundreds of miles away by now.

"I'm going." Laurence headed for the door.

"Should I expect you back, or must you continue straightaway on your journey?"

He paused. "I don't know. I can't think."

"All right. Take this." She handed him a purse full of coin. "Fare well, dear. You'll have my help when you need it."

"Thank you." Laurence pocketed the money and left to follow the dwindling scent trail as fast as his preternatural speed would let him. He raced into the surrounding pine forest and uphill, all the while cursing himself for ever letting Remy out of his sight.

The witch was naive to the world outside his village. He wouldn't make it long on his own without his magic. Surely he wouldn't risk using his powers. Why would he leave the protection of Livia's cottage?

Not much farther, the aroma of smoked meat lingered in the air. Spotting the remnants of a campfire, Laurence sniffed, sorting through various smells until he'd homed in on Remy's. Traces of his scent blazed a tingling path from his nose straight to his gut. A neat pile of discarded bones indicated Remy had caught his own rabbit and built a cooking fire, though the ashes had long since grown cold.

If Laurence weren't worried sick, he'd be proud, but there was no time to dwell on the witch's accomplishments. He dashed past the makeshift camp onward through evergreens and into an old-growth deciduous forest where pine needles gave way to broad leaves. Scanning the area, his eyes found no clues, but his nose remained on the trail. The witch's scent grew stronger as Laurence ran, covering Remy's footsteps with powerful strides.

Thoughts of the Marshland Pack discovering the witch before he could invaded his mind. They could tear him to pieces. They'd enjoy it. But Remy would use his spells to protect himself in an emergency, wouldn't he?

Remy's scent grew stronger. Narrowing in on his location, Laurence's gaze swept over the copse of trees until he discovered a telltale pile of disturbed leaves. If his heart still beat, it would be racing. He lunged for the pile, muscles tense as he flung the leaves out of his way.

Remy appeared beneath them, and Laurence couldn't stop himself. He grabbed the witch by the shoulders and lifted him, holding him close.

"What?" Remy startled, sputtering, body rigid in his grasp. Laurence only pressed him tighter to his chest.

"Laurence?" His voice came out muffled and confused. "What are you doing here?"

Nose in Remy's hair, breathing deeply, Laurence allowed himself to relax a fraction. "Are you all right?"

"Course I'm all right." Remy pushed back. Their eyes met. "What's wrong with you?"

Letting him go, Laurence stood. Worry receded and anger took its place. "What's wrong with *me*? You disappear in the middle of enemy territory and have the nerve to ask what's wrong with me?"

Remy stared up at him, eyes taking on a defiant sheen. "Enemy territory? But Livia—"

"Livia does not rule these lands!" Laurence gestured wildly to the forest surrounding them. "The Marshland Pack do, and if you think they wouldn't kill you on sight, that would be your last mistake. Dagna's pack are sweet cakes compared to Marshland's. How foolish could you be?"

Remy cringed. "I didn't know—"

"Right, you didn't," Laurence raged. "Which begs the question, why would you leave without me? The world isn't safe. You might have been slaughtered!"

"Stop yelling," Remy pleaded.

Fuming, Laurence took a step back. He'd been terrified of finding Remy hurt or dead, and now he felt like killing the little witch himself. How dare he? After all Laurence had done to protect him, why would he risk himself? For what? A whim? "Why did you leave?"

Amber eyes wide, Remy shouted back, "I could hear you! Did you want me to listen?"

"Hear what?" But as soon as the question left his lips, Laurence realized what Remy meant.

"I know you aren't interested in me that way, but that doesn't mean you can expect me to stay put while you fuck someone else. That isn't a fair thing to ask."

Remy's clenched jaw and intense stare proved too much for Laurence. He averted his eyes. The knowledge that Remy'd heard him with Livia bounced around his brain, an uncomfortable thought.

Remy exhaled. "It wasn't my intention to worry you. I'd meant to return before nightfall, but as you can see, I fell asleep."

"You could have been killed over nothing," Laurence murmured, the fight seeping out of him.

"It didn't sound like nothing," Remy sniped.

Laurence met his gaze. "You must have left right away. We didn't continue. I excused myself and slept in my own room." *I would not hurt you like that.*

Remy's brows knitted together, and it would have been comical if this weren't so serious. Laurence itched to pick the leaves from his hair, but Remy would not welcome his touch just now.

"I thought…" His voice came quiet, hesitant. Remy shuffled to stand, trailing bits of twigs and leaves along with him. He brushed them off. "I thought you and her…"

When Remy didn't finish, Laurence explained, "We've been lovers in the past, but I didn't sleep with her last night."

"Oh." Remy's mouth framed the word and paused like that. His gaze not quite meeting Laurence's, but instead focused somewhere over his shoulder. "But, why not?"

That question required a complicated answer, and not one Laurence could form with ease, even in his own mind.

Remy is a man full grown Livia had said, but Laurence hadn't really thought of him as such. The witch was his charge—vulnerable on enemy soil—and needed his protection, but also…a man full grown, who Laurence should trust to know his own desires. And whom Laurence desired in return.

"I thought you might wake." Laurence took a step closer. "I wanted to be available if you needed me." Not the entire truth, but enough.

Remy's shoulders sank slightly. He'd been hoping for a different answer.

Laurence sighed and tried to relax his posture. He felt bad for shouting. Remy had not deserved such treatment. Tentatively, he filled the silence. "Well, despite all odds, you seem to be all right."

Remy nodded. "Yes, I'm fine."

"Good." Laurence stepped back. "No harm done, then."

Finally meeting his eyes, Remy said, "I'm sorry to have worried you."

Some of the tension Laurence had been holding in his shoulders released at the words. "I'm sorry I upset you."

Silence yawned between them. A coyote's howl echoed through the hills. Remy wiped the sleep from his eyes and stretched.

"I saw you caught your own supper," Laurence offered.

A little closed-mouth grin curled the corners of his lips. "I did, thanks to your lessons."

"Well done."

"It was delicious." Remy gathered his things and shouldered his pack. "What now? Back to Livia's?"

"No, she's already agreed to help. We can continue on our way. We'll need to be careful, and to pick up our pace for the next few days."

"Why?"

"The Marshland Wolves. We are skirting their borders. They are a hostile pack and won't take kindly to finding us in their territory."

Remy began to walk. "How do you know them?"

Laurence fell in step, and they made their way through the trees. "Only in my capacity as messenger, but they won't welcome my presence uninvited."

"So we try to pass through undetected?"

"Right."

Forging ahead with Remy at his side now felt familiar. In the past, he'd always been alone on these trails and could move much quicker. Remy's presence demanded a slower pace. Laurence found himself enjoying the change. With more time to take in the scenery, he noticed different things: the lush greenery of sprawling ferns as they cascaded down the hillside, old trees bent ages ago by man to mark the way, an army of frogs calling at every lowland. Normally, he'd blaze by so fast he'd miss the forest's majesty.

Observing Remy as the witch noticed these small miracles became its own pleasure. Remy's face hid nothing of the wonder he experienced. His bright, curious gaze missed little as they scanned the surroundings.

Those caramel eyes flashed to Laurence, shining in their brilliance as Remy drew breath to say something. Laurence found himself holding his in anticipation.

"I had the most wonderful dream," said Remy, his clear voice filled with joy. "Would you like to hear it?"

In that moment Laurence could think of nothing he'd like better. "Tell me."

Listening to Remy speak of summers with his grandmother made Laurence remember the time before he'd become a vampire. Warm sunny mornings spent tending the garden, and late evening suppers with his wife after a hard day's labor. It wasn't often he let his thoughts wander that direction. Normally too painful, but only the good memories drifted through his mind as the witch spoke.

"Did she ever tell you more from the vision she had that day?" asked Laurence when Remy finished his tale.

"She never did, though I've always been curious." Remy had a tendency to slow his pace when deep in thought. He strolled lazily, gazing sideways at Laurence. "You think she foresaw the arc?"

Laurence gave a nod. "I do. And I wonder what else."

"Me too," Remy murmured.

They tromped along under the cacophony of midnight forest sounds; crickets, nightjars, leaves crunching underfoot. Laurence's thoughts circled back to his past. Remy had shared so much during their time together, but Laurence—almost nothing. He let out a deep breath and began.

"I was married once…before I was turned."

Remy stopped in his tracks. Laurence chuckled and continued walking. Remy had to scurry to catch up. "Sorry, you were saying?"

"Her name was Hannah. She had hair like yours, but that is where the similarity ends," said Laurence, the laughter still in his voice. "She was at peace on our small farm and satisfied to do the same chores day in and day out. Hannah made things simple. Easy."

"You must miss her," said Remy carefully.

He should, shouldn't he? But he didn't. Those times were another life, long evicted from his emotions. She didn't deserve what happened to her. Someone should miss her. The old guilt crept out from its hiding place and made itself at home in his gut. "She was murdered."

A startled gasp escaped Remy's throat. "What happened?"

Laurence had known Remy would ask. When he started the story, he'd intended to tell it all, but reluctance flared.

The witch picked up on his hesitancy. "That is, if you want to tell me. I'll understand if you'd rather not talk about it."

Steeling himself, Laurence forced the words out. "The one who made me, my sire, he killed her, though I didn't know at the time. I found her dead in our chicken coop. She'd gone out before dawn to gather eggs for breakfast. When she didn't return, I went searching. Her lips and fingers were blue."

Remy reached out and took his hand, palm warm against Laurence's. "I'm so sorry."

Laurence shrugged and gave the hand in his a gentle squeeze. "It was a long time ago. I didn't know what happened. The town doctor thought I'd done it. Strangled her. I thought maybe she'd suffered an attack of the heart. But I was the only one there, you see. So, when word spread to her family, to the rest of the town, I had to flee. They all thought I'd killed her."

"Oh, Laurence…"

He hadn't told this story to anyone in nearly seventy-five years, but somehow, he kept going. "I lost everything. My wife, my home, my work, the farm. All of it. It's what he wanted."

When Laurence didn't continue, Remy asked, "Who was he?"

Their gazes locked. "My sire's name is Valeri."

Remy's mouth hung open. "But why did he do it? If he cared enough to make you a vampire, why would he want you miserable?"

"Oh, he didn't want me miserable." Laurence let out a pathetic laugh. "Not really. At least not for long."

"I don't understand."

"You must excuse me; it's been so long since I've told this story. I haven't told it in order. When Hannah died, I'd never met Valeri. If I'd seen him in a crowd, he'd have been a stranger, and I'd look right past him. But he knew me. He'd been stalking me from afar. Valeri wanted a companion, and when he chose me, he simply destroyed everything that stood in his way."

The next words were bitter on his tongue. "Valeri stole my life so he could take me for himself. He swooped in and played the rescuer. Turned my miserable world upside down. Gave me something to live for again."

Remy gave a slow nod. "I see. You'd have never agreed to join him otherwise. You'd have been loyal to Hannah."

"Yes, you've got the right of it."

"How did you find out what he'd done?"

"I didn't at first. Not for years. In the beginning, he was enamored with me. Devoted. He treated me like a prince. Life with Valeri was a dramatic change from life on the farm. I went from worrying if the food would hold out all winter to having every luxury I could think of at my fingertips. But the scales eventually fell from my eyes. He saw me as little more than a possession. In the end, he confessed his sins all on his own, so convinced of my reliance on him that he thought nothing would stand between us. I'll never forgive him for what he did to Hannah. To me. I escaped the first chance I could. Livia helped me get away."

Remy squeezed his hand. Laurence squeezed back. Their footsteps were the only sound. Laurence's heavy and sure. Remy's a pitter-patter next to him.

"I am glad you have Livia," said Remy with a hint of sadness.

"She is a good friend. And now, so are you," said Laurence, grateful the witch hadn't prodded with more questions. The tale had taken something out of him, and the telling of it had turned the mood solemn. But he welcomed Remy's comforting presence, and the smaller hand in his own.

"Thank you for sharing this with me."

Laurence nodded. As they walked, the mood lightened. It felt good to have taken Remy into his confidence. The trail sloped gently through the ruins of old homesteads. Unkept stone walls crumbled back to the earth.

"There is an old grain silo not too far ahead," said Laurence. "It's abandoned. We can rest there for the day."

"Lead the way," said Remy.

With hands still joined, they made for the cluster of overgrown crop fields. Laurence had never seen Marshland Pack patrol this section. They should be safe for the day.

10

If Remy thought sleeping in ancient mausoleums had been vexing, then the abandoned grain silo was the fodder of nightmares. He'd never been so glad to leave a place.

Eerie echoes bounced off the round walls when they spoke. The stale air reeked of mold and decay. As they slept, an afternoon storm had rolled in. A sharp clap of thunder startled Remy awake. Fierce winds battered the structure. When hail began pounding the metal roof with such ferocity the entire silo threatened to collapse, Remy had burrowed deeper into Laurence's side beneath their blankets.

The vampire held him until the storm subsided, but Remy hadn't been able to fall back to sleep. Thankful to be on the road, he hoped to never see that place again. A yawn overtook him as they walked.

He glanced at Laurence. "Do you think we could stop soon?"

Laurence scanned their surroundings. Remy followed his gaze. The trees there were the short and scraggly variety known to wetlands. They'd left the mighty oaks behind. Loons sang their melancholy notes into the wind.

"If we're quick about it." Laurence took the pack from his shoulder and led them off trail.

Dumping out what was left of the food, Remy frowned. Hard bread and nuts. He could catch something, or ask Laurence to, but the vampire was obviously wary of spending too much time there. With a sigh, he tore off a hunk of stale bread. It would have to do.

Remy sat with his back against a thin tree, swatting away bugs. They'd been tromping through the damp lowlands of Marshland Pack's territory. Laurence thought it less likely they'd run into patrolling wolves there along the more undesirable section of their lands. The marshy ground played host to numerous biting insects. Magic would keep them away, but Remy couldn't risk it. Instead he tucked his legs under himself and used one hand to eat, the other to shoo pests.

"How's your side?" asked Laurence.

"Fine." The wound no longer bothered him but for the faintest itch now and then. The soreness had faded, and the skin healed around the stitches. He'd need to have them out soon. "How are you feeling?"

"Fine," Laurence echoed. He remained standing, posture rigid, his whole presence radiating vigilance.

"Are you hungry?" Remy asked as he ate faster, shoveling a handful of nuts into his mouth.

"I can wait."

"But you are?"

"Some," admitted Laurence.

Remy tipped his chin, exposing his neck. "My offer stands." The need to contribute flared strong, but Remy would be fooling himself if he believed it was only that.

Gray eyes darkened to slate as Laurence's pupils dilated. The expression on his face sent a shiver rippling under Remy's skin. Energy sizzled between them. The vampire looked away.

"Thank you, but no." He pitched his rumbling baritone low, as if he didn't want to be overheard.

Remy searched his sprawling tendrils of awareness for signs of trouble and found nothing. He cocked his head to the side. "What is it?"

Laurence met his gaze, eyes shining with intensity. "Only a bad feeling. Don't fret."

Impossible not to when Laurence said something like that. Remy packed up the food. "I can wait too, then."

"You're certain?"

"Yes."

"I know you prefer to walk, but I think I should carry you. We'll make better time if I run. Maybe get out of pack lands before dawn."

Remy did prefer to walk, but whatever had Laurence worried was enough to gain his compliance. "All right. Give me your bag."

Laurence handed it over, and Remy shouldered both before climbing on his back. Arms wrapped round the vampire's chest, thighs squeezing his waist, Remy could think of worse concessions, though he hated to feel like a burden.

"Ready?" asked Laurence.

"Yes." Remy held on.

The vampire took off at a run, racing to the trail through the stunted treescape. Air rushed past Remy's ears, sweeping his hair back to tangle in the wind. He clung tight, his chest to Laurence's back, and watched the world pass by from over the vampire's shoulder. Once in a while his cheek would brush against Laurence's soft raven hair. It smelled of snowfall and sent a shiver down Remy's spine despite the warm night air.

They moved with such speed, trees and shrubs blurred. A sense of awe bloomed warm in Remy's chest. Laurence's breath remained calm though he sprinted fast as a racehorse. Vampires were incredible that way. An effort like this would tire Laurence out eventually, but not before Remy's muscles grew shaky from clinging to his back.

If only Remy could thank him properly, but he didn't have much to offer, and what he had offered, the vampire refused.

Laurence's confident stride beat a fast metronome along the forest floor, broken by the occasional leap over streams and roots. The bags rustled against Remy's back. Only the stars stood still.

An inkling of awareness tugged for Remy's attention. Probably nothing, but he followed it, casting his extra sense broadly and attempting to narrow his focus on the source. When he couldn't pinpoint a singular cause, a spike of anxiety rose from his gut. Remy stamped it down and concentrated.

Flickering hints of threat began to surround them. An ominous circle formed wide along their perimeter. Remy caught a trickle of ill intent with alarming clarity.

He stiffened. "Laurence!"

The vampire ground to a halt. "What is it?"

"An ambush."

Laurence looked left and right. He turned to check behind them. "How many?"

The oppressing silence of calm before a storm rose the small hairs on the back of Remy's neck. "Dozens."

"From where? How soon?"

"They have us surrounded. Minutes. Maybe less."

Laurence set Remy on his feet and faced him. "You cannot use your magic."

"I have to."

"You don't. I'll face them."

"Laurence—"

"Don't give in unless you are about to be harmed," said Laurence, his voice stern. "I can take more damage than you'd suspect. Do not use your magic to protect me, only to protect yourself if it becomes clear I cannot." Gray eyes lingered, wary, awaiting confirmation.

Remy clenched his jaw. "I won't let them hurt you."

"You must!" Laurence took his shoulders. "I can fight were-wolves, but not without taking hits. You'll need to hold back."

Remy could not promise that. "How can I help?"

Laurence took in their surroundings. Remy noted the flat land with no high ground to be had. Scattered trees, but not dense enough for cover. Rocky terrain.

"I'll need you out of the way," said Laurence. "In a tree. Come."

The likeliest of candidates stood taller than the others, but the trunk was no wider in circumference than a milk maid's bucket, the branches a skinny man's thigh.

Remy eyed it suspiciously. "Give me a boost?"

Cupping his hands, Laurence made a cradle for him to step in. Remy reached for the branch as the vampire lifted. He grabbed hold and hauled himself up. It felt sturdier than it looked, though he was not much higher than a man's head. At least his perch would give him a good view, and if he needed to intervene with magic, it would be simple from this vantage point.

"Hand me the knife," said Laurence.

Remy drew the skinning blade from the pack and passed it down. Laurence tucked it into his belt, his gaze flicking behind them. Remy heard it too. Animals galloping.

The wolves were closing in.

"Quick, toss up some rocks," said Remy. "I've good aim."

The vampire didn't argue, just chose a few hefty specimens and sent them up. Remy found the most secure position he could manage, rocks piled in his lap, one hand clinging to the trunk, the other ready with a rock.

"Stay put," said Laurence as pounding footsteps thundered from all sides.

"I will. Be careful!"

He wouldn't promise not to use his magic, though staying in the tree suited him fine. Panic edged along his senses, but instead of letting fear overwhelm him, Remy used it as fuel. He concentrated and gave what information he could.

"There are fewer than I thought. Fourteen. All in wolf form. The true alpha hangs behind. The leader is his second. A female. She comes from the north."

As Remy pointed, she burst into view, racing toward them with two others on her heels. A sleek brown wolf, packed with muscle, she flared her nostrils and snapped at the air, teeth clacking. Others filled in on all sides.

Laurence dropped into a fighting stance, knees bent and loose, arms up.

But the wolf didn't attack. She came to an abrupt stop as the pack surrounded them and shifted to her human form.

Confident, tall, and naked, she stood casually and looked Laurence up and down. Rust-brown hair hung to her waist but did little to cover her pert breasts or the twin set of muscular ridges covering her abdomen. "Vampire, you harbor an enemy."

"Stand down, wolf."

Her smile shone like a razor's edge in the moonlight. "You're in no position to give orders."

Laurence advanced on her. "The witch is not your enemy."

She stepped back but raised a brow. "That's not what Dagna's messenger said. We have you surrounded. Hand him over, and you can go free."

"I will not."

She lifted one shoulder in a casual shrug. "Have it your way." Lifting a hand, she signaled to the others. "You both die."

The wolves flanking her launched into the air.

Remy held his breath.

Laurence spun, plucked one from mid-flight, and flung him against the tree.

The branch under Remy shook with the impact. The wolf yelped and sank to the ground.

Remy held back; Laurence didn't need his help yet. The vampire grappled with the second wolf, but in seconds, the fight was won. The two injured wolves fled to nurse their wounds.

The female growled and shifted to join two more from the crowd. They attacked at once. Remy's heart clenched as their snarls echoed with fury. He gripped a rock with white fingers but didn't have a clear path to throw it.

With both hands, Laurence grabbed the first wolf and slung him against the second. The she-wolf bit deep into his shoulder and hung on. The vampire wailed.

The alpha wolf hung back and observed, his yellow eyes intensely focused. He watched Laurence fight as Remy watched him.

Laurence delivered a rib-cracking kick to a downed wolf trying to rise, then wrapped fingers round the foreleg of the she-wolf at his shoulder and yanked.

Bones crunched.

The wolf's jaws released, and she fell screeching to the ground. She hurried to right herself and slunk away with a pronounced limp.

Remy chucked a rock at an oncoming wolf. It hit square in the temple and the animal stumbled backward.

Another raced past and leapt for Laurence's back.

"Watch out!" cried Remy, but Laurence was already in motion. Spinning, he kicked. The heel of his boot knocked the wolf sideways, but the animal growled and leapt again.

Laurence ducked, pulled the knife from his belt, and nearly split the wolf's belly in two.

Blood poured from the wound and copper tinged the air with its heavy metallic scent. Laurence's gray eyes blackened to ebony as he switched deftly from defense to offense, lunging at the huge gray wolf that lingered on the sidelines.

The alpha.

The massive animal had been ready. Tight muscles uncoiled as he launched to meet Laurence, aiming for the throat.

The vampire threw an elbow in his way. With the other hand, he swiped the knife across his flanks.

Remy tore his eyes from the scene to catch another wolf preparing to join the fray. He chucked the next rock with all his might, bashing the animal's forehead. The wolf staggered back but did not go down. Remy threw another, hitting the same spot, and the wolf went still.

His eyes flit back to Laurence. While the vampire grappled with the alpha wolf, the female had found her feet and prowled close. She lingered just past Laurence, so Remy had no clear shot. Clever bitch.

The rest of the animals stood at the ready, bodies tense, teeth bared. Maybe five who could still fight. Remy fisted the last rock in tight fingers.

The alpha snarled, snaring Remy's attention. He watched in horror as the creature tore a chunk from Laurence's thigh.

Laurence collapsed with a cry.

The sound tore at Remy's heart. He gathered energy to attack with his magic, uncaring if it meant his fellow witches could trace him. He had to protect Laurence.

Preparing to cast the spell, he noticed a stalking wolf too late. The animal dug powerful hind legs into the dirt and leapt for the tree. Remy kicked, and missed.

A jaw full of massive teeth latched onto his pants at his calf, tearing the fabric but missing his flesh. Swiping claws dug trenches in the tree branch.

Remy thrust his free leg against the wolf's shoulder and shoved. The animal fell to the ground.

A booming rumble from the alpha demanded their attention. *Laurence!* Was Remy too late to help?

They battled in a bloody tangle of limbs, the wolf snarling,

Laurence still clinging to the blade. With no opening to use the weapon, the vampire resorted to wrestling the beast to the ground, desperately trying to avoid his wildly nipping jaw. Laurence couldn't take another bite.

Just as Remy began the spell again, the vampire rallied. He flung the wolf off him and palmed the knife.

Growling, the alpha took a defensive posture, creeping low, muscles coiled.

While the wolf pack watched, the two predators circled each other before diving in.

The alpha lunged, teeth snapping viciously.

Laurence struck out with the knife, jammed it into the alpha's neck, and sliced deep.

A crimson arc sprayed from the wound, painting Laurence in red.

The alpha sagged to the ground.

With a ferocious echoing howl, the female launched herself at Laurence.

The vampire threw the knife with a flick of his wrist.

The blade hit its mark with a sick thud, sinking into her chest before her body barreled into him.

Laurence fell to his back beneath her weight. With her dying breath, she went for his throat. Teeth snagged skin as he thrust her away. He retrieved the knife and staggered to his feet, bleeding.

"Your alpha and his second lie dead," Laurence bellowed to the remaining wolves. "Go now or join them on the other side!"

The group scattered backward.

All but one. The lone wolf began to shift.

Remy watched the transformation with tempered awe. Slower than the female, who'd been a wolf one second and a woman the next, this one seemed to take effort to make the change. Legs straightened and elongated, tail shrank back, fur receded to skin, and snout became mouth and nose. The man unfurled from all fours and stood, arms out, palms up—a gesture of surrender.

The other wolves cowered behind him, anxious to leave.

Despite his smaller stature and his place on the losing side, the man squared his shoulders and looked Laurence in the eye. "What of our dead?"

"You can collect them later, when we've cleared your territory."

He shook his head. "I cannot just leave them here."

"You can and you will. Until the witch and I reach safety, you will get out and stay out."

"Let me send the others away and remain by myself. One wolf is clearly no threat to you. Please, do not begrudge our pack this."

Laurence's lips pressed to a fine line. Blood seeped from his shoulder, thigh, and neck. Remy longed to go to him but would wait for the standoff to end. He'd promised.

"All right," said Laurence. "Get the others out of my sight."

The man turned to the remaining wolves and nodded. They didn't wait to be told twice and raced into the distance.

"Stay back. No sudden moves." Laurence glanced from the last wolf standing to Remy. His eyes caught on the torn pants leg. "Are you all right?"

If he weren't terrified for Laurence's wellbeing, Remy would have rolled his eyes. Of course he was all right. He'd stayed in the blasted tree as Laurence had ordered. "I'm fine. You're hurt."

"It's not as bad as it looks."

Remy didn't believe him for a second. "I'm coming down."

Laurence reached to help, grimacing as his shoulder stretched with the movement.

"I've got it, Laurence. Step back." Remy descended from the tree without trouble and stood before the vampire, checking him over with wide eyes.

The lone wolf remained immobile, glowering at them in silence.

Blood caked along Laurence's shoulder and down his bicep. The vampire stood heavily on one leg, favoring the injured thigh. Clothes and flesh ripped away, Remy could see the exposed muscle bathed in red. Though the injuries must be excruciating, Laurence bore them stoically.

"What do we do?" asked Remy.

"We leave. Quickly, in case they send reinforcements."

"Can you travel like this?"

"Yes, and I can carry you as well." He bent to one knee. "Come."

Remy took his elbow and gently pulled him up. "No. I'll run if you think we must, but I won't be carried." He shouldered both packs. "Lead the way."

Laurence shook his head. "If you won't let me carry you, you should go first. Set the pace—one you can maintain—don't sprint. I'll follow." He pointed to the direction they'd been traveling before the attack.

Remy didn't like it, but what choice did he have? Magic tingled along his fingertips. It flowed under his skin. Not using it felt wrong. But he'd not let Laurence's actions be in vain.

He caught the vampire's eyes and nodded. "Call out if you need to stop."

"Aye."

A glance to the remaining wolf indicated he wouldn't cause trouble. The man stared at his fallen comrades, the fight in him traded for sorrow.

With a deep breath, Remy took off at a jog. He had enough adrenaline coursing through his system to run all night.

They ran until Remy heard Laurence collapse behind him.

11

Darkness smothered Laurence with icy vapors and hulking shadows. He struggled but couldn't free himself from its harrowing grasp. A damp chill crept from his fingers and toes inward, threatening to consume him. He'd always hated the cold. Shivering, Laurence fought to wake.

Warm hands bracketed his cheeks. Breath ghosted over his face.

"Laurence." Remy's cry broke the dark hold. "Laurence!"

Light filtered in from fluttering lids. He opened his eyes.

"Oh gods! Are you all right? You fell," said Remy, his face so near it appeared blurry. His hands stayed put, their warmth a comfort.

Laurence leaned into the touch and mentally took stock of his surroundings. Somewhere near the north border of Marshland Pack territory, approaching Keeper's Pass, but not yet out of harm's way. He'd lost too much blood. Pain flared in his leg as he stirred.

"Don't move," ordered Remy. "You aren't well."

They must keep going. The pack was fragmented without their leader or his second but still dangerous. And Laurence couldn't fight again until he'd fed and had a day to sleep and recover.

"Laurence." Remy kneeled over him, his pretty face blocking the world from view. That was fine. He'd rather look at Remy. Which must have been what the witch wanted because he kept saying his name. "Laurence, focus. What should I do?"

Right. Focus.

Laurence took a deep breath and concentrated. He needed blood. A rabbit wouldn't be enough, but better than nothing, and Remy had proven he could catch them. "Hunt for me. I need to feed."

The witch gave an exasperated sigh and pressed his wrist to Laurence's lips. "Then feed."

Oh.

He shouldn't. But the soft, delicate skin with its alluring heat was a temptation difficult to resist. Difficult—not impossible.

Never drink from a witch.

All vampires knew that rule. Witches could control you after, or so the lesson went, though Laurence had never known a vampire controlled by a witch in all his years. Did Remy know? Is that why he was so eager for Laurence to drink from him?

"Can't," muttered Laurence.

"Why not? Why won't you take what I offer?" Remy's expression turned vulnerable, but his wrist still hovered over Laurence's mouth. "Do I revolt you so much?"

"No, not that. Never that." Laurence looked the witch directly in the eye, willing him to believe it. He found Remy anything but revolting. "Not supposed to drink from a witch. You could take my free will."

"What?" Remy's amber gaze widened in disbelief. "That's not true. At least I think it's not. I've never heard of such." The crease on Remy's forehead deepened. "Why would I do that? Do you think me a monster?"

Laurence sighed. "Of course not."

"The only things I want from you have no value at all if not given of your own free will," Remy said softly. "Trust me."

Laurence turned the words over in his mind. What he knew of Remy suggested the witch told the truth, and whether he did or not, Laurence believed him. Remy was far too caring to hurt him in any way.

Pulsing blood sang to him from beneath Remy's delicate skin. A siren's song beckoning to his core. Hunger churned and seethed, gnawing at his gut and demanding to be sated. The freckled flesh and thin blue veins of Remy's wrist begged to be plundered.

"Drink," said Remy, his eyes shining with sincerity.

Laurence took hold of the offered wrist, opened his mouth, and bit.

With a breathy gasp, Remy leaned in. "That's it."

His fangs sank into soft flesh. Laurence moaned as hot copper nectar hit the back of his throat. Sweet like the scent of roses on the breeze and more addicting than the opium of a poppy flower, Remy's blood filled a need so primal Laurence burned for more. He groaned around the punctures, his lips fastened flush against smooth skin.

Swallow after succulent swallow, the delicate ambrosia filled his stomach and began to heal his wounds.

With a moan of pleasure, Remy collapsed onto his chest. Laurence wrapped his free arm over him and pulled them tight together. The witch pressed his hard length against Laurence's hip in a slow, steady motion, lost to the delight of feeding a vampire.

Even as he relished every mouthful, Laurence knew he must stop. He couldn't deplete Remy and leave him vulnerable but tearing away from the most delicious blood he'd ever known wasn't easy. He'd thought himself too old to be this affected, but there was something different about Remy. A force drawing him in that he couldn't resist.

Though reluctant, Laurence withdrew his teeth and tongued the wounds closed, using his saliva to stop the flow. He kissed the precious flesh beneath his lips and settled Remy's arm at his side.

Remy let out a needy whimper that went straight to Laurence's groin.

Their breath mingled, Laurence's deep and satisfied—Remy's short and desperate with arousal.

It would be such a delight to flip him over and take care of his need, but Remy deserved more than a hasty affair on muddied soil. Laurence wouldn't take advantage, though the witch presented endless temptation.

His wits restored, Remy stopped thrusting and settled heavily against Laurence, hiding his face in the vampire's chest. Laurence stroked his back, gliding hands down his spine and back up to his shoulders with gentle pressure.

"Curses," said Remy. "I did not expect that to be so..."

"Intense?"

"Erotic," Remy corrected with a full body undulation that emphasized all the places they touched—chests, stomachs, legs, ankles. They were connected at every place Remy could manage given his smaller frame.

Laurence chuckled and gripped his waist.

"Don't laugh at me," came the soft reply muffled against his shirt.

"Oh, Remy. I'm not. I wouldn't. You've affected me very much." Laurence shifted just enough for the witch to feel the solid evidence for himself. "See?"

Remy lifted his head, golden hair falling over his brow, amber eyes blazing. Every instinct in Laurence demanded he tug the witch down for a kiss. He fought it. The lust was just fueled by blood anyway.

The little nymph boldly stole the decision away.

Remy claimed Laurence's lips and ground against him with a greedy whine. Wet heat consumed the chill from his mouth with each flick of Remy's tongue.

Laurence opened for him—it was that or be bitten until he complied.

Remy licked past his teeth, found his tongue and wrestled it to submission. All Laurence could do was give in, and the surrender brought soul-deep satisfaction. Remy's blood warmed his veins while his mouth stoked the fire of longing Laurence had struggled to contain.

Needy whimpers rose between kisses. Was that him making those sounds?

This was more than bloodlust, more than a body's need for release...Remy had stolen his heart. He adored this witch squirming in his arms.

Laurence could stay like this forever, kissing Remy, feeling the swell of his backside beneath his palms.

But they shouldn't.

Danger loomed. These lands weren't safe. Remy wasn't safe.

Overcoming great reluctance, Laurence tore away from their kiss, leaving Remy gasping. Above them, the arc glittered in the sky, reminding Laurence of Remy's power and of his vulnerability.

"What," the witch sputtered. "What did I do wrong?"

Laurence squeezed both cheeks. "Nothing. You're perfect. That was marvelous. I want to do that for hours."

Confusion danced in Remy's eyes, pupils grown wide with lust. "Then, why?"

"Not here," Laurence explained. "It's not safe."

"Bollocks," huffed Remy.

Laurence kissed the irritation from his expression. Remy melted back into him until Laurence pushed him up. "Come. Up you get. We must go."

"I'm beginning to hate werewolves," he grumbled as he rose, offering his hand.

Laurence took it and let the witch pull him to his feet. "That makes both of us."

"How are you? I was so worried. You just...fell." Remy studied him from head to toe.

"Much improved, thanks to you. I'm fine now, honest." The infusion of blood from Remy coursed through his system, much stronger than anything he'd drunk prior. His wounds, though still tender, had closed. After a day's sleep, they'd disappear. Most importantly, he could run again.

"That's really quite astounding." Remy's gaze fixed on the worst of the wounds, the one on Laurence's thigh. "I did that?"

"Aye." Laurence adjusted himself in his pants, the effects from Remy's gift still raging in his groin.

A sly grin crossed Remy's face as he did the same.

"Come, we must go." Laurence picked up their packs, handing one over. "Another hour will bring us to a hidden cave. We can take cover for the day."

Remy arched a brow. "A cave, you say? How could I resist? Lead on, dear vampire."

"This way," Laurence guided them forward at an even jog.

As he left, he heard Remy hum and murmur, "Mmm...Never been fucked in a cave."

Laurence narrowly avoided collapsing for a second time.

12

Remy trotted after Laurence, his body tingling with unspent energy, heart full to bursting. Relief that the vampire was all right battled with frustration that they weren't kissing anymore.

He channeled the frustration to fuel the run. One more hour. Remy could wait one more hour, couldn't he? He'd waited ages, but now that Laurence had finally come around, a second longer was a second too much.

Every inch of his skin buzzed. Feeding the vampire left him exhilarated. When Laurence's fangs slid razor-sharp into his flesh, Remy had expected pain, not pleasure. From his curled toes to his hard cock, no part of his body remained unaffected. And best of all, Laurence had responded in kind.

Laurence had kissed him back.

Vigorously.

And kissing was all Remy wanted to do for the foreseeable future—well not *all* he wanted, though it would make a delightful start. Instead, he consoled himself by staring at Laurence's finely shaped ass while they hurried out of Marshland Pack territory. To a cave. The vampire knew of many secret little hideaways. Places tucked away and safe from daylight nestled along their route. A career's worth, Remy assumed, wondering how long Laurence had been a messenger for the ruling vampires.

The thought spurred a prickle of anxiety. The vampires of The Dozen. Remy would meet them soon and petition for protection. That line of thinking threatened to overwhelm the hum of arousal lingering from Laurence's kisses. He steered his mind elsewhere.

The early morning hours boasted chirping insects and bird-song. Soon the midnight navy sky would lighten to gray, and they'd need to take cover. Remy's stomach churned. He'd hardly eaten tonight, and exhaustion hung heavy across his shoulders. The backs of his legs were tight from near constant walking, but he liked the strength he'd gained. He felt powerful in a different way now. Like a man who climbed mountains.

His next summit would be Laurence.

How long had the vampire returned his feelings and not said anything? And why, when Remy had made his desire so painfully obvious. He vowed to ask all these questions that dangled between them like exotic delicacies waiting to be tasted, and he wouldn't be put off by Laurence's dodging.

They veered off-trail and sideways through dense brush, their fast clip slowing to a walk as leaves and branches were shoved aside.

"Almost there," said Laurence.

Relieved, Remy shook out his tired legs and followed closely, letting Laurence do most of the work. Making their way to a steep rock face, they walked alongside until the opening of a small cave appeared. Smaller, in fact, than Remy had imagined.

"Don't worry, it's larger than it looks," said Laurence, reading his mind.

"That's what they all say." Remy smirked and resisted the temptation to pinch the vampire's hindquarters as they lowered to crawl inside.

Laurence threw a glance over his shoulder, one brow raised. "You're incorrigible."

Once past the entrance, the cave opened wider, tall enough to stand with plenty of room overhead. Remy heard water flowing from deeper inside. He took in a lungful of the earthen scent of stagnant air.

"Can you see?" asked Laurence. A slight echo hinted at hidden depths beyond.

Though the interior was nearly pitch black, he could. Thankful for decent night vision, he replied, "I wouldn't want to try to read, but yes, I can see."

"Good." Laurence shrugged off his pack and spread the wool blanket on the sandy rock at their feet. "When the sun comes up, it lightens. Not enough to bother me."

Remy followed his lead, taking out their second blanket. He'd need it. The air was damp and chilly. With any luck, Laurence would warm him soon enough. Remy's gaze roamed the vampire's handsome face. His crooked nose. His lovely dark hair that Remy wanted to run fingers through. His broad shoulders, one still covered in dried blood.

"How are the bite wounds? Are you in pain?"

Laurence shook his head. "Tender, but no pain. They'll mend as we sleep. It's already happening."

"That's amazing." Remy knew vampires were fast to heal, but he hadn't realized one day was enough.

"Your blood did this. I'd not have made it here without you."

"My pleasure." A broad smile spread at the thought. "And I mean that in every sense of the word. I want you to drink from me whenever you thirst."

Eyebrows drawn, Laurence frowned. "For what reason?"

"Because it feels good. Because I want to give back to you. Because I can't bear the thought of you drinking from someone else."

Laurence's heavy expression lifted. His eyes widened.

Perhaps Remy should have held that last bit back, but no, that wouldn't be in keeping with his style.

"Not because you want to control me?" said Laurence, his tone tentative. "I know it sounds crazy. It isn't something you'd do, but I feel I have to ask."

"I honestly don't think it's true." Remy kicked off his boots and began to peel away his shirt.

"We don't know that," said Laurence.

"I certainly don't feel as though I could make you do anything." Remy glanced up through his lashes. "Shall I try?"

Laurence squared his shoulders, his face entirely too serious for what Remy had in mind. "Aye."

Remy flung his shirt aside and unfastened his pants.

Still waiting for whatever he thought the witch might make him do, Laurence ignored the mood as it shifted and morphed between them.

Remy pushed down his pants and smallclothes at once, leaving him bare. Lids lowered, he purred, "Fuck me."

Laurence's mouth fell open. So caught up in superstition, he'd failed to anticipate Remy's ploy.

"Well," said Remy, hand on a hip he cocked to the side playfully. "Is it working?"

Laurence's irises darkened as he looked Remy over from head to toe, lingering somewhere in the middle.

"It's working." The vampire advanced on him, swept him up with hands gripping under his thighs, and growled.

Remy opened his legs and wrapped them around Laurence's waist. Pinned against the cave wall, the hard stone cool against his back, he shuddered and sank his fingers into the soft black tresses that had been tempting him all night. Laurence kissed him.

Finally.

Remy surrendered in glorious triumph. Lips parted, welcoming tongue and teeth, he yielded with a whine of pleasure. Laurence took him, groaning against his mouth as he plundered.

Remy's naked cock lay trapped between them, pressed with delicious pressure to the answering hardness behind Laurence's breeches. The rough fabric chafed his sensitive skin. Leaning into the sensation, he ground himself tighter. He squeezed Laurence between his thighs and threw his head back to allow access to his neck.

"Please," Remy whispered to the ceiling.

"What do you want, poppet? I'll give you anything," Laurence sighed out, mouth moving along his throat.

"Bite me."

Laurence's lips curled to a smile against his skin.

Remy wanted teeth. Fisting two thick handfuls of hair, he held the vampire in place. "Here."

Obliging, Laurence took a mouthful of flesh and muscle and clamped down, but he didn't break skin.

Remy whimpered and writhed in his arms. He pressed in for more.

Letting go of one thigh, Laurence brought his hand between them.

Cool fingers wrapped securely about Remy's shaft, and he forgot to be bothered by the lack of blood drinking. Expert strokes threatened to hurtle him to the edge all too quickly. His balls sat tight against his body, warm and tingling with tension.

"You're good at this," Remy managed, basking in sensation.

Laurence released him from the faux bite. "You're lovely to touch."

Leaning back against the stone, Remy watched as Laurence

pulled his foreskin back to trail blunt fingers over the plump flushed head. A bead of pre-cum swelled and was swiped immediately. The tip glistened as Laurence swirled the moisture in teasing circles.

The vampire was impossibly strong. To hold him like this with one hand under his rump and the other working his cock while Remy flailed in his grip. He wished for a mirror so he could watch properly.

Laurence leaned in to kiss him again. Remy greedily sucked the invading tongue farther into his mouth.

Heat collected in his balls. Remy ground them against Laurence's hard cock, still tragically trapped behind clothes.

Long, rhythmic strokes pulled sparks of desire from his core. Remy thrust into the sultry ring of Laurence's fingers, aching for release.

"Gods. Harder," Remy pleaded as he approached the point of no return, toes curling.

The grip around his shaft stiffened. Laurence had him.

Remy bucked mindlessly, chasing his peak. Laurence's eyes, dark as ink, locked on his. Remy shook, overcome with fervor, vibrating out of his own skin. As he quaked and came between them, hot seed slicking his abs, he couldn't look away, lost in the vampire's hungry gaze.

Remy grinned and panted, coming down from the blissful high. He couldn't stop a giggle of pleasure from bubbling forth, even as the vampire continued to stroke gently. He'd known it would be good. He hadn't known it would be *that* good.

"Oh Laurence," Remy gushed. "You're magnificent."

"As are you." Laurence swiped a bit of cum from his belly and held it to Remy's lips.

Remy opened for him and tongued it from his finger. He swallowed around the digit in his mouth, then circled with his tongue and sucked.

Laurence watched with obvious yearning. Remy squirmed

against his cock until Laurence gave a tantalizing thrust of his hips. The vampire took back his finger.

"Put me down and take off your clothes," ordered Remy the second his mouth was free.

Laurence set him on his feet. "You don't have to—"

"Do not finish that sentence!" Remy snapped. "Of course I don't have to, but if I don't see you naked this instant I'll be forced to use my magic and once your clothes have vanished I don't actually know how to bring them back, so if I were you—"

"All right." Laurence toed off his boots and unfastened his pants. "You're a bossy thing."

"And lie down for me. I can't stand after that. I'm all wobbly." Remy sat on their blankets.

Laurence finished undressing while Remy watched with eager anticipation. Each layer revealed a new treasure. First the smooth ridges of his abdomen, then the layer of dark curling hair on his chest, and two pert nipples Remy couldn't wait to taste. When the vampire's pants hit the floor, Remy had new sights to admire. Thick muscular legs and a perfectly proportioned cock, heavy balls hanging behind. His mouth watered.

Laurence joined him on the blankets, allowing himself to be guided to his back as Remy pushed and pulled him into the desired position. Having Laurence pliant under his touch sent a rush of power coursing through his veins. The thrill of possibility stirred energy in him, causing a full body sensation he desired to share. Immediately.

Bending over, he pressed a kiss hard and fast to Laurence's mouth before moving to his nipple. As he tongued the nub, the vampire's hands landed on his back and slid from shoulder to rump. How did every shift of Laurence's hands feel so good?

When the first nipple had pebbled, he moved to the next and licked it to matching hardness. Then he sat back and admired his work. Twin flushed peaks stared back at him, shining with saliva and begging to be tweaked. So he did.

Laurence let out a gasp, arching into the touch. "Again," he demanded, fingers squeezing Remy's sides. Remy complied with a grin, harder this time.

One day, he'd spend hours lingering over the vampire's magnificent, furred chest, but today he had a cock to become acquainted with and wouldn't be delayed any further.

Settling between two powerfully muscled thighs, Remy gazed at his prize. The rosy, pink phallus curved proudly to rest on Laurence's abdomen, waiting for Remy to demand its offering.

"For me?" he purred.

Laurence was beyond words, squirming deliciously under Remy's appreciative gaze.

Remy licked a long slow stripe from base to tip and back before taking the thick, twitching cock into his mouth.

Above him, Laurence's groans echoed off the cave walls, filling Remy's chest with heat. He took the hefty balls in hand and palmed them gently while working the shaft deeper into his throat. God, it felt good to have what he'd longed for all this time. Laurence under him, moaning his pleasure, Remy teasing him to climax. Even his dreams were not this exquisite.

Laurence's fingers had found his hair and clenched. Not as hard as Remy would have liked, but enough to draw a whimper from his throat.

Allowing Laurence's thrusts to set the pace, Remy hummed around the cock in his mouth. His throat hugged the spongy glans, ready to swallow. His lids fluttered closed in pleasure.

Laurence lay a heavy calf over his back, heel against his ass. Remy liked the way it felt, to be held in place by solid muscle.

"So good, Remy," Laurence murmured between moans.

Quivering under him, Laurence hovered close to the finish. His balls drew tight, and his hips stuttered. Remy gave all his lover needed with enthusiasm, eager to taste the results.

A burst of liquid hit home as Laurence came while buried

deep in Remy's throat. Milking him for each drop, Remy swallowed around the pulsing shaft. Laurence gave one last thrust and stilled.

As Laurence began to relax—the tension from his muscles releasing, his respiration slowing to normal—Remy let his cock slip from his mouth. He gave it a kiss and rested his head on the vampire's stomach.

Hands stroked his hair. His cheeks. Fingers brushed his lips, and Remy's tongue darted out to greet them. They lay together in the glowing aftermath of pleasure, basking in the intimacy it offered.

Remy's other senses slowly woke. It had lightened in their little cave. The sun must be up. The scent of sex faded and was replaced with earthen smells of dirt and rock. Laurence's soft, steady breathing would have lulled him into a stupor were it not for gentle hands tenderly wrapping beneath his armpits to haul him up.

Remy grinned and settled heavily against Laurence's side. "Darling."

"Darling, yourself." Laurence pulled the blanket over them and snaked his arms under to hold Remy close. A satiated smile spread lazily across his face. "You've done that before."

A fit of laughter escaped Remy's lips. "I'm five and twenty! You thought I hadn't?"

"I didn't know," said Laurence, his tone earnest.

"Because you never asked." Remy ran a fingertip down his crooked nose and over his lips. "I would have told you. Does it matter?"

Trailing a cool hand over Remy's spine, Laurence left a patch of gooseflesh in its wake. "Of course not."

Remy shivered and curled in tighter. "Why didn't you ask?"

"I thought it inappropriate. I'm so much older."

"Is age of any importance to a vampire?"

Laurence gave a slight shrug. "You needed someone to protect you."

Remy chose his next words carefully. "I'm forever grateful for your protection. But what I want from you is your love."

Laurence pressed a kiss to his forehead.

The kiss would have to be enough for now.

13

Laurence approached Keeper's Pass with Remy panting heavily behind him. The arduous ascent had taken longer than he'd anticipated. If they didn't pick up their pace on the descent, they wouldn't make the outskirts of Wyckshire before dawn.

Keeper's Pass crossed the ridgeline between two towering summits, Crown and Hawk. The well-worn trail soared over the valleys it connected and was the preferred route from pack territories to human towns and finally to lands under vampire rule. The journey up and over the pass shouldn't take more than one night, but they'd gotten off to a slow start.

Laurence had woken in their familiar position, with Remy clinging to his side, only for the first time they'd been naked. Leaving the bed proved difficult with so much freckled skin on display. When Remy pressed against him, tongue to his ear, Laurence forgot why he'd wanted to get up anyway.

Once both were satisfied, Laurence had laid Remy flat and set to work on the stitches. Their knife was too large to cut the careful rows, so he bent and used his teeth. He'd snap the line with a precise bite, then gently pull the entire row free. There were four rows, and the process should only have taken a few minutes, but with the way Remy squirmed and giggled, claiming ticklishness, they'd had a late start indeed.

As they neared the top, the ground leveled out. Remy's curious gaze drank everything in while Laurence assessed their situation. Crossing would be quick, the road being free from other foot traffic. As long as they didn't dawdle, the timing should work out.

"Remy?"

The witch glanced over his shoulder, cheeks pink from exertion. The urge to feel their heat against his lips surprised Laurence with its intensity. No time for that. And no place either.

"Yes?" Remy's attention flicked from their surroundings to home in on Laurence.

"We're moving too slow. I'm afraid we won't make it to shelter before dawn unless we speed up. Or I could carry you again?"

With a sigh, Remy gazed back to the trail. "As much as I'd like to have you between my thighs, could we try going faster? I'm enjoying the exercise."

Laurence chuckled. "Aye." At least their thoughts were aligned.

They cleared the treeline where the path opened wide enough for them to walk shoulder to shoulder. Dense fog didn't allow for much of a view—the summit of Crown barely visible between clouds and Hawk completely obscured. Winds raced through grassy fields, creating a whistle that, combined with the fog, lent the atmosphere an eerie mood.

"You've made this trip before?" asked Remy.

"Many times."

"I suppose it's much faster without a tagalong."

"Indeed, though I prefer it with you." That earned him a smile.

"Charmer," said Remy. "What happens if you don't make it to a shelter in time? In all your traveling, has it happened before?"

"It has, though it matters little when I'm alone." Memories of days spent sleeping in the cold earth filtered through his mind. "I can rest in the ground when needed."

"In the ground?" said Remy, voice loud, wide-eyed with intrigue.

Laurence wondered what the witching elders had actually bothered to teach him, as the ways of the world clearly never made the curriculum. "Yes, all vampires can do it. It's not a secret."

"Can I do it?" asked Remy, his tone far too excited for a subject Laurence previously thought dull. Relearning the world through the eyes of a sheltered witch transformed the mundane into the magnificent.

"I've never heard of a witch going to ground. How would you breathe?"

"I suppose I'd need a vent. What do you breathe when you're in the ground?"

"Dirt," said Laurence, his lips curling into a smile.

"Oh." Remy giggled. "I suppose I should have guessed that."

"I prefer to sleep in a bed." It would be divine to share one with Remy. Perhaps they would when they reached Bran Vigny.

"I imagine so." Remy's shoulder bumped Laurence's. A lovely little grin graced his face. "Still, useful trick."

"In a pinch," said Laurence.

"How long have you been in service as a messenger? What does it entail, beyond the obvious?"

Once Remy started with his questions, dissuading him was next to impossible. Laurence's reluctance to share had faded as his trust in Remy grew. Though he'd prefer not to discuss himself when he could listen to Remy's pleasant chatter instead, the more he could teach the witch before life inevitably forced them apart, the better.

"Going on forty-five years. I'm well suited for the work. I enjoy travel." Laurence glanced to the path ahead. How many miles of foot trails like this one had he covered in his time? Thousands, surely. Tens of thousands? "It means how it sounds. I deliver messages."

"Why work for your rulers at all, when you could do anything you want?"

"I volunteered my service to The Dozen in return for their protection."

"From what?"

"Valeri." Laurence found simply saying the name of his sire repulsive. It passed from his lips like bile, rancid waste to be buried and forgotten. "He can't touch me as long as The Dozen forbid it."

"Has Valeri threatened you?" Remy's voice distorted with alarm.

"In the past, yes. He still thinks I belong to him. He wants me back, and because he's my sire, he has some influence over my will. That influence lessens with time, but until I'm free of it, I prefer to remain under the protection my service offers."

"Is it often so dangerous?" asked Remy. "They did send you to the front lines of a war after all."

"Not often. Usually delivering messages is simple. This was a different sort of assignment."

"Well, what was the assignment then?"

"Protect Dagna's pack. Lead them, if it came to that. Win the war."

"Will you be in trouble for leaving them?"

Laurence gave a shrug. "I don't think so. The wolves hardly need my protection now; you saw to that." He glanced through the dissipating fog to the opal sheen of Remy's arc. "Vampires would have preferred to stay out of this conflict between your species and the werewolf packs."

"Why? And why choose the side of the wolves?"

Laurence couldn't help but laugh. "One question at a time, please."

"Oh, sorry. I'll be quiet," said Remy, grinning sheepishly.

The flush of color suited him, thought Laurence as he continued, "I shall start from the beginning. We had no dog in the fight, so to speak. At least not at first. Your elders sought the natural riches found on territory belonging to wolves—rare plants, herbs, game animals and such. Rather than continue to barter peacefully and share the bounty, which had worked for centuries, witches began to govern those lands. Wolves live by their own code and leave others alone. Naturally they resented witches putting rules in place and expecting them to be followed. Thus, the conflict began."

Remy listened with his usual intensity. Laurence wondered how his people's version went. One thing he'd learned in his years, guilty parties generally don't care to admit their guilt.

"Wolves were quick to remind the witching elders who the land belonged to, but witches had grown accustomed to using the space. They no longer accepted the boundaries and saw the land as their own. Squabbles broke out. Tensions escalated. You're familiar with the execution of Dietrich Bennet?"

"Yes. He stole from the elder's coffers and burned the old school building to ashes."

"Werewolves tell a different tale. After his death at the hands of witches, they sought reinforcements from neighboring packs, and war began in earnest."

"Wait, how does the story go from their side?" asked Remy.

"That he stole from the coffers is admitted—a minor amount and to prove a point—but he died swearing his innocence in relation to the fire. In any event, neither offense is punishable by death according to werewolf code, and yet…"

"Our elders executed him," Remy finished.

"Packs protect their own. Werewolves and witches have been killing each other ever since."

"Yes, they ransacked our village in retaliation. Wards were put in place after that. I learned to see to their maintenance as part of my schooling."

"I'd wondered what made the curriculum, as it seems much did not," said Laurence gently.

"A lot of what I know of other cultures now seems skewed. If other vampires are like you and Livia, well…I've been lied to. I thought you all to be bloodthirsty demons."

"Perhaps that's part of the reason why The Dozen chose to side with werewolves over witches. That, and werewolf territory lies between our two lands. If witches acquired that land, if they governed werewolves like they want to, who's to say they wouldn't try to conquer vampires next?"

"I see. Yes, I suppose it makes sense you'd side with wolves."

Remy pondered that in silence. They were nearly across Keeper's Pass and the fog had receded. The twin summits of Hawk and Crown sliced the scattered clouds. Remy's keen eyes took it all in. Laurence had seen the crossing before, and though the view was stunning, he preferred to watch Remy. The moonlight cast beams on his golden hair, highlighting the long waves. His amber eyes scanned the horizon thoughtfully.

Laurence gave him the time he needed to think as side by side they began the descent.

"Laurence." Remy's clear voice pierced the cold night air. "How does one become a vampire?"

The subject change threw him. "You weren't taught anything about other species, were you?"

"Not enough and not accurately. Will you tell me?"

"Aye, very well, but we must pick up the speed. You go first. Set a pace you can maintain."

Remy took the lead at a quick clip with Laurence on his heels.

"Vampires are turned through a blood exchange. It's rather simple. The chosen must be drained so completely as to ensure death, but before the heart beats its last, the vampire opens a vein. The chosen drinks their fill, and transformation begins."

"How long does it take?"

"That depends. If done well—nearly all the blood drained, then promptly given back in its entirety— it can happen in minutes. If done poorly, the change could take hours and could require a second try or could fail all together."

"But why should the transformation fail?"

"If the chosen wasn't on the verge of death after all, the attempt might not take. They could recover and remain unchanged...or they may still die. If the vampire is unwilling or unable to offer enough blood back, death could claim the chosen for herself. Mind you, I've only ever seen the transformation successfully completed. The stories of failure are secondhand."

Remy glanced over his shoulder, tripped, and caught himself. "Have you made another vampire?" His tone pitched higher than usual.

"I have not."

"Then how—"

"I've seen Livia do it."

"Oh."

Remy trotted briskly down the mountainside. They were under the cover of a tunnel of trees once more, and it was darker as a result. A human would have trouble seeing. Laurence's crystal-clear night vision allowed him to pick out even the smallest movement. Bats diving as they hunted, the glowing eyes of a possum in the distance, bugs crawling along tree trunks. If Remy noticed these things, Laurence couldn't tell.

"Why haven't you made another vampire?"

"I've no desire to uproot anyone from their life. There are plenty of vampires; the world doesn't need more of us."

"You're not lonely?"

How did they come to this subject? Laurence fielded questions of war with relative ease, but the subject of companionship teemed with pitfalls. When he didn't answer fast enough, Remy turned to search his face.

"Eyes on the trail or you'll fall," said Laurence.

Remy pressed forward. "I just wonder, in all your years, what has kept you from finding a mate?"

"A mate?" Laurence balked at the term. Mate sounded so…*permanent*. "Is that what you call it?"

Remy shrugged. "I suppose not. Witches marry, so husband or wife, that's what I call it."

"And yet you said mate."

"Werewolves call their partners that," Remy pointed. "What do vampires call them?"

Some vampires did use the term mate, Laurence knew, others said partner, husband, wife…*lover*. "I've known vampires to marry and use the traditional words. I suppose any of the relevant terms. One isn't more broadly used than another. What makes you ask?"

"Curiosity."

Laurence chuckled. He should have known.

"Did it hurt?" asked Remy

"Did what hurt?"

"Being turned into a vampire?"

"It wasn't painful, no." Laurence paused to find the right words. "It felt like slipping into a dream—easy, inevitable, surreal."

"Do you know any witches that've been turned into vampires?"

"I don't, though I wouldn't be able to tell unless they'd told me. I don't think there are many. We're taught it isn't safe to drink from you."

"Right, and we're taught never to allow ourselves to be turned. Witches who are made into vampires lose their magic. What happens if a werewolf is turned into a vampire?"

"That is also rare. To my knowledge, I don't know any. They lose their wolf half, so naturally they'd be reluctant."

"But if a vampire falls in love with a werewolf, or a witch, wouldn't they want to turn them?"

"I don't think it happens often. The species rarely mix."

Remy went silent again. Laurence was glad of it. The conversation veered too close to introspection for comfort. He would never turn someone into a vampire and curse them to an existence of endless nights and little else.

Better to live one lifetime fully than limitless lifetimes of emptiness.

14

Wyckshire, a bastide town, sprawled on both sides of its towering stone walls. They'd slept in an abandoned vegetable cellar not far from the main gates, and made entry while people still bustled about the gridded streets. The heavenly scent of candied nuts drew Remy toward the colorful market stalls as merchant's closed for the night.

Remy eyed the sticky, honeyed treats wrapped in paper cones. His mouth watered as he shifted his gaze to Laurence. "Could I?"

With an indulgent smile, Laurence handed him a bulging purse. "Help yourself."

Remy marched up to the vendor, an old man, slender and short, with hard, hazel eyes. "How much, please?"

The man looked him over. "Four lira."

As Remy dug for the money, Laurence stepped in. "Two, and that's one too many."

His shoulders lifted in a shrug. "Two."

Remy gave over the coin and took the paper bag of nuts. "Thank you," he said to both men absently, concentrating instead on the sweets. He popped a nut into his mouth with a satisfying crunch. Cinnamon and sugar burst along his taste buds. He'd have moaned if Laurence didn't already have the most amused expression on his face. Heat crept along his cheeks at being the reason for that smile.

"Good?" asked the vampire, a hint of laughter in his voice.

"So good. I wish we could share them."

"Look on the bright side, more for you."

"Indeed," said Remy around a mouthful.

"Don't spoil your appetite. There will be a good dinner where we're going."

"Right." Remy took a handful of nuts to snack on, folded the paper over the rest and pocketed them for later.

The town's center square was a thriving sea of movement. Bone-weary field workers returning to their homes within Wyckshire's walls, jovial clumps of men seeking ale from the pubs, tidy storekeepers closing up shops for the night. Remy glanced this way and that, taking it all in. Scents of curry-smoked meats and human sweat mingled thick in the air. He took a deep breath, loving the activity of a human city, even the grimy bits.

"I know an inn where you'll be safe," said Laurence. "There is a pub that serves food and ale well into the evening. We'll be there soon."

Remy dreaded this part. Laurence had filled him in on his plans, and Remy's stomach sank at the idea. He did not want to be separated. But the vampire insisted on getting The Dozen's permission before Remy entered Bran Vigny. Remy would stay in Wyckshire while Laurence went ahead to speak on his behalf. With any luck, Livia or one of hers would already be there paving the way.

"Do you have to leave already?" asked Remy as they rounded a corner from the main thoroughfare onto a quieter side street.

Laurence's gray gaze landed on him with surprising intensity. "I don't have to. I could stay tonight and go tomorrow night."

Remy's heart seized at the possibility even as his mind and mouth said, "No. I'm sorry. I shouldn't have asked. You must go. I've no way of knowing how much longer the barrier will hold, and we'll need a plan for when it fails."

Nodding, Laurence shifted his eyes to the sky, posture rigid. "Right. Of course."

The arc overhead, its magic holding strong, glimmered between them and the moon. Remy thought of the elders, of Emmeline and Helewise, back home scheming up ways to tear the barrier apart. At least he'd left them no trail by which to hunt him. Any traces of his magic were long since dissipated, and he'd gone for weeks without casting spells. Remy was a needle in a haystack, and without him, they'd need a new strategy for their war. He wanted no part in it.

Passing closed shops, Remy peered into windows. He took a whiff of leather from the saddlery shop then gazed longingly at the beautiful wares of potters. Each shop with its own treasures to be discovered, but it was the booksellers that snagged Remy's eyes and held them. Stacks of books shelved floor to ceiling beckoned with their siren's call. He would have to stop in tomorrow. At least he'd have something to look forward to while Laurence blazed ahead.

In a stroke of luck, the inn stood less than a full block from the booksellers. Laurence held the massive wooden door open for him, and they stepped inside. A large, dimly lit room filled with tables greeted them. Cooking aromas wafted through the air along with the scents of ale and sweat. Men chatted and laughed, the din of jovial noise rising to meet their ears. Remy scanned faces, excited to be around so many humans at once.

Laurence approached the bar toward the back and Remy

followed. The crowd ignored them, but a serving lass already noted their presence and hurried behind the bar to greet them. With her red hair and more freckles than even Remy boasted, she was pretty if a little frazzled around the edges.

"Welcome," she said as Laurence took a barstool. "What will ye have?"

"Two plates, two ales, and we'll be needing a room. Is Berhan about?"

"Aye. I'll fetch yer things and let 'im know yer here."

Remy took the stool next to Laurence and eyed him sideways. "Two plates, two ales?" he asked quietly.

"Suspicious to only order one, and I've seen you eat. You'll manage."

"You haven't seen me drink," said Remy, brows raised.

Laurence gave a small laugh. "Can't hold your ale? Will I be carrying you off to bed later?"

Remy lowered his lids and gazed up through his lashes. "If my luck holds."

Laughing outright, Laurence took coins from his purse and laid them on the counter. "Hush, you strumpet, or someone will notice."

The serving lass returned, two plates balanced neatly on her arm and an ale in each hand. She set the lot on the bar and scooped up the coins. "Thank ye. Berhan will be right over."

Laurence nodded in return. He grabbed his cup and lifted it to his lips.

Remy watched as Laurence pretended to drink. He mimed it well. Must be used to this sort of playacting. "Do you spend much time with humans?" Remy took a swig. The ale was decent, yeasty with an oaken aftertaste he could get used to. He took another deep swallow.

"Some. Not much." Laurence gestured to the food. "Eat."

"Gladly." His plate contained a bowl of stew that smelled

delicious—mixed vegetables and lamb. There were potatoes on the side and a hard bread for dipping that smelled of rosemary. Remy dug in.

As he ate, a man approached. Laurence greeted him in a friendly manner, clasping his wrist with a smile. "Berhan. Good to see you."

Berhan was a stout man, short of stature, probably no taller than Remy. Black hair salted with gray hung to broad shoulders. Muscles bulged beneath a muslin tunic with shirtsleeves pushed up to reveal a myriad of burn scars. Remy pegged him for a blacksmith.

"Likewise," said Berhan. "What brings you my way?"

"Passing through. Need a room for a few nights, if you please."

"Course. Your usual?"

"If it's available, thank you."

"It is," Berhan handed over the key. "How long will you stay?"

"At least a few nights." Laurence gestured to Remy. "And it's for my charge here until I can come back and collect him."

The man offered his arm, and Remy took it. "Berhan."

"Remy. Happy to meet you."

"If you'll be needing anything while you're here, let me know. Find me at the forge, two streets south."

"Aye, thank you," said Remy.

"He could use a good skinning blade," said Laurence. "I'll send him along with coin on the morrow."

"Got plenty of those," said Berhan. He tipped his head to Remy. "We'll be seeing ye soon then, lad. Rest well."

As Remy watched him leave, he couldn't help but be excited about the idea of his own knife. In the elder village, they lived communally. All things were shared. And while Remy had never minded much, the thought of having a knife of his own, and from Laurence no less, made him giddy.

"Go on," said Laurence. "Finish eating, you've mine to manage when yours is gone."

Remy tucked back into the food. Hot and delicious, it wouldn't be a burden to overindulge this once. Not when the savory stew was near to heaven on his tongue, settling warmly in his stomach. He chased the dry bread with another gulp of ale.

"I noticed a bookseller on the way here," said Remy. "I'd planned to go there, too."

"You like books? Never mind, actually, that doesn't surprise me at all. Buy whatever you like."

Remy set the ale down with a thud. "I hope you know I didn't mention it so you'd offer to buy me things. I only want to look."

Laurence waved away his concern. "I did not think that at all, though really, the money is of no consequence. Besides it's Livia's. She'd be delighted to know she'd bought you books."

Remy thought about that. Laurence was over one hundred years old and Livia over one thousand—plenty of time to amass a fortune. "Is she rich? Are you?"

"She is certainly. I've no concerns about money, so there's no need to be frugal. Though whatever you buy, you'll have to carry on your back. There's your limit."

Polishing off the first ale, Remy swapped it for the second. In his life, he'd always been provided for. Food, shelter, clothes... he'd never gone without those basics. But there had been few luxuries, beyond books, and the idea that he could go into a store and choose whatever he liked was intriguing.

"You really don't mind?" asked Remy.

"If you buy things? No, I really don't. I'd like you to. Perhaps a nicer set of clothes as well. The vampires you meet will be richly dressed."

"All right, thank you." The drink made him warm. His belly

near to full, he started in on Laurence's. "I'm afraid I'm going to fail you. I couldn't possibly finish this."

Laurence laughed, held the empty cup in his hands and looked for all the world like an ordinary human enjoying an evening at the pub. "Don't worry about finishing it. Just eat what you like then I'll show you to the room."

Remy frowned. "Then you must leave."

"Aye, but I'll be quick. I'll get a horse from the livery. The journey won't take long."

Normally Remy would be thrilled to have a few days in a human town to meet people and explore, but he'd grown accustomed to Laurence at his side and would miss him like his own right arm. Pushing the food away, Remy set his eye on the last bit of ale. Why not? He finished Laurence's cup. Already the alcohol caused a pleasant tingle behind his eyes and over his lips.

"Chin up," said Laurence, judging his mood. "Come, let's get you upstairs."

Remy followed through the dwindling crowd, past a large stone fireplace and up worn, wooden stairs to the second level. Down a narrow hall and to a door dead center. "This is Berhan's only windowless room. As it's cramped, he lets this one out last, so it's usually available unless he's full up. I've told him I can't sleep without the darkness."

Cramped was an understatement. No bigger than a closet, the room contained a single bed, a lopsided chair, and a nightstand for the water basin.

"Lovely," said Remy.

"We've stayed in worse." Laurence shrugged. "At least there is a bed."

"I've no complaints..." A thought occurred to Remy, bolstered by all the ale in his belly. "Well one, I've one potential complaint."

Laurence raised a brow. "What's that?"

"We've a chance to fuck in a proper bed. This one is smaller than I'd like, but I believe in us." Their gazes locked, gray on amber. Remy let his eyes go wide and hopeful. "See me off properly?"

Laurence shot him a smoldering look and locked the door.

15

Remy lay naked and boneless on the thin bed. He was alone; Laurence had left for Bran Vigny. The dark little room smelled of damp and sex and offered little comfort without the vampire's arms around him.

If Remy shut his eyes he could still feel Laurence on his skin, so he squeezed them tight and relived each moment.

They'd clung to each other, the vampire's weight a welcome trap pinning him to the bed. Remy had clenched his thighs tight for Laurence to thrust between, the bed rocking precariously with each stroke. Teeth scraped sharp at his collar bone, but despite Remy's begging, did not break the skin. Blissful rocking sent bolts of arousal to his length, hard and twitching with need as it lay trapped between their bellies. Laurence came with a moan, his desperate spasms slowing to helpless little trembles. Then the vampire slid down Remy's body to finish him off with his mouth.

Though the memory threatened to rouse him again, Remy lay sated and sleepy, dreaming of next time. He would insist Laurence fuck him properly. Oil went on his mental shopping list for tomorrow.

A pillow made a poor substitute for the vampire's chest. Remy curled up under his blankets and fell into a light doze which must have turned into a deep sleep, because he awoke to the sound of servants getting on with the morning's chores.

The backward sleep schedule left him groggy, but the promise of daylight beckoned. So he readied the best he could, washing from the basin on the dresser and throwing on his dingy clothes—with a new set, he could get these laundered. With that in mind, he set out for a day's worth of exploring and errands.

First stop, a street vendor for something to eat. Wyckshire was a lively town boasting plenty to choose from. With a hot meat pie in his belly and sunshine on his shoulders, Remy's fine spirits soared even though he missed Laurence at his side.

The vampire would be sleeping now, whether cooped up in some hideaway or already at the castle Bran Vigny, Remy didn't know. He promised himself not to dwell on Laurence's absence —not when he had money in his pocket and a bookseller to visit —but each time his eye caught something interesting, he'd open his mouth to tell him, then fight off the wave of disappointment that Laurence wasn't there.

Remy saved the bookshop for last. He'd chosen new clothes —basic layers but of a fine quality fabric, grays and blacks to look nice next to Laurence's—then he sent the old ones to the inn to be washed. At the grocer's market he purchased dried snacks for his travel pack and that vial of oil he couldn't wait to put to use. Then he'd gone to Berhan's forge and chosen a knife with the man's help, a small skinning dagger with a dark wooden handle that felt as if it were made for his hand. After all that, the bookseller's storefront called like a cool drink on a hot summer's day.

A large cloth sign hung outside advertising samples of script the local scribe had mastered for those wealthy enough to order something custom. Remy admired the twirling letters, but he would not have time to wait on anything custom. He'd choose from whatever the owner kept in stock.

As he walked through the front door, a little bell over the threshold jingled. Soon after, a young woman about Remy's age appeared from behind the stacks.

"Good day to you," she said, her voice cautious but friendly. She wore a green apron stained with ink over a faded brown dress and appeared a bit frazzled.

He smiled back. "And to you, my lady."

Color flushed her cheeks at the greeting above her station. With brown hair and eyes to match, she would have looked plain but for the way her face lit up for a customer. "How can I help you?"

Remy scanned the shop. Drawers for manuscripts lined one wall with scrolls neatly arranged on top. Shelves with second-hand wares, choir tomes, and Latin textbooks stood floor to ceiling. Old tablets with a scrawling script he didn't recognize were displayed on a table by the window. Thin pamphlets on tatty parchment and bound with string overflowed from straw baskets set on the floor. Hardly any space was left unoccupied.

The smell was heaven—paper, ink, and leather—Remy took in a pleasing lungful. A treasure trove of goodies awaited his attention, and he wished to spend the rest of the day perusing every nook and cranny.

"I simply don't know where to start!" he answered with no lack of enthusiasm.

She laughed. "I take it you like to read then, *my lord?*"

"Very much, though I don't often get the chance. You?"

"Aye." She wiped her hands on her apron and held one out to Remy as a man might. "Always loved the written word. Name's Clara."

He clasped her wrist. "Remy. Pleased to meet you, Lady Clara."

Clara gave a half-curtsey and gestured for him to come

farther inside. "Schooling type texts this way, and here's the religious section if you prefer it." She swept her hand from one row of shelves to the next. "I've Latin over here, you look the sort. And in the baskets, gutter filth not worthy of gentleman such as yourself."

Remy raised a brow, eyeing the baskets. "Gutter filth you say?"

"Terrible stuff," said Clara, plucking a pamphlet from the bin and handing it over. "Tales of ghosts, demons, and vampires out to terrorize young maidens and old spinsters alike. You'd hate it." Her lips curled to a sly grin that rose to glittering brown eyes.

Vampires. Remy took the pamphlet with a sly wink. "I would certainly hate it though I should probably buy several. To be sure, that is."

Laughter spilled from her lips. "As many as you like. Ten lira apiece. Feel free to read a bit before you buy."

"Thank you, and tell me, what have you for my grandmother who can read the Latin? Secular, not religious."

If such a thing were possible, her delight increased tenfold. "Has she read any Virgil? The Roman poet?"

"I've no idea, but doubtless she'd enjoy her own copy either way."

Clara led him past one row of shelves and to another with a bounce in her step. She carefully pulled a small volume from her stock. "Here then, this one is called Eclogues and is a collection of pastoral poems in the original Latin."

"Perfect, you have my thanks again. Perhaps I'll just take a moment to choose between the terrible stuff for myself, then I shall pay for everything at once."

Clara tipped her head. "I'll wrap this one up for you."

Remy chose several of the leaflets from the baskets, the ones which professed to be tales of vampires. He thought they'd amuse Laurence and liked the idea of reading a story of vampires to his vampire as they settled for bed.

"Could I impose on you further?" asked Remy.

Her eyes narrowed, her gaze turning cautious. She'd wrapped the book he'd chosen for Evanora in cloth and was tying it with a bit of blue ribbon when she froze at his words. "That depends. What do you want?"

Remy glanced at the floorboards. "I only meant that it's nearly time for supper, and I am staying at the inn up the street. If you've no plans, I thought perhaps we could dine together? I don't know anyone here."

"Dine together." Her voice had gone flat.

Perhaps she thought him forward. "I see it was a poor suggestion. My apologies, I'll take the books and leave you in peace."

"Sixty-five lira." She pushed the package his way. "Why would you want to dine with me?"

Remy dug out the coin and laid it on the counter. "Conversation. I meant nothing by it."

Clara's gaze softened a whisper. "You're at Berhan's place?"

"Aye," said Remy hopefully.

Her jaw tightened, and she stuck out her chin. "I close shop in two hours. I'll meet you there after."

Remy wasn't sure what had put her off or what had changed her mind, but he'd love to have her as a dinner companion. "That would be a pleasure, my lady."

"Clara."

"Clara," Remy amended. He took the package and bowed to her before leaving.

Outside the air had grown warm and humid. Remy retreated to the inn with his treasures, thinking perhaps he could steal a quick nap before dinner. He found his old clothes freshly laundered and folded on his bed. What would Laurence think of the new garments? It would be obvious he purchased them to match the vampire. Would Laurence care? Would he poke fun? No, it wasn't like Laurence to tease, at least not harshly.

As Remy lay down and shut his eyes, thoughts of their lovemaking on this very bed danced repeatedly across his mind. He reached into his smalls to stroke his cock and imagined it was Laurence's hand that worked him. A short time later he nodded off, hand still sticky with evidence of his lust. Dreams of the handsome vampire filled his head.

His stomach woke him in time for dinner, rumbling its discontent. Remy washed, attempted to tame his hair, and headed down to the pub to meet Clara.

He didn't have to wait long. Clara strode into Berhan's like she owned the place, shoulders rolled back, head held high.

Remy stood to escort her in.

One of the men who'd been shoveling mouthfuls of barley cakes down his trap hollered at her. Beside him, another man jeered.

Remy hurried to her side, appalled at their behavior.

Clara set her eyes on his, firmly ignoring the rude men.

"Bitch," one of them muttered, none too quietly. "Watch your back."

Remy's magic gathered at his fingertips, ready to defend her, but he reined it in. He couldn't risk leaving a trace and working spells in front of humans was prohibited unless it was a matter of life and death. Name calling, though hurtful, wouldn't kill her.

Clara stalked past him with purpose and dropped heavily into a chair.

Remy sat across from her. "What was that about?"

She shrugged. "They don't like me."

"But why?" Remy asked, caught himself, then backtracked. "I'm sorry, that's none of my business."

"It's fine." She waved off the apology. "They don't think a woman should run a shop on her own. They like to threaten just to hear their own voices. I say sod them all."

"Well, yes. Sod them all then." Remy signaled to the barmaid for ales. The woman nodded and went to fetch them. "It's your shop? That must be nice, to peddle books, that is."

"I'm the lead scribe as well." Pride sparkled in her eyes. "The book you bought for your gran? That's my work."

"My goodness, that's remarkable!" Remy could write, all witches were taught their letters, but his messy scribble would never be fit to sell. "How do you find the time?"

Her shoulders lifted in a slight shrug. "I like to keep busy."

Their ales arrived, two mugs and a tankard to share between them. "Thank you, mistress. Could we have two plates as well?"

"Aye," said the barmaid as she retreated, but not before glowering at Clara. Did everyone in this town hate the bookseller? No wonder she'd been so suspicious about his invitation.

"Would you tell me how you came to own a bookshop? I must say, I'm desperately curious what it's like. To spend your days among so many stories. Are you an author?"

"You ask a lot of questions," said Clara, the crease on her forehead deepening.

She reminded him of Laurence. "I do, don't I? I'm endlessly curious. You don't need to answer, we could talk about something else."

The barmaid set a plate in front of each of them. Barley cakes with leak and onion soup. It smelled lovely. "Thank you," said Remy with a nod.

Clara nodded her thanks as well but kept her eyes on the food rather than the disapproving serving woman. The barmaid left with a huff. Remy ignored the foul attitude and dug in.

"My father owned the shop," Clara answered out of the blue. "S'pose he'd have liked a son to leave it to, but there was naught but me. He was a good teacher, though. Taught me all I know. We ran the shop together until he passed, solstice last."

Remy frowned. "I'm sorry."

"Thank ye," Clara said into her soup bowl.

"The shop is magnificent. You obviously do a grand job with it."

"What brings you to Wyckshire anyway?"

None of the answers that sprang to mind were things he could share with Clara, and Remy had never been good at falsehood. He stuck as close to the truth as possible. "I'm traveling with a friend, but he's gone ahead for a few days. So I'm here alone. I felt put out about it until I saw your shop, then I knew I'd something to look forward to. Now I have vampire stories to read before bed."

"If they give you nightmares, don't say I didn't warn you!" She lifted her ale and took a drink.

"You don't like vampires then?"

"Oh, I adore them. If I ever met one, I fear I'd swoon. Tall, dark, and handsome with an appetite to die for. What's not to love?"

Remy raised his mug with a grin. "I'll drink to that!"

16

The sure-footed, black courser Laurence rented from Wyckshire's livery maintained a fast clip to Bran Vigny. An easy journey on horseback—the quicker the better because he was already eager to reunite with Remy. He felt each mile of distance between them like a punch to the chest, stealing air from his lungs.

Remy had been nearly asleep as Laurence said goodbye. He slipped out with one last glance at his lover sprawled naked and glorious on the little bed. He'd keep that picture in his mind forever.

"Whoa." Laurence slowed the big horse to a walk as they passed through the castle gates.

"Ho there," said the stable boy, taking the reins.

Laurence dismounted and gave the black gelding a pat on the neck. "He's a smooth goer. Give him a few extra carrots for me, will you?"

The boy scratched the horse behind the ear. "Aye, of course."

Leaving the courser with the attendant, Laurence flagged down a page. Her face lit with recognition as she trotted down the main steps and crossed the courtyard to greet him.

"Back so soon, sir?" she greeted. "What can I do for you?"

Laurence didn't know her by name, but he recognized her face. A young vampire, not ten years turned and still under the care of her sire. "Have someone prepare my room, if you please, and a bath. Do you know, is Livia of Rome in attendance?"

"She is. Shall I fetch her?"

"Just let her know I've arrived, please, and invite her to my rooms if she's not otherwise occupied."

"Yes, sir." She skipped back up the steps and off into the castle.

Laurence followed at a slower pace, eyes scanning the yard. Bran Vigny loomed tall, dark, and imposing over heavily manicured gardens. Greenery spilled forth from the entryway to the gates. A maze of curved pathways sprawled amongst the lush vegetation. The castle itself was built upward more so than outward, as if straining for the clouds.

He'd called Bran Vigny home off and on for forty-five years. He wondered what Remy would make of the soaring castle and looked forward to finding out, hopefully soon. Assuming The Dozen would allow it.

Climbing the steps two at a time, Laurence made his way inside. Usually the place gave him a sense of calm, but anticipation clawed at his nerves. If The Dozen extended their protection to Remy, what would they demand in return?

Regardless, he'd need to clean himself up and check in with Livia before requesting an audience. His rooms were on the sixth floor, with long-ranging views of the forest that surrounded Bran Vigny's boundaries. He opened his door to find Livia had already made herself comfortable. She stood to greet him, unfolding her elegant limbs from their reclined position on his lounging settee.

"Hello, dear, welcome back." Livia gifted him with a slow smile. Dressed head to toe in gold velvet, her stunning gown clung tight at her top and hung loose in folds around her ankles. The color brought out her golden-brown eyes.

"Thank you for coming." Laurence greeted her with a kiss.

"Heavens, you look like something a cat would drag in. What's happened?"

He indeed looked rough. His pants, torn in the fight with the Marshland Pack, were tatty and covered in grime. His shirt, thankfully black, hid most of the dirt but was worse for wear. At least he'd been able to wash off the dried blood at Berhan's. "I need a bath."

Her gaze traveled from his head to his toes. "You may need two of them. The servants are drawing one now. Does your witch fair well?"

Laurence undid his belt and began to peel away his ragged clothes. "Aye. Remy is well. Safe in Wyckshire."

Livia followed him through the sitting room and into his bedroom. "And the barrier?"

"He knows no more than we do. The arc holds for now though surely his elders are struggling to overcome it as we speak. Remy doesn't know how long it will hold."

She leaned against the wooden rails of his bed as he dug through the wardrobe for proper clothes. A servant emerged from the washroom and curtsied. "The water is ready, sir, madam."

"Thank you, sweeting. You're dismissed," said Livia with a graceful wave of her hand. The serving girl left them alone; the door slid shut behind her.

Laurence laid the new clothes on the bed and shucked off the rest of the dirty ones, piling them in a heap on the floor.

Livia toed them farther away. "Those should be burned."

"I won't argue. Come keep me company and fill me in?"

"Of course." She led the way into the washroom.

The stone floor was cool against the soles of his feet. A brass tub stood near the fireplace, just large enough for Laurence to submerge himself fully. Livia perched on a little wooden stool as he climbed in.

Enveloped in warm water, Laurence closed his eyes and let out a sigh. He thought of Remy and wished the witch could be there to enjoy this luxury. Remy all loose-limbed and flush from a bath would be a temptation he could lose himself in for hours. Maybe once he arrived—

"Ahem," Livia coughed, bringing him back to reality.

"Sorry, only thinking."

"I'm sure." Her lips curled to a smile. "You're bedding him now, then?"

"Why is it you always seem to read my mind? And yes, you were right about that."

"I often am." It would have come off as boastful from anyone else, but from Livia the sentiment only sounded sincere.

Laurence grabbed the soap and got on with washing. "Have you spoken with The Dozen?"

She exhaled. "Extensively."

"And? What's the news?"

Livia crossed one leg over the other and leaned in. "My sense is that Remy will be welcomed. They're wary but will offer to extend their protection. In return, of course, they'll expect his help on certain projects."

Laurence went to object, but she raised her hand. "They won't tell me which projects. Or you, for that matter. They'll discuss it with Remy when he arrives. If he refuses, they offer safe passage through to human lands in Benton and their well-wishes for his continued good health. He can part from our rulers on friendly terms but without their protection. It's no use pushing for details. I've tried, and they won't budge."

"You told them if he performs spellwork, his kind can track him?"

"Yes, though they knew that. There is a witch here who can teach him to cloak his magical trail. That lesson will come first.

Don't look so suspicious, this is good news. Let's wait to hear what they ask Remy to do before we fret."

Laurence wracked his brain for an inkling as to what projects The Dozen would want Remy's help with. Nothing good came to mind. He dunked his head beneath the water and ran fingers through his hair. Surely Remy wouldn't agree to anything that would endanger his safety. Perhaps he'd be wise to grab his witch and flee straight for Benton. Forget the whole business of war and battle—a tempting possibility.

He broke the surface to find a guarded expression on Livia's face. "There's more, isn't there?"

She nodded. "You aren't going to like this."

"What?" Concerns for Remy's security flooded his mind. Maybe he shouldn't have brought the witch there after all.

"Valeri is here."

Dread seized his chest. "But—"

"He asked to return to court. His petition was granted on the stipulation he leave you be. The Dozen are well aware of his transgressions and of their commitment to you for your service, but it has been forty-five years. They believe he's paid his due and earned a chance at redemption."

"Earned?" Laurence spluttered. "How?"

"He brought intel from overseas. Don't ask me, I don't know it. Only that whatever he's learned was enough to put him back in their good graces. Valeri knows better than to come for you."

"Does he?"

Her jaw tightened, a little twitch. Someone that didn't know her as well as Laurence did might not have noticed. "I won't let him harm you. Or Remy."

Remy.

Gods, what had he done? Brought Remy within miles of the filthy grasp of his sire. Valeri would never let Laurence go after he'd rejected him, and if he learned what Remy meant to

Laurence, he'd seek to destroy the witch. Or possess him, which might be worse.

"You're overthinking," said Livia. "He isn't concerned with you. Hasn't asked of you. And he's brought along a new fledgling."

"Slave, you mean." Laurence knew how Valeri treated fledglings once the shine wore off.

"We can hope Valeri has finally moved on."

"I won't risk Remy's life on hope."

"Never. You have me, and I've promised to protect your witch, as I have protected you in darker times."

Her words meant something to Laurence but didn't completely ease the fear that gripped his mind.

Livia took a piece of soap from the tray. "Lean forward, I'll wash your back."

Laurence would convince Remy to take the safe passage offered. Get out of Bran Vigny and away from Valeri's sphere of influence.

When he failed to budge, Livia put her hand to the back of his neck and tugged him forward. "Your back?"

He let her move him how she wanted. She lathered soap across his shoulders and down his spine. Her familiar scent of magnolia blossoms wafted along the air between them. Livia's touch would ordinarily soothe or excite him, but he was in no mood for either. "Thank you," he said when she'd finished.

"You're welcome. Please don't worry. Let me handle Valeri."

Dirt ringed the tub. Laurence stood and climbed out, taking the towel Livia held out for him. "What should I tell Remy? That I've brought him to a house of vipers? That he's in more danger now than before we'd met?"

"Stop this dreadful line of thinking. Would he even be alive if it weren't for you?"

No.

Remy would have died the night he created the arc. Werewolves would have killed first and asked questions later. The thought wasn't exactly comforting. "What have I done, Liv?"

"Your best." She cupped his face in her hands. "And your best is more than most. We will keep him safe. Valeri can hardly accost either of you at Bran Vigny."

That much she had correct. With The Dozen in attendance, Bran Vigny remained a safe haven, even if evil lurked its hallways. The faster Laurence got on with his business there, the faster he could go back to Wyckshire and collect Remy. He dried off with haste, and they returned to the bedroom.

"I'm sorry for disrupting your life with this," said Laurence. "Thank you for being here."

"You're welcome." She picked up his tunic and shook it out. The cloth smelled stuffy, having been folded in a wardrobe unused for so long.

Laurence dressed quickly. He wasn't fussy about his clothes, but he had chosen the black and gold to compliment her gown. They'd make a handsome pair when petitioning the ruling vampires.

Thankful for Livia at his side, Laurence remembered his first time in front of the court. She'd been there for him back then, too. Ever faithful. He'd been scared—constantly living with Valeri's threats on his shoulders—and he'd asked for protection with hopes they'd execute Valeri. He knew better now. Vampires weren't permitted to slay their own, regardless how heinous the crime. Legions populated the dungeons below as a result.

Livia straightened the fabric of his collar and smoothed her hands from shoulder to bicep. "Much better."

Laurence set his mind to the matter at hand and extended his arm. "Shall we?"

Livia took it. "We shall."

They exited his rooms, walked down a mountain's worth of stairs, and headed for the Great Hall. Glowing yellow sconces and multi-colored tapestries lined the walls. Their footsteps echoed on the bare stone floor.

Other vampires went about their business, servants too. Laurence ignored them. He had practiced his speech in his head as he'd ridden, but things were different with Valeri present.

Livia's fingers at his elbow gave him courage. Their gazes met as they approached the carved double doors that stood between them and The Dozen. She nodded, and Laurence returned the gesture.

He noticed the door's carvings. A great horned devil looming over his subjects as flames licked at their feet. Their faces rendered frozen in terror for all eternity.

Chest tight, gut churning, Laurence tore his gaze from the hellish scene and thrust open the door.

The rulers assembled behind a massive oval table, eight in total though twelve made up this council. Mahu, the eldest, was noticeably absent. All eyes turned as they entered. Livia was elder to at least half their number, and well respected, having turned down a post on their court more than once. Laurence had served them faithfully for decades. Even without Mahu, they presented an intimidating front.

Incense burned in braziers on smaller tables against the walls. Smoke wafted by, scented of sandalwood and jasmine, smells Laurence associated with this place and these vampires.

Corinne rose from her center seat, a striking woman with fair hair and skin but irises dark as cinder. Her voice rang clear and high. "We have been waiting for you. Welcome, Livia, Laurence."

"Mistress," they answered in unison. Laurence bowed while Livia only inclined her head.

Gesturing to the empty chairs with bejeweled fingers, Corinne resumed her seat. "Please, join us. We've much to discuss."

The others nodded their greetings as Laurence pulled a chair out for Livia, then took one for himself.

Not for the first time, Laurence would place his fate in The Dozen's hands. He'd tied Remy's destiny to their whim for better or for worse. Laurence could only hope he would not come to regret this decision.

Corinne steepled her fingers, her gaze falling heavily on Laurence. "Tell us about the witch."

17

The next day, Remy dropped into Clara's bookshop eager to gush over the story she'd sold him. The riveting tale of a demonic Lord Vampire terrorizing a town full of farmers had kept him up half the night. Remy had cast Laurence not as the vampire, but as the town hero, a brave farmer standing up for the weak among his flock—and dying for them, unfortunately.

The bell jingled pleasantly as he stepped inside. Remy stopped short at the threshold with a gasp as he took in the interior. One of the ground-to-ceiling bookshelves lay sideways across the floor. It had destroyed a table on its way down. The baskets of pamphlets were smashed amongst the scattered mess of books and papers. Their mistress was nowhere to be seen.

"Clara?" called Remy, alarmed. What if whoever did this had hurt her too? "Clara!"

He picked his way through the wreckage, stepping carefully to avoid damaging the books further. "Are you here? It's Remy."

Clara emerged from the back room, arms folded, shoulders set. Her watery eyes blazed with anger. "It was that brute, Aktis. He wrecked my shop and threatened to send in his goons!"

"Are you all right?"

Clara huffed and untucked her arms. In her hand she brandished a knife not unlike the one Remy had purchased from Berhan. "Fine. He couldn't lay a hand on me while I had this. But he'd no trouble attacking my books."

Remy stood next to her, and they surveyed the damage together. "Damn. Who's Aktis? Why would he do this?"

"He's my landlord's son. The old man's got frail so he sends Aktis 'round to collect nowadays. He's one that don't think I should have the shop on my own. But he can go to the devil because I pay my rent."

Clara's fingers gripped the knife's handle, knuckles white. Her rigid posture radiated tension. She turned to Remy, her eyes cold. "Aktis fancied me when we were younger. He was a bully back then too. Used to pick on the smaller kids. Won't take no for an answer. He's had it out for me ever since. And now the rest agree. They don't like seeing a woman fair better than them."

Remy reached forward and gently peeled her fingers from the knife. "Put this away. You won't need it while we clean up."

Her brows crept up. "We?"

"Of course. It will go much faster with two people. Meanwhile, what is there to do about this bully Aktis? Can we report him to someone?"

Her shoulders lost some of their tension and began to sink. She gave a laugh that held no mirth. "Who? Wyckshire has no sheriff. Berhan's the closest thing we got to a watchman, and he already knows Aktis is a prick."

"Won't he help?"

"He does what he can. Not much to do when the crowd agrees with Aktis."

They continued to scan the wreckage. The obvious starting point was to clear and right the shelf. Remy longed for his magic. A tingling sensation pulsed at his fingertips, ready to put the shop back to right in seconds. But no, they'd do this the hard way. "Well then, let's get this sorted, and we can think of a plan as we work."

Her face displayed her skepticism. "A plan?"

"Indeed. You can't go on like this, it isn't safe." Remy knelt to begin moving books out of the way. He wished Laurence were there. The vampire could simply intimidate Aktis until the brute agreed to fuck off.

Clara plopped down next to him and followed his lead. She gave a long, tired sigh.

"Hey," said Remy. "No more of that. When my friend returns, he'll help us. He'll know what to do."

She topped off a stack and slid it aside. "Who's this friend of yours anyhow, and why has he left you behind?"

"His name is Laurence, and he had to leave to do me a favor." Remy shoved his pile of books next to hers and began another. "I'm in a bit of a tight spot myself. He's set out to fix it."

"Oh? What's happened? You all right?"

"It's a long story."

"Long stories are my business, go on."

With the books cleared, they could right the shelf. The task would give Remy a moment to think. This would be easier if he could tell Clara the truth. "Lend me a hand first."

She stood, and they each grabbed a corner of the shelf and heaved. The solid wood behemoth was heavy and awkwardly shaped, taller than either of them. Remy grunted with effort. Clara was stronger than she looked, and together, they shoved it upward and back against the wall.

"I could never have done that on my own," she said, wiping her hands on her dress.

Remy let out a chuckle. "We hardly managed it together."

"Why don't you hand me books, and I'll put them where they belong while you tell me about whatever tight spot you've gotten yourself into?"

"All right," said Remy, wondering how he should put it. He grabbed a stack of books. "Well I've done something, you see, and my, uh…village isn't so thrilled with me so I've had to leave. I suppose that makes me homeless."

She placed one book after another back on the shelf. How she remembered what order they went in was magic in itself.

"Laurence is helping with living arrangements. That's what he's doing now in the next town over."

Clara turned to him sharply. "But the next town over is abandoned! You can't stay there."

He gathered another stack for her to shelve. "Abandoned?"

"Do you mean the ruins of Bran Vigny? Or the town past it, because Benton is a long way off. Your friend may not return for weeks if he's gone there."

Remy had meant Bran Vigny, of course, but Laurence had made no indication the place was in ruins. Though it could be spellwork making it appear so to humans. Enchantment wasn't a skill of Remy's, but Emmeline could manage it. Thinking of her raised the little hairs on Remy's neck and arms. He shook it off. Were there witches at Bran Vigny?

"Now that you mention it, I'm not sure, though he led me to believe he'd return soon."

The sympathetic look she threw him morphed into resolve. "Stay in Wyckshire. I've rooms over the shop. You could work for me."

Remy grinned as he imagined being a bookseller's apprentice, helping around the little shop. Delightful. He sighed. In another life perhaps, but he couldn't stay. When the arc fell, it wouldn't be safe. "That's very kind of you. I'd better wait to see what Laurence says when he returns."

She grabbed the last book from his arms. "Who is this Laurence fellow to you, because your eyes go all dreamy when you speak his name."

His grin broadened to a full-on smile as he picked up the

next stack. "I rather like him. We've only just met a few weeks ago, but he has quite charmed me already."

"A beau then?"

Remy's cheeks heated. "Indeed."

"He treat you nice?"

"He does." Remy set his voice low with a conspiratorial whisper. "And he kisses like he's starved for me. It's positively seductive."

Her face lit with warmth. "Good for you. I'm glad. I look forward to meeting him."

"I can't wait to show him the story about the vampire. He's going to love it."

Her eyes widened. "You've finished already?"

"Aye, last night. Kept me up hours. I had to know how it ended."

Clara paused her sorting of books. "You want to know a secret?"

"Of course I do, what?"

She studied his face. "I wrote that one."

"No!" Remy's mouth hung open. "Really? It's magnificent. Your Lord Vampire is such the ghastly villain and yet I found myself rooting for him just a bit. However did you manage it?"

Clara gave a humble shrug and turned back to her work. "I've always loved stories."

"Me too. You must sell me another. I want to read everything you've written. I've no idea how you find the time for all this."

They finished setting the shop back to rights, all but the table, which was irreparably broken and had to be counted as a loss. Afterward, they swept the floors and cleaned up dust that had been scattered everywhere in the scuffle. By the time they were through, they both needed a wash. But first, Clara put on a pot of tea and fixed a plate of biscuits.

Remy collapsed into the chair across from her, tired and happy. It felt good to help someone else and to make a new friend in the process. He hoped one day it would be safe to visit Clara and her bookshop again. He could relax there, among the stacks, curled up with a good story.

Just as he lifted a jam-filled biscuit to his lips, a zinging snap crackled through his every nerve. He felt it like the downpour from a summer storm—sudden and fierce—the sky opening up and rain tearing down from above. His magic stirred in response, at the ready, chomping at the bit, but Remy could do nothing.

He froze, his hand with the biscuit poised before his mouth.

Clara stared at him, eyes wide. "What's wrong?"

What's wrong?

Everything.

His great magical barrier shattered around them, silent and invisible to Clara, but loud as a thunder crack echoing in Remy's ears.

Remy may as well paint a target on his back, because the arc was no more.

A disparate sense prickled at Laurence's awareness as if the air itself was irrevocably altered. A bad feeling churned in his gut. He shoved the sheets aside and rose from bed. Crossing the room with dread clinging to his chest like ivy, he unbarred the shutters and hurled them open. A gasp escaped his lips as he peered at the stars. The opalescent sheen had vanished.

Remy's arc was gone.

Urgency drove Laurence through the motions of dressing and packing his bag. With the barrier gone, getting Remy to the relative safety of Bran Vigny was paramount. The Dozen repeated the same offer to Laurence as they had to Livia. They would grant Remy sanctuary in exchange for service, the parameters of which would be discussed with the witch alone. The secrecy, though irritating, was the best offer he would get.

Grabbing his pack, he flung open the door with the intent of informing Livia before he left. In a stroke of luck, she was already heading toward him.

Clad in only her silver sleeping gown, she hurried forward on stockinged feet. "The barrier–"

"–has collapsed. I know. I'm off to fetch him now."

"Shall I come along?"

"No, stay here. Keep an eye on Valeri. I'll be quick." He leaned in and kissed her goodbye.

She gave his shoulders a squeeze before letting him go. "Travel safe."

"Aye."

Laurence strode purposefully down the steps, through the labyrinth of hallways, and out the castle doors. He cast a longing glance at the livery. He'd prefer to ride back to Wyckshire but could run the distance faster. The decision wasn't an easy one— riding would leave him fresh on arrival, which may prove useful, but ultimately he prioritized speed.

With the moon at his back, Laurence swallowed the distance by foot. As he raced, so did his mind. Remy would be safe. The witch knew to wait and not use his magic. They'd expected the arc would fail eventually; this wasn't a surprise. Laurence only wished it had happened *after* Remy was safely ensconced at Bran Vigny.

Arriving in Wyckshire near midnight, Laurence went to Berhan's straightaway. He sidestepped a group of men huddled on the street by the inn, went through the pub, and up the stairs to the small, windowless room. He expected to find Remy asleep.

Knocking lightly, Laurence called out in a strained whisper, "Remy?"

Silence. He knocked again then concentrated on listening. Steady heartbeats and even breathing came from folks sleeping in the nearby rooms, but nothing from Remy's. Without a key, he'd have to break the door down. It would be loud, maybe wake other people, but it couldn't be helped.

Laurence forced it open, quiet as he could be while still knocking the door off its hinges. Wincing at the awful screech, he peered inside. Empty.

Where would Remy have gone?

Wait…not empty. Remy's things were gone, but a note lay folded on the center of the bed. Laurence snatched it with clumsy fingers, nervous in his rush to lay eyes on the witch.

L,
You can find me at the bookshop.
-R

Laurence turned on heel with no idea why Remy would have left Berhan's for a bookseller's, but he didn't care. He counted himself lucky the witch had had the presence of mind to leave a note. Glancing both ways down the hall revealed no disgruntled guests. He hurried down the stairs and back outside.

As he made his way to the bookshop, still working out how he'd wake Remy without attracting the attention of everyone nearby, the ear-piercing sound of shattered glass rang out in the night.

The flailing body of a man flew through the air and landed with a thud in the street, surrounded by shards of glass. Not seconds later, another body followed. Laurence nearly collided with a third as he leapt through the space where the window used to be and into the bookshop.

There stood Remy, arms outstretched, clearly channeling magic from his fingers toward the fourth man. A woman huddled behind him, wild-eyed and panicked. Remy flung the man past Laurence and out of the shop.

"Remy!" What was he doing using his magic?

"Laurence!" Remy looked relieved to see him.

Any minute now, people awoken by the disturbance would peek out their windows, open their doors, and maybe wander outside to see what the ruckus was all about. Laurence assessed the situation with haste. No one would believe Remy had fought four men and won, but they might believe Laurence had.

He cast his gaze back to Remy. "Are you all right?"

When Remy nodded, Laurence left the shop for the street.

Two of the men were trying to stand, but something held them down. Laurence turned. "Remy, cease."

The witch's expression shifted to shock, and he dropped his hands to his sides. Two men crawled to their feet, the other two still lay amidst the glass.

Laurence stood over them. "Stay down."

"Who the fuck are you?" said a man covered head to toe in cuts and scrapes from the glass. The coppery tang of blood scented the air, reminding Laurence it had been too long since he'd fed.

"Quiet." Laurence punched him in the jaw.

One of the others took a swing at him, dagger clutched in straining white fingers.

Laurence dodged, kicked the man in the back of the knee and dropped him back to the ground. "I said, stay down."

Onlookers began to cluster.

Berhan rushed from the inn, his face flushed red. "What's going on?"

Remy and the woman emerged from the shop. People stared from open windows. To stall while he came up with an explanation, Laurence rubbed his knuckles as if they were sore.

"They attacked us," said Remy. He nudged the woman at his side. Her eyes took on a fierce intensity Laurence had to admire after what she'd just witnessed.

"They've been threatening to rob me since Pa died. Never thought they'd go through with it. Lucky for me my friends stayed over." She glanced at Laurence.

He gave her a faint nod. Laurence thought they'd intended more than robbery, but he kept his mouth shut.

One of the would-be-robbers bolted, followed quickly by a second.

"Oh no ye won't," said Berhan, giving chase.

Careful not to reveal preternatural speed or strength, Laurence joined the chase. Another townsperson leant a hand and together they caught the runaways. Laurence held the man with one arm locked behind his back.

A small crowd had formed; people huddled on stoops and watching the whole thing. Nothing like the threat of a street brawl to bring out the neighbors.

A glance at Remy revealed an alert glare and a carefully poised finger obviously keeping the two men who hadn't run from moving. He really needed to get Remy out of here before someone noticed the unnatural restraint.

The man in his grasp struggled and whined. Laurence yanked his belt from his waist and tied it round his wrists. "What do I do with this one?"

Berhan, dressed only in his nightclothes, his hair standing in every direction, somehow still managed an air of authority. "That's Aktis you got there. I imagine his pa won't be none too pleased. Bring him in, I'll hold them till morning."

Laurence dragged the struggling man into the inn and left him in the cellar at Berhan's instructions. Afterward, with the help of another man, they brought the last two in. With that done, he made to go, but Berhan spoke up first.

"I didn't know you knew Clara," said the innkeeper. "Fine lass."

Laurence didn't know Clara, but apparently Remy had made her acquaintance. He shrugged. "I like to read. She sells books."

Berhan accepted that answer well enough. "Good thing you were there."

"I should go talk to her, make sure she's okay."

"Aye, go on. I'll deal with this lot."

Laurence nodded and took his leave. The onlookers dawdled only briefly, then began to lose interest. He found Remy and Clara huddled together inside the shop, Remy holding her shoulders and whispering frantically. Unshed tears welled in her wide eyes.

"Don't be scared. I'm so sorry. I didn't mean to frighten you. I'd no idea what else to do, and it all happened so very fast you see so—"

Laurence stopped him with a hand to the small of his back. Remy whirled and sank into his chest. "Oh Laurence. What have I done?"

With one arm around Remy, Laurence looked to the woman. "Are you both all right?"

Her nod came slow and silent. Remy straightened. "I'm fine, but I've scared the wits out of poor Clara and blown our cover too. Laurence, we must go. They could be here any minute."

"Your people can trace you that quickly?"

Clara's eyes darted from Remy to Laurence and back.

"Maybe, maybe not. Depends quite a lot on luck. One set of witches will scry for my location, then another will arrange a portal. It could take minutes or days, there's no way of knowing."

"Of course there isn't," said Laurence dryly. This was rotten luck. And the girl looked torn between insisting they all go to hell and fainting where she stood.

"Witches?" she asked.

Remy turned back to her. "Are you all right? Please tell me you're all right."

Clara raised her eyes to Remy's, voice shaky but clear. "What are you?"

"I'm a witch. He's a vampire—"

"Remy!" said Laurence, but the witch kept talking as if he hadn't protested at all.

"—but we'd never harm you, I swear it." He grabbed for her hand, and she let him take it. "I won't let anything bad happen to you."

"Oh, the devil," said Laurence. "We'll have to bring her along."

"Of course we will," said Remy, as if it were rather obvious. "She can't stay here; it's too dangerous. Those vile bullies will never let her alone after tonight."

Laurence shook his head. That reason was all well and good, but Clara had seen magic firsthand, and with Remy's admission, she could not be left a loose end to rail on about witches and vampires. Bran Vigny would be her home now, whether she liked it or not. He hoped she'd come easy.

Laurence glanced to Remy. "Do you have your things? We should hurry."

"Right, I'll get them. Can you help Clara pack a bag?"

Yes, help a young woman pack her underclothes, perfect. "Just go."

Remy scurried from the room. Clara still looked mildly dazed, but she collected herself enough to protest. "I can't leave. This is my shop."

"Was your shop," said Laurence and immediately felt bad for being so blunt when her face fell. "Clara, I'm sorry, but you can't stay here. You must see that. I realize you've been through quite an ordeal, but I really do need you to gather your things so we can leave. I can have someone pack up your books and send them along once we're safe."

Her eyes scanned the shop in a wide sweep. "All of them? You can do that?"

"You have my word. The essentials only for now. Please hurry to collect them."

Her lips pressed to a fine line and a determined expression took hold of her features. In a strong voice she said, "I'll only be a moment." Then she swiped a handful of pamphlets from a basket and took off in the direction Remy had gone.

Laurence put a hand to the bridge of his nose and pinched. What in the seven hells had he gotten himself into?

19

Remy kept Clara close while they crossed through Wyckshire for the stables. As the shock of the attack wore off, the ramifications of what he'd done began to set in. Fear crept up his spine. He'd had no choice but to use his magic; the men had brought knives. And now he'd given Emmeline all she needed to find him. She wouldn't stop until he was back in her clutches. If she had to go through Laurence, she'd do it.

Not for the first time Remy wondered if the world would be safer had he died creating the arc.

Clara's voice snapped him out of it. "Is he really a vampire?"

"Yes, though he's nothing like Lord Vampire, I promise. Laurence is kind." They followed behind him. Remy thought perhaps he should tell Clara that Laurence could hear them no matter how much she kept her voice down, but she had enough information to process already.

"And you're a witch." It wasn't a question. She'd seen for herself, after all.

"I would have told you, but it's forbidden," Remy explained. They turned a corner from one cobbled lane to another. In the dead of night, the streets were quiet. Remy had Clara's hand, guiding her as surely she didn't see as well in the dark as he did.

"What will happen, now that I know?" she asked.

"Nothing bad, I'll make sure of it. But I don't know what it's like at Bran Vigny; I've never been there."

Her brows rose. "We're going to the ruins?"

"I've been led to believe the castle's intact, though vampires stalking around moldering ruins would be lovely fodder for your novels."

In spite of their circumstances, she managed a smile, her eyes glittering. "I'll bear that in mind."

Laurence brought them to the livery by the town's gate. He turned to Clara. "Can you ride?"

She shook her head. "I never have."

Laurence's gaze shifted to Remy. "Can you?"

"I've ridden." What he didn't say was that it had been nearly a decade since he'd been on a horse. It was probably fine. He liked the beasts.

"There's one bit of luck. I'll just get two; Clara can ride pillion."

Laurence disappeared into a large barn and emerged a few minutes later leading two massive, intimidating animals by their halters. Remy swallowed. When Laurence went to hand off a horse to him, he had to struggle not to balk.

"This is Poppy." Laurence patted the behemoth of a brown courser on the shoulder. "I'm told she's an easy goer."

Remy took her reins and stroked her neck. With any luck, she wouldn't sense his unease. Giant black eyes gazed down on him with a quiet calm. "Hey, Poppy. I wish I had a carrot to bribe you with."

The horse let out a whicker, and Remy's unease settled.

Next to him, Clara watched intently. "Do you think she'd let me pet her too?"

He nodded and stepped out of the way. She stroked the

horse from neck to shoulder as Remy had. Poppy's gaze remained soft, her ears forward and relaxed. Surely they'd woken her up, and he felt sorry for that.

Laurence's gaze shifted from Remy to the horse. "Mount first. I'll give Clara a leg up once you're settled."

"Honestly, she's better off riding with you." Remy cast an apologetic smile to Clara. "I only half know what I'm doing."

Laurence nodded and moved their bags from his horse to Poppy. Then he mounted in a fluid movement Remy doubted he'd be able to match. The vampire extended a hand to Clara. Her gaze flit to Remy.

"Go on," Remy encouraged. "Laurence won't bite unless he's half dead and you beg. At least that's my experience."

Clara, though wide-eyed and likely overwhelmed, managed to chuckle. "If you say so." She took Laurence's hand, and he lifted her onto the great gray beast as if she weighed no more than a toddler.

"It's easier for the horse if you ride close," Laurence instructed.

Clara adjusted her skirts and scooted forward against Laurence. He took her hand and wrapped it around his waist. Remy would not let himself be jealous of an innocent human woman they'd uprooted and were currently snatching away from everything she'd ever known. Instead he climbed onto his horse with a grunt and a bit of a wobble. Poppy, bless her, put up with his clumsy effort without protest.

Laurence was still speaking gently. "Try to keep your legs still and your hips loose as we go. Let your body move with the horse. Ready?"

"As I'll ever be," said Clara in a clear, brave voice. The more Remy knew of her, the more he liked her.

"We won't be going fast. Riding double like this, and at night no less, we'll keep the horses to a walk. There's nothing to fear."

Except a marauding group of vengeful witches, thought Remy, knowing better than to say it out loud lest it come true.

Laurence made a clicking sound and urged the horse forward. Remy gave Poppy a gentle squeeze, and she followed behind. So far so good. He was glad for the distraction of remembering good horsemanship, else he'd be dwelling on one of several pressing concerns. Instead he focused on communicating with Poppy as they exited Wyckshire's gates and rode through the fields beyond.

The vast night sky appeared darker without his barrier glistening between them and the heavens. A crisp chill added bite to the rolling breeze. Farm smells hung heavy in the air, damp soil and manure. The forest beyond beckoned with its canopy of trees. Their leaves would begin to turn soon, but it all looked the same in the dark.

The slow pace gave Remy too much time to think. He was glad for the breaks they took to water the horses, glad for words with friends to drown out the misery of his thoughts. Anyone near him would be in danger. He should reject an offer of sanctuary at Bran Vigny and move along to face destiny on his own. It would be the brave thing to do, but Remy wasn't sure he could muster up that kind of courage a second time.

A glance to Laurence told him he could. The vampire freely offered a wide smile, his gray eyes locked on Remy's with affection. When Clara disappeared through the trees to take care of her own business, Laurence pressed in for a quick stolen kiss. The touch lit a spark of desire to Remy's core. He grinned.

"You look very handsome in your new clothes," said Laurence, putting some space between them.

"Thank you." Remy promptly closed the distance. "She knows about us by the way."

Laurence's brows lifted. "She does?

"Yes, so she won't be shocked when you kiss me again." Remy stood on his toes to meet Laurence's lips. He opened his mouth to the kiss, inviting the vampire's tongue to play. When Laurence held back, Remy whined and pressed forth with his own.

Sharp twin razors under his tongue made kissing a divine dichotomy of pleasure and pain. Remy lanced his flesh on purpose, and the coppery tang of blood welled between them. Laurence groaned and sucked Remy's tongue farther into his mouth. Hands gripped his sides, holding Remy in place. He leaned in for more.

"Ahem," Clara gave a polite cough to announce her return.

Laurence pulled away immediately. Remy could only follow, so lost in kissing he didn't care who watched. He fell into the vampire's chest and enjoyed the rumble of his voice. "I apologize, my lady."

"Not on my account, you don't," said Clara. "But I thought you should know, there's a halo 'round the moon. Means a storm's coming. We almost there?"

Laurence tipped his head, alert, perhaps listening for tell-tale winds or a rumble. "We won't arrive tonight, not at this pace. I'd planned to stop at the ruins."

"All that's left are ruins," said Clara. "At least that's what they say. I've never left Wyckshire."

"An enchantment obfuscates the road that leads to the castle some miles past the ruins. It would look only like dense forest to passersby."

"Magic?" asked Remy.

"Yes. I suspect you'll meet the witches who maintain the spell. The court will likely want you to work with them."

"Oh." Well he'd expected conditions, but with the arc gone and himself exposed, he wouldn't expect that offer to stand. "The danger to harbor me under their roof has increased tenfold since you made the request. Emmeline will track me here."

"Who's Emmeline?" asked Clara, her eyes growing sleepy. They'd kept her up all night, poor thing.

"I'll explain it all to you after we've slept," said Remy. "Let's hurry to shelter. If you're right about the storm, I don't want to be caught in it."

Clara *had* been right about the storm. They made it to the ruins just before the skies opened and a deluge pelted the landscape. The water beat against the old stone with muffled thuds. Poor Laurence got soaked caring for the horses, but Remy and Clara remained dry in the remains of an old castle vault.

The air was musty and stale, the wide expanse of the vault nearly pitch-black. He led Clara by the hand. "You must be exhausted."

"Fairly, yes," she said with a yawn. "And part of me is terrified, but this is also the greatest adventure I've ever had. Already I could write a book. I cannot believe your beau is a vampire. And you a witch! How did you meet?"

Remy began the tale as they unpacked their blankets and settled. Clara listened, but her attention waned. She needed rest. For that matter, Remy did too.

"Shall I tell the rest when we wake?"

She gave a sleepy nod and curled up on her side. Remy tucked the blanket around her and leaned back against the crumbling stone. Clara's soft breath soon evened to rhythmic snoring.

When Laurence arrived, dripping wet and scowling, Remy rose to greet him. "You alright? What's happened?"

"Aye, fine. Nothing. Only I'd wished for better circumstances for the horses. There's naught left of a barn to speak of, so they're in the castle proper without anything to graze on and only the grain I'd brought for them to eat. They'll want more before we leave."

Remy did feel sorry about that. Poppy had been lovely and

cooperative for all he'd asked of her in the middle of night, sweet creature.

"I could turn them out for a while, during the day," offered Remy.

"That's not a bad idea." Laurence turned to go. "I'll be back shortly."

Remy reached for his elbow. "Wait, why? Where are you going?"

Laurence covered Remy's hand with his own. "I need to feed. I won't be long."

"Don't go," his voice came quick and annoyingly desperate. "Drink from me."

"I shouldn't. I don't want to weaken you. You need your strength."

"Did I seem weak to you last time?" Remy argued and watched with some amusement as Laurence realized what they'd got up to after the last time he'd fed. "Besides, I can draw from you while we sleep."

The crease on Laurence's forehead deepened as he considered the proposal.

"Drink from me. I insist." Remy let his head fall to the side, blatantly offering his neck. He saw the moment he'd won as Laurence's expression transitioned from one of resistance, to one of hunger.

"Let me get these off first."

Remy watched with greedy eyes as Laurence peeled off each layer of sopping wet clothes until he was down to his smalls. The broad expanse of his furred chest made Remy's fingers itch to touch. Before he could make a move, Laurence swept him up into his arms, the breath huffing from Remy's chest in surprise. He clung to the vampire's shoulders, head lolled to the side, eager for the stab of pain and the ecstasy that would follow.

A long sweep of Laurence's tongue wet from collar bone to ear. "You taste marvelous."

"Do it," said Remy, full of breathy anticipation. "Please."

Delicious pressure, followed by sweet stinging pain and then a deep, gut warming pleasure overtook his senses. His whole being reduced to the point where Laurence's teeth broke his flesh; awareness spread to the rest of his body like the stroke of a lover. Passion vibrated from his veins to the vampire's mouth, peaking with every swallow.

Remy let his body go limp in Laurence's firm embrace. The sensation was easy to drown in, a peaceful death he'd gladly give himself up to, but as his eyelids fluttered closed, Laurence stopped. Teeth slid from his flesh and the tongue returned, laving the area thoroughly.

Remy whimpered his protest. "More."

Laurence chuckled against his skin. "I've had plenty. Why don't we save the rest for later, hmm?"

Sweet kisses dropped along his throat, up to his ear. A deep need to rest welled at his center. "If you say so."

"Let's get you to sleep." Laurence laid him down and settled next to him, pulling the blankets over them both.

Remy curled against Laurence's side, running his palm over the captivating skin of the vampire's abdomen. "I'm not *that* tired you know, we could—"

"Yes, you are." Laurence tugged him closer. "Hush. Go to sleep."

"You could take a lesson or two from Lord Vampire," Remy muttered, already drifting off.

"Who?" Laurence's deep rumble faded with the pelting of the rain.

Without a thought to what dangers they might face upon waking, Remy grinned as sleep claimed him from reality for another day.

2 0

———————

With only a few miles to go before they reached Bran Vigny, Laurence glanced back at the chattering pair behind him. Clara rode with Remy, who trusted Poppy enough at this point to be comfortable riding double. The two had been in conversation since they'd set out from the ruins. Laurence found the distraction from the growing threat of danger welcome. Nothing they could do would stop Emmeline's pursuit, so dwelling on it wasn't helpful.

Clara's endless questions reminded Laurence of Remy, who patiently answered everything she asked. With so much similarity between them, it was no surprise they'd bonded quickly. Remy filled her in on his people, the war, what he knew of vampires and werewolves, and their journey to this point. Laurence had listened as he thought over their predicament, but now they were close enough to be overheard.

"We're nearing the gates," Laurence cautioned. "Perhaps the conversation should veer to less sensitive matters."

Remy's features tightened, anxiety evident in the rigid line of his spine, the firm set of his shoulders. "Right, thank you."

Rounding a corner, dense forest opened to field and Bran Vigny's grand elegance came into view. Clara let out a gasp. If Remy was impressed, he was too nervous to show it. Laurence wished words of encouragement came easier for him. He'd have liked to offer assurances, to tell his lover everything would be all right, but the truth was, anything he could offer would be a platitude. Quite possibly, this could all go horribly wrong.

As they made their way inside, Laurence called for the stablehands and sent a page to fetch Livia. He helped Clara from Poppy's back and placed a comforting hand on Remy's shoulder. He only let the touch linger for a breath, but the muscle underneath his palm softened at his touch.

Remy said goodbye to the horse as a boy led them off. Then his eyes met Laurence's. "Your home is lovely."

Lush courtyards lined either side of the main road to the castle steps, fragrant summer blossoms scented the air, and the towering spires reached for the stars. Clara stood near to Remy gazing upward. "Your home is rather tall."

Laurence smiled at her words. "It is, isn't it? As if the earth were not enough, vampires wanted to conquer the sky as well."

Her eyes sparkled. "Oh I'm definitely putting that quote in my next book."

"Ever glad to be of assistance," said Laurence. "Shall we?"

Clara clutched Remy's hand and nodded. For all the world, she looked more confident than the witch at the prospect. Laurence offered Remy his arm, and the three of them strode side by side up the stairs. Keeping an eye out for any signs of Valeri, Laurence scanned his periphery and found none.

As they reached the top, Livia appeared to greet them, concern coloring her gaze. She reached for Laurence first, then Remy, gracing them with kisses. When she made it to Clara, her lips parted and her pupils widened. Clara had a similar look on her own face.

Livia wore a gown of gleaming blue satin, well fitted, with

rainbow-colored jewels sewn lavishly into the bust line. Clara would have never seen anything like it, but the woman wasn't focused on the dress, she met Liv's golden stare with bold interest.

Laurence stepped in to introduce them. "Livia, this is Remy's friend Clara, a bookseller from Wyckshire who's had a bit of an incident." He glanced to Clara. "Clara this is Livia, my friend who is here to help Remy and I out of our sticky situation."

A warm smile curled broadly across Livia's face and was met with a sunny expression from Clara. The two women joined hands and exchanged kisses on each cheek.

"My pleasure," purred Livia into Clara's ear. She wrapped an arm about her shoulder and pulled her from Remy's side to her own. Clara went without hesitation. "Shall I take charge of dear Clara then while the two of you seek audience with the court?"

"Yes, thank you, that would be helpful," said Laurence. "As long as it suits Clara."

Clara nodded without taking her eyes off Livia. Well then. Laurence would have laughed if their situation weren't so dire.

"Come to my rooms when you are done," said Livia as she swept Clara into the castle.

Laurence was left alone with Remy, the witch's hand clung snug to his elbow. "Are you ready?"

"Any last words of wisdom?" asked Remy, his amber gaze intense.

"Don't agree to anything you aren't comfortable with."

"Excellent advice. We'll see if I can manage it."

"You can. Come." Laurence led them inside and to the Great Hall. The Dozen would have known of their arrival and anticipated their entrance. "I'll introduce you, then I expect I will be asked to leave. I'll be right outside if you need me."

Remy lifted his chin, silently asking to be kissed. Laurence granted the request, lips against soft lips to calm both their nerves. Never long enough. He exhaled, then pushed open the door for Remy to walk through.

He had that same look about him that Laurence remembered from the night he cast the arc. Powerful and concentrated, but vulnerable all the same. Dashing in his new gray and black clothes, with his honey-blond hair hanging loose round his shoulders, a young witch in the precarious position of being hunted. Laurence fought the urge to sweep him away from danger and flee for distant, unknown lands to start over. But Remy wouldn't have it. He'd set out to end a war, and somehow, they must do it.

Ten chairs were filled this time, nearly the entire court gathered for this interview. What did they see when they eyed Remy? A pawn, a tool to be used for their own ends, or a powerful ally in his own right? Laurence hoped for the latter.

He walked behind Remy, allowing the witch to stand on his own. Remy didn't need to cling to Laurence for this.

Corinne stood. "Welcome, Remigius of the Elder Village, we've been expecting you. Laurence, you may leave us now."

Remy didn't turn to watch him go. His voice rang clear and steady. "Thank you, madam. It is an honor to make your acquaintance."

"You may call me Corinne. To my right is Ash. If you decide to stay, you'll be working closely with him. Ash handles our liaisons with your kind. Enough introductions for now. Please, have a seat."

And that was the last Laurence heard before the door closed behind him. His stomach clenched with worry. He didn't know Ash, and he didn't relish the idea of Remy interacting with vampires he couldn't vouch for. A part of him hoped Remy refused the offer and they could flee while there was still time.

How long before an army of witches descended on Bran Vigny looking for their wayward star pupil?

Laurence sat on a tall-backed wooden chair in the outer

chamber. From here, he could see the doors of the Great Hall and down the hallways on either side of the entrance. The chair was more for show than for sitting, and it felt like it. Hard and straight and covered in dust.

He wished for Livia's reassuring presence but was thankful to her for looking after Clara. Their first meeting had given every indication that Livia would take the lost girl under her wing. Good for them. Livia had a way with needy strays, lord knew she'd been there for Laurence.

Casting his gaze down the long corridor, over statues and past portraits down the length of the wall, he noticed a figure approaching and went rigid as the chair he sat in.

Valeri.

Anxiety raced from his spine, tightening his ribcage and stopping his breath. He saw the moment Valeri recognized him. The vampire stopped in his tracks. A wicked grin curled the edges of his lips. He hadn't changed in eighty-five years. He still wore black leather from head to toe, with his chestnut brown hair combed back from his face. Arching cheekbones and deep-set eyes gave away his Slavic origins. His nostrils flared, scenting Laurence with obvious relish.

Memories rushed back and threatened to engulf him. Valeri compelling him to act against his own will, cackling as he suffered. Valeri's threats and torments as punishment for not loving him enough. For not allowing him the complete control he demanded. The feeling of being hopelessly dependent on a cruel, murderous master.

Laurence forced air into his lungs. Valeri could not hurt him here. Bran Vigny was safe and the bastard knew it. Laurence stood and faced him.

At a distance of forty paces they glared, Laurence's gaze angry and defiant, Valeri's...something else. Laurence couldn't tell. It looked like longing, but Valeri could lie through a gaze, so Laurence couldn't trust the interpretation.

Valeri knew better than to approach. Not with Laurence under the protection of The Dozen. To come forward would be to risk punishment, and Valeri was cocksure, not stupid. He couldn't advance, but he didn't have to turn around and leave either. The standoff stretched uncomfortably. Valeri cocked his head a fraction. Licked his bottom lip and let his mouth part.

Laurence took a step back before he'd realized what he was doing. Valeri's grin turned to a glinting smile, like a flash reflecting off a dagger's blade. The bastard knew he'd won that round.

Jaw tight, teeth clenched, Laurence forced his shoulders down from his ears and lowered himself back into the blasted chair. Valeri could go to the devil. He tore his gaze from his maker to stare at the doors of the Great Hall. The carved demons stared back. In his periphery, Laurence saw Valeri turn on his heel and stride away.

Good riddance.

Laurence had begun to calm down when the door creaked open, and Remy came into view. Ash loomed tall over his shoulder, one possessive hand on Remy's neck.

A growl rumbled from Laurence's throat at the sight. He was on his feet collecting Remy from Ash's grip in the blink of an eye.

Ash had the nerve to chuckle. "Easy, old man. I meant nothing by it."

"The hell you did." Balancing on a razor's edge, Laurence tucked a willing Remy behind his back and bared his teeth. "Don't touch him."

Ash raised a white-blond brow. Trouble danced merrily in his cool blue eyes. "Why," he purred, "is this one yours? Tell me, will you claim him?"

Remy's hand at his elbow brought Laurence back to earth. "He belongs to himself."

With a casual shrug, Ash turned and sauntered back to the others. Laurence led Remy away, the witch trotting to keep up.

"What was that about?" asked Remy.

"I don't know, but I don't like it."

Remy huffed. "You aren't going to like this either."

Laurence focused his gaze, searching Remy's face. "What?"

"They want me to help Valeri."

They want me to help Valeri.

Laurence let the words sink in. He grimaced. What the hell had Valeri brought from overseas that would put him into The Dozen's good graces and warrant the assistance of the most powerful witch these lands had ever known? Though his mind raced, he came up empty. Regardless, the halls of Bran Vigny were no place for this discussion. He needed to get Remy alone.

"Did you hear me?" asked the witch.

"I wish I hadn't," said Laurence, guiding them to his private rooms. They climbed the stairs. "Give me a moment."

Next to him, Remy nodded. His face showed frazzled nerves, yet his endless curiosity could not be stymied. The witch's busy eyes took everything in even as Laurence hurried him forward. What must Bran Vigny look like to Remy who only a few weeks prior had never left the bosom of his people's territory?

Over the centuries, vampires had amassed a huge collection of paintings and sculptures which now hung along the walls and sat on nearly every available surface. Given time, no doubt Remy would study each piece: rich landscapes done in oils next to stuffy old portraits of counts and countesses long since dead, and nude gods carved in stone. Laurence hated to rush him, but he needed to know The Dozen's conditions. With Remy's elders like bloodhounds on his scent, time was a luxury they didn't have.

"This way." They'd reached Laurence's floor and veered left to his rooms. The soft yellow glow of sconces lit the way.

Remy's hand at his elbow gave a little squeeze before releasing so he could precede Laurence into the sitting room.

Laurence half expected to find Liv and Clara there, but was glad of their absence. He wanted Remy to himself. The urge to wash Ash's scent from the witch's neck rose unbidden. He shouldn't be so petty, so possessive. Remy did not belong to him. But neither did he want another vampire staking a claim—especially not Ash.

He shut the door and bolted it behind them. "Let's sit, and you can tell me what's happened."

Remy had a peculiar look on his face as his eyes searched Laurence's. "Kiss me."

Laurence's lips parted of their own accord. He'd not expected the sweet demand, but now that it was made, he could do nothing else.

Pinning Remy to the wall, Laurence took his lips. Honey-sweet from those candied nuts he'd hoarded and soft as velvet, Remy's mouth opened for Laurence's tongue. The witch moaned into the kiss, and his arms came around Laurence's waist to cling tightly.

They pressed in close, and Laurence knew the urge to bite and be bitten. He held back, gentled their movements and dropped little kisses along Remy's jaw.

"That's better," said Remy, lips moving against Laurence's cheek. "Now we can talk."

That drew a welcome chuckle. "Now? Now that I want to

strip you bare and have you in a proper bed? Now you want to talk?"

"Well no, not if *that's* an option." Remy slid a hand under Laurence's tunic to find skin. "Your suggestion is much better. I hereby concede to your judgment in these matters."

Laurence groaned and untangled himself from Remy's grasp. "You're too much. Talk. What have they asked of you?"

Remy settled on the lounge with a sigh. "It's complicated."

Laurence took the spot next to him. "I'm listening."

"They're confident they can protect me from Emmeline and the witches who support her. I did not reveal Helewise's powers or their ultimate plan to use me to spread poison. Maybe I should have. Emmeline deserves whatever punishment they inflict, but Helewise and I were friends as children. She had a kind heart at her core, and she's being used in the same way they'd like to use me but with less ability to fight back. I got out. She could not. I don't want to sign her death sentence."

Laurence dropped a hand to Remy's thigh and gave a comforting squeeze. "I understand. Wise of you to hold back."

"I think your rulers underestimate the threat my people present, particularly when I'm certain other ranking members among the elders will back Emmeline's gambit—maybe all of them."

"That's concerning."

"Indeed. And therein lies the bad news. Once they've quelled the threat from my people, if they do, I'll be expected to protect Valeri in turn—"

Laurence stiffened. "No."

"He's been tasked with a dangerous mission, and a witch with my strengths would help ensure his success."

"Absolutely not," his voice came clipped and harsh. Anger that The Dozen would make such an outrageous request flared, burning cinders in his chest.

Remy covered Laurence's hand with his own. "Listen. If they

do this. If they protect me from my people, put an end to the ongoing conflict and ensure the elders won't pursue me, I'll owe them something. We've always known there would be a debt to pay. And with free rein to use my powers as I see fit, Valeri is no threat to me."

"You don't know that," Laurence growled.

"I do." Remy's stare hardened. "You've seen me cast. I can take care of myself, and you as well, should you choose to come with me. That's up to you of course." His intense gaze softened, lips curling into a hopeful smile. "And I've never been on a ship. We'll be sailing north."

"Remy," said Laurence, a sick feeling churning in his gut. "My god. You have not already agreed to this, have you? Please tell me you haven't."

Words weren't necessary, Remy's expression held the answer Laurence dreaded.

"No! You must take it back. We can still leave for Benton and be rid of these problems that were never ours to begin with. You cannot consort with Valeri. He's vile! A viper hidden amongst the weeds. We've no way of knowing what he's scheming."

Remy leaned in, taking Laurence by the shoulders and holding tight. "Laurence, wait. Think it through. Valeri could not have planned this. He'd no way of knowing a witch of my capability would fall into your rulers' laps at just the moment they needed that particular miracle. Further still that I would be your lover, or that you'd be in the castle. This is all coincidence, not some plan of Valeri's to trick us. And the mission itself is honorable. The information we seek could save the vampire you know as Mahu."

Laurence shook him off and stood. What could Mahu possibly need saving from? He was the eldest member of the council and not yet...oh. Had the madness begun to claim Mahu? But that didn't matter. "It's a terrible idea. They should never have asked it of you."

"I don't have all the details yet. Can we wait to be enraged about it until after Emmeline has been dealt with? I'm rather more concerned with the threat she presents than the threat of Valeri, at least in our immediate future. She could be here any second, and she won't be satisfied until I'm in chains doing her bidding and packs of werewolves lay dead at her feet."

Pinching the bridge of his nose, Laurence shut his eyes. Unthinkable. The nerve of The Dozen to throw Valeri into the mix after everything he'd done.

"I saw him tonight," Laurence confessed.

"Valeri?"

"Yes." Laurence shot Remy a glance. "If you'd seen the way he looked at me, you would doubt his motives too."

Remy came to him then, arms open, but Laurence didn't want to be coddled. He stepped out of his reach.

"I'm sorry," Remy whispered. "Are you angry with me?"

Laurence laughed with no mirth. "Oh, I'm angry."

Remy flinched. The gesture made him look smaller. Helpless. But Laurence knew better. Remy was right: given free rein with his magic, the witch could protect himself. Even from Valeri.

Laurence sighed. "Not at you. None of this is your fault, though I wish to the devil you hadn't agreed without speaking to me first."

Remy shuffled from one foot to the other. "I did not feel as though I had a choice."

"No, I imagine you didn't." Laurence opened an arm to him, and Remy claimed the space at his side with a look of relief. "The Dozen are masters at what they do."

Remy encircled Laurence's waist in a tight embrace. "I suppose I'll come to learn that for myself after this."

"For good or for ill."

The witch glanced up, amber eyes glittering. "Look on the bright side."

"There's a bright side?" asked Laurence.

"Emmeline could always get me first, then we won't have to worry about Valeri after all."

"You accursed imp." Laurence pinched Remy's rear just hard enough to hear the witch yip. "That isn't funny."

Remy pinched him back. "It's a little funny."

"It isn't." Laurence brushed a wild strand of hair behind Remy's ear. "And stop arguing with me. When did you become so insolent?"

Remy gazed up through his lashes, licked his bottom lip. "Someone should probably teach me to behave."

"Impossible. Besides, I like you as you are, cheek and all."

Remy turned in his arms and pressed back. "Best consider all my cheeks then."

Laurence rocked into the contact, his groin against Remy's backside. "You devil. We were discussing something important."

"Were discussing. Now we're not. Take me to bed, then tell me again how you like my cheeks."

Scooping Remy into his arms, Laurence carried him to the bedroom and deposited him on the plush mattress. "This will require thorough research," he said, climbing over him.

Remy flung his arms over his head in submission. "Swear it?"

Laurence sat astride his hips and pinned his arms where they lay. "I give you my word."

Arching, Remy murmured, "I want your cock."

"You shall have that too."

Naked and desperate, Remy'd had enough of Laurence's tormenting light touches. "Please," he whined, his fingers clawing the vampire's broad back. "The oil."

Laurence sucked on his earlobe, teasing the delicate skin with hints of sharp incisors. Remy wriggled beneath him on the soft feathered bed, wrapping his leg over Laurence's backside and pulling him in for more friction. Aching and hard, their cocks jutted against one another, trapped between them with nothing slick to ease the way because the vampire couldn't be bothered to—

"Get the damn oil," Remy huffed.

Laurence chuckled, his breath humid against Remy's jaw. "Yes, dear." He dropped a wet kiss on Remy's mouth then rose from the bed to rummage in the wardrobe.

Remy stroked his cock as he waited. Slow, languid pulls because any more than that and he might spend. On edge since the vampire had laid hands on his flesh, he'd never been as eager for a lover as at this moment.

The bed dipped on Laurence's return, rocking Remy with it.

Laurence's gaze fell heavy on Remy's length as he worked himself. "I could watch you all night."

Remy let go and reached for his lover's cock instead. "I'm going to need more from you than watching. I've been waiting for this since that night in the cave." He gave a gentle tug.

"Me too." Laurence's voice came out husky. "Turn over."

Remy obeyed in one swift motion, flipping to his stomach, legs slightly parted, exposed, and vibrating with anticipation. The black satin sheet beneath him was already warmed from his body heat and smooth against his skin. He drove his hips forward for the luxurious glide of his shaft against the silken fabric.

Laurence's cool palms came down on his shoulders and slid along the curve of his spine to rest on his backside. Remy pushed into the touch. He laid an arm under his head so he could glance over his shoulder. Laurence's slate-gray eyes roamed his torso. Remy felt his gaze as much as he saw it, such was the weight of his lusty stare.

Writhing and moaning as Laurence prepared his body, Remy banished thoughts of war, of elders, werewolves, and The Dozen, of sanctuary and debt—all of it—from his mind.

He focused on Laurence's talented fingers. On each place where their skin touched. On the sounds that slipped past his lips unbidden, from little whimpers to outright groans as the vampire coaxed him open with tantalizing efficiency.

When Laurence finally covered him with his body and pushed in, Remy's every nerve tingled with urgency. The weight of the vampire against his back provided welcome grounding as he basked in the stretch of being filled. Chest hair tickled his sensitive skin. Laurence dropped open-mouthed kisses along his neck.

"Good?" asked Laurence as he bottomed out.

Remy shivered beneath him, drowning in the sensation of so much contact. "Yes."

Laurence alternated between shallow and deep thrusts, leaving Remy a quivering mess. He fought a wave of pleasure threatening to crest too soon, biting into his own arm to stop it.

"Too much?" Laurence rumbled in his ear.

"Never. Keep going," he sighed out, prepared to beg for more. It had never been this divine. The vampire was a generous lover, playing his body like an instrument, each note higher than the last.

Laurence grabbed Remy's hand and laced their fingers together. Squeezing tight, he began to move in earnest. The bed rocked with each thrust. Every press and retreat sparked a new flare of arousal. Remy's cock dragged and leaked against the slippery bedding. The decadent joining forced a long groan from his throat.

"You feel amazing," gasped Laurence against his neck. "Perfect for me. So eager."

Remy writhed under him, matching each thrust, moaning his need. "More, Laurence. Harder."

The vampire slid an arm beneath his hips and hauled him to his knees. The new position drove Laurence deeper. Remy's thighs shook.

Laurence wrapped fingers around his shaft and stroked.

"Oh!" Remy cried as bliss hurtled him to the pinnacle.

Laurence kept him there, dancing on that knife's edge between too much and not enough. Stretched and filled and fucking into the vampire's tight fist. Lost in this luxury of sensory overload, he barely registered the fangs at his throat, but his body knew what it wanted. He tilted his head to give Laurence the access he needed.

"May I?" Two desperate words, huffed out between thrusts.

"God, yes. Do it. Please," Remy begged.

Twin lances slid into his flesh, tearing a keening wail from Remy as he spilled into the vampire's palm. Shaking with the force of his release, Remy pressed into the sensations, his ass against Laurence's hips, his neck against the invading teeth. Ecstatic ripples of euphoria claimed his body, radiating out from the points of contact until he felt tremors even in his toes.

Remy submitted to all of it with elation. Having Laurence like this, in all the ways he'd wanted him, sent his spirits soaring high as the rest of him.

In the grip of climax, Laurence tensed and shuddered. The pressure of his bite intensified as the vampire came inside him, pulsing and vibrating his pleasure. Remy panted, delightfully trapped in his embrace, beneath his weight with sharp incisors still buried in his throat. Aftershocks rocked him with their thrilling pings of exhilaration.

Laurence hummed against his skin, his hunger demanding to be heard as well as felt. While the vampire drank, Remy's breath slowly returned. A metallic tang hung in the air. Laurence guided him back to his stomach, his fangs retreating and his tongue coming to replace them. Then he settled them on their sides, still licking Remy's neck with long, tender strokes. Remy let himself be moved like a rag doll. It felt wonderful to be in Laurence's arms like this, under his care.

They lay nestled against each other, coming back to themselves in stages. Remy took a deep, satisfied breath. He brought Laurence's hand to his lips and sucked a finger into his mouth. He'd be content to lounge together for the rest of the night, but the world with all its problems would come crashing back eventually.

Laurence pressed a kiss to the top of his spine. "That was…"

When his lover didn't finish that thought, Remy twisted to look at his face. He grinned at the lovestruck expression he discovered. "A long time coming and positively worth the wait?"

"Yes, in fact. And terribly delightful. I will ache for you constantly now."

Remy turned in his arms and tangled their legs together. "Good. I want you to."

Their lips met, mouths open, tongues caressing. Laurence tasted of copper, and Remy found he liked it. He pressed deeper for more. They kissed until Remy had to pull back for air.

"We could leave," Laurence blurted, his gaze intense. "We could go to Benton. Pass it. Keep going. Find our own place."

Remy's chest expanded with longing. The idea was tempting, tugging at his will and threatening his resolve. But no, he couldn't give in. "I need to finish what I've started, Laurence. And then I must follow through with what I've agreed to do."

Laurence let out the breath he was holding. He shut his eyes, but not before Remy noted the disappointment there.

His heart sank. "I'm sorry." He trailed his fingers through Laurence's thick, dark hair and planted another kiss on his lips.

"Don't be, your courage is one of the many reasons I admire you," replied Laurence without opening his eyes.

Remy dropped featherlight kisses on each eyelid and another between his brows. He was about to jokingly ask after the rest of the reasons when a knock sounded on the outer door. Remy concentrated, cast his senses outward, and smiled.

"It's Livia. And she's brought Clara. We should dress." Remy squirmed to untangle himself from Laurence's hold, but the vampire tightened his grip.

"One more." Laurence leaned in for a kiss.

Remy granted it. "Now let me up, you big goon. We've guests."

Hurrying to dress, Remy wondered how Clara was getting on and found himself glad the women had come even if staying in bed for the foreseeable future was an inviting temptation. Laurence had thrown on a robe then gone to the door to stall, while Remy wrenched his whole set of clothes back on.

He nodded to Laurence to let them in, all the while intensely aware the vampire wore nothing beneath the flowing crimson. The sight was almost sexier than seeing him completely naked.

Almost.

Livia led Clara and a serving girl into the sitting room, the young miss carrying covered dishes. The aroma drifted to Remy and reminded him he hadn't eaten enough. Whatever it was, it smelled divine.

"Thank you, Rebecca, there is fine," said Livia, directing the girl to leave the trays on the table.

"I'll be back for the dishes in a bit, Mistress. Will there be anything else?"

"No thank you, dear."

Rebecca found her way out, leaving Remy to watch Clara carefully. The bookseller sported a secret little grin and shining eyes. Remy wished they had time for a tête-à-tête.

"Have a seat, darlings," said Livia. "I shall serve while you educate us on your goings on. Not *all* of them, mind you, only the relevant bits."

Remy felt his cheeks flush.

They settled in the sitting room; there was no dining table for eating, why would there be? So Remy made do with holding his plate in his lap. Livia had piled the porcelain dish high. Roast bird, carrots, dried fruit and spiced bread. His mouth watered as he contemplated where to start. The reaction drew a laugh from Livia.

"How I enjoy observing mortals with their food." She watched as Remy dug in. "Perhaps Laurence should fill us in while you concentrate on chewing. I assume he has the details?"

Remy nodded as he swallowed a piece of duck. Tender and juicy, the morsel melted in his mouth. He washed it down with a nutty brown ale and listened with half an ear as Laurence caught Livia up on their situation.

"You don't want him to go," said Livia, not even a question. Laurence's tone had made it obvious.

"Of course not, it's too dangerous. Maybe you could talk to them. Get him out of it?"

Remy was about to pipe up when Livia said, "But he could save Mahu. Valeri's mission is his only hope."

"What's happened to Mahu?" asked Laurence.

Livia's eyes cast downward. "The aging sickness. It's begun."

Remy had not been filled in on the details of his mission with Valeri. One crisis at a time was enough for him. He turned to Clara. "You all right?"

She nodded. "Yes, Liv's spent the night showing me around. I got the grand tour. This castle's incredible."

"I'm jealous, I've yet to receive a tour."

"Apparently you've had more important things to do." Clara eyed Laurence suggestively, and Remy felt the flush return to his traitorous cheeks.

"Indeed." He gave a sharp grin. "Very important."

Her smile morphed and her face took on a serious expression. "Are your people really coming to kill us all?"

Remy exhaled sharply. "They're coming, and not to borrow a cup of sugar. Though beyond getting me back, I'm not sure what they'd be aiming to accomplish. Historically, there's been no quarrel with vampires. Only recently the vampires sided with werewolves against us. Emmeline wants to win the war. She won't care how many have to die for her to do it."

"Maybe you should run," Clara whispered, keeping her voice low as Livia and Laurence continued their own discussion.

Remy clenched his jaw. "That's what Laurence wants."

Clara rested her hand on his knee. "Why not listen to him?"

Remy shook his head and gazed into her concerned eyes. "I have to finish this. I think I'm the only one who can."

23

Gasping for air, Remy bolted upright in bed.

Oh, no.

Beside him, Laurence was jarred to wakefulness. The vampire met his eyes and took his wrist in hand. "What is it?"

Remy's heart thundered in his chest. "They're here."

The war had come for him. Emmeline had come for him. Whatever happened, Remy had to protect Laurence.

A resounding boom shook the castle walls. The bed they shared vibrated beneath them. A mysterious quiet followed, only to be interrupted by another blast.

Remy flung the covers off. "I have to go."

Laurence, sluggish due to the high-noon hour, hung onto Remy's elbow. "But you can't."

"I must." Remy forced out the words between clenched teeth. He didn't want to leave Laurence unguarded, but Emmeline was his responsibility. He couldn't let her destroy the castle and its residents along with it.

"It's daylight," warned Laurence, desperation edging into his voice. "You can't go now!"

Remy pressed a kiss to his lover's lips, hard and hurried, then left the bed to get dressed. "They will not wait for Bran Vigny's occupants to rise before they attack. They've chosen daytime on purpose. I must go."

"But there is no one to protect you." Laurence's firm baritone was betrayed by his stricken expression as he struggled from the bed. Vampires weren't meant to function this time of day.

"There is." Remy tucked his new knife into his belt, though if anyone got close enough for him to need it, he was already dead. "Evanora is here. I feel her presence. And the castle witches. I have protection."

Laurence's eyes darkened to slate. "But *I* cannot protect you!"

"Nor do I want you to." Remy reached for Laurence's face, cupped his cheeks and leaned in. "Let me protect you this once. Please."

"No, I won't allow you to risk yourself again." Laurence's voice rose an octave, hands firm on Remy's biceps. "Let Bran Vigny's witches fight without you. You and I will join at dusk."

Remy shook off the vampire's hold and stuffed his feet into his boots. "My grandmother is out there," he pleaded, willing the vampire to understand. "I'm going."

"It's too dangerous!" Laurence reached for him to hold him back, but Remy dodged.

Fighting reluctance, he cast a spell, sending the vampire back to the bed. "I'm sorry, Laurence. But this is my war to end. With any luck, it will be over by twilight." He waved his hand in the air, creating a barrier so Laurence couldn't follow.

"Remy, don't go," Laurence bellowed, struggling against his invisible prison. "Don't do this. Let me loose."

Remy forced a calm into his voice that he didn't feel. "Trust me. I can beat her."

"Can you beat all of them?"

He couldn't answer and wouldn't be delayed any further.

Turning his back on Laurence was the hardest thing he'd ever done. Tuning out his lover's pleas, a close second. He flung open the door with a quick spell and flew to the castle's exit. Evanora would need him in order to switch sides safely. He must hurry; the battle had started without him.

"Hand over the boy-witch Remigius." Emmeline's screech resounded unnaturally loud, her voice enhanced with magic. "And we will leave Bran Vigny unscathed."

Outside, daylight stole Remy's vision for a terrifying second before his eyes began to adjust to the brightness. Static rolled in heavy waves through the air. Magic everywhere. Remy's body hummed with it, his fingers tingling with unspent power.

The sun hung high in a cloudless sky, and an army of witches floated in formation above the castle. Their flowing robes gave the appearance of dancing silhouettes in the air. Behind them, low to the ground, a giant portal blazed a blue and purple oval back to his village.

A sense of longing bloomed and wilted in Remy's chest. He couldn't go home, maybe never again.

Emmeline hovered front and center, auburn hair swept into a tight bun, one hand in the air, poised to attack. Behind her, the Elder Village's witches waited for orders. The core group close to Emmeline, perhaps seven in total, shared her fierce determination. Nerves clung to the others like ivy, twitching under their muslin robes.

Remy scanned their line for Evanora and found her along the left flank. Behind her, a gaggle of like-minded witches who probably planned to defect with her when the opportunity arose. Emmeline wouldn't suspect, so fervent she was in her ploy for victory.

A calm voice answered from the battlements. "The witch you ask for is under our protection and does not wish to go with you."

Remy glanced behind him and to the top of the soaring castle. A cluster of maybe thirty witches stood at the ready, postures rigid, but they were outnumbered nearly five to one. A tall, muscular woman in Amazonian leather armor, her flowing red hair whipping in the wind, held the center. A witch made for battle. It was she who'd spoken.

By now, Emmeline had spotted him, a lone witch on the lower steps of the castle's entrance, seemingly unguarded. Remy sensed all eyes shifting his way. An eerie quiet drifted between the adversaries.

Remy gathered courage to address his elder. "You've gone too far, Emmeline. The wolves you seek to control want only to be left alone. The vampires whose home you threaten never wanted to be a part of your war to begin with. Even your own people long for the peace we had before an appetite for power overwhelmed you and the rest of our elders. Go home."

As Remy spoke the words, he felt her rage bubbling to the surface, a warning he could not heed. Emmeline wouldn't back down. She'd fight to the death.

And so would Remy.

"Traitor!" Emmeline spit, her eyes gleaming with fury. "Do you know what you've cost us?"

She thought she would win. Remy believed he would. The time to find out whirled toward them like a tornado. How much damage could he avoid in the maelstrom?

"You will pay for what you've done," Emmeline yelled, gathering magic in her outstretched palms until light flickered orange between them. "And you'll do your part for your people, like it or not."

She hurled a fireball straight at him. Remy burst straight up from the ground and into the air. It struck the stones where he'd stood and burned a vibrant red deathtrap before sputtering out. His only defense against a fire-witch like Emmeline was to move. His talent with particles did nothing.

From the battlements, another fire-witch threw her own flaming mass in counterattack. Emmeline dodged, then Helewise re-routed the blaze away.

Floating in midair with Bran Vigny's witches at his back, and Emmeline's larger troupe at his front, Remy readied his power in hopes of avoiding this showdown. He glanced to Evanora. She nodded. She'd have known to expect something like this but attacking a group when it contained his own grandmother caused a tightness in his gut. He ignored it. He had to.

Calling every fleck of dust, every bit of twig or leaf, miniscule stones and grains of sand alike to do his bidding, Remy raised his hands and shoved the invisible mass at the opposing army.

The entire line, every witch, was knocked from the air like a set of dominoes, swept back and flung to the canopy of treetops below. The portal flickered and sizzled as the witch who'd cast the gate struggled to keep it open.

"Go home," said Remy quietly, though his voice could be heard loud and clear as though he'd shouted from the castle spires.

The portal held. Already Emmeline's troops were recovering, as Remy hadn't actually meant to harm anyone—this time. He'd only sought to give them a taste of what they were up against, a chance to retreat.

Some of Emmeline's number panicked, moving farther back after his show of strength, but the lead witch herself only became more enraged. She signaled to two women at her side, who flew forth, heading straight for Remy.

The twins. Remy knew them from childhood lessons, they'd always beaten him at spellwork. They wouldn't fear him now.

Behind him, the castle witches prepared a defense. Remy would need it. He felt their magic coalescing at his back and hoped their spell would be enough to hold off his boyhood rivals.

Ivy erupted from Sabni and Sebni's palms and spiraled outward at an alarming rate. Remy threw his hands up to defend himself, but it was too late. Their clinging tendrils latched on and squeezed. As quickly as he could snap one vine, four more formed in its place.

From behind, a surging wave of humid, salty air pummeled the ivy and Remy both. Remy staggered, struggling with the weeds, using his power to detangle vine after vine. The counter-attack gave him enough leverage to free himself. He risked a glance over his shoulder in thanks, eyes connecting with the red-haired woman, then dodged a second attack hurtling his way. In his periphery, Emmeline and her cronies prepared more fireballs.

Sweeping a massive lot of ether to do his bidding, he sent Sabni and Sebni crashing back through the shimmering portal with twin popping sounds. If they knew what was good for them, they'd stay gone.

Remy whipped around in time to see the battlements catch fire. The castle witches swarmed to contain it.

"Stop this!" Remy howled, fingers splayed to gather more power.

Emmeline grinned, a crooked smile glinting with wicked intent. "Give yourself up, and we'll leave with no further harm done."

Remy didn't want anyone to suffer on his account, but cowing to Emmeline's wishes wasn't an option. With Remy under her control, she'd be unstoppable. He raised his arms, calling on his gift, and slung a web of particles to contain her.

Emmeline dodged, impossibly fast, and signaled to her troops. They readied to attack with varying degrees of speed. Remy had shaken their confidence, all but the women closest to Emmeline, who shared her zeal. Helewise glared with beady eyes, still devoted to her mentor.

The portal crackled loudly, catching Remy's attention. Werewolves emerged by the dozen, stalking the ground beneath the battle and gnashing their teeth.

Emmeline's brow knit together in frustration. She waved a hand to close the portal, but Remy blocked her efforts, curious what the wolves would do and unwilling to take away their avenue of retreat.

Stuck pacing below the action, the animals prowled as a unit, a cluster of packs surveying the landscape, searching for their line of attack.

Though these wolves were likely on his side, Remy didn't need the complication. Neither, apparently, did Emmeline. She motioned for a cluster from her troupe to attack the newcomers. They peeled off and blazed toward the ground.

Torn, Remy glanced to the witches on the battlements. With the redhead in front directing their defense, the group held their own. So he raced to protect the werewolves. He couldn't let Emmeline massacre a pack of wolves for the ill-judged decision to follow her through a portal.

Remy cast a barrier around them to keep them off the board. They snarled in protest.

This could go on for hours, the back and forth, the struggle for dominance. Witches from both groups would suffer. Wolves would suffer. Remy needed Evanora and her lot safely on his side, and then he would do his damnedest to end this, no matter the cost.

Without turning his back on Emmeline, he joined the guard on the battlements. If only they'd had time to plan tactics before this. Remy wasn't sure they'd take direction from him, a male witch and a traitor to his village.

Emmeline sent a new batch of women to the front line, and they gathered magic between them. That Helewise was among their number was concerning.

"They're preparing a poison," Remy warned Bran Vigny's fleet.

"Leave it to me," said a petite brunette. The redhead gave her a nod, and she leapt off the battlements to intervene.

Remy continued quickly. "My grandmother and her friends are here for me. I'm going to send for them, please let them join without trouble."

The red-haired woman answered, her clipped voice full of authority. "Do it. We'll cover." Power radiated from her in a swollen tide Remy felt to his bones. He would not want to be her enemy.

"Thank you." Remy shot a glance to his Gran. The smile she sent in return beamed even from afar and looked both out of place in a battle and comforting in a way Remy needed desperately. She signaled to her friends, and as one, they sprinted for the battlements.

Emmeline shrieked and flung a flaming disc in their path, but the red-haired witch sent it whizzing away with a casual flick of her fingers.

A second disc hit one of the deserters in the shoulder. She cried out and began to falter. Evanora grabbed her and dragged her along to safety.

Remy sent a burst of his own power at Emmeline, keeping her busy until Evanora and company were safely among their number. Eight witches in total, and though it didn't even out the odds, Remy would be stronger with Evanora at his side. They'd practiced combining their powers since he was a boy of twelve, and their skills were about to be put to the test.

Her arms came around his shoulders. Remy leaned into her embrace, inhaling the familiar scent of rose soap from her hair. He dropped a kiss on her cheek, then forced himself to pull away. "Thank you for coming."

"I said I'd be here, didn't I?" She winked.

Her vision…had it included this moment? By the devil, what else did she know? But it didn't matter, she wouldn't say a word until after the dust settled. Visions, revealed too early, were fraught with danger.

Evanora's defection wrought dissention in Emmeline's ranks. The witches squabbled amongst themselves. Helewise, her first attempt at poison thwarted by the brunette, refused to attack again.

"I won't be a part of killing Evanora," cried Helewise.

"I'll do it myself!" Emmeline shoved her out of the way and raced forward, gigantic fireball poised at her chest. Her aim focused not at the witches on the battlements, but at Bran Vigny's grand entrance.

Remy had only a second to react. He couldn't let her burn Bran Vigny, not with all the vampires trapped inside.

Laurence was in there!

Evanora touched his shoulder. Remy drew from their combined strength, amassing more magic than when he'd built the arc. Power coalesced between his palms. He set his sights on Emmeline, gaze intense. This battle would begin in earnest.

Remy would save Bran Vigny, if it was the last thing he ever did.

24

*L*aurence pummeled the invisible wall that held him prisoner. Whatever Remy had done, the magic held despite Laurence's great efforts to break it. He gritted his teeth and tried again anyway. Fury coursed through his veins. Remy had better survive the battle because Laurence wanted to kill the witch himself.

Twilight approached, bringing the inevitable triumph of darkness over light only to be swapped again until the end of days. Would he be free of Remy's cursed trap at dusk? Laurence bided his time on a blade's edge, anxiety his only companion.

Outside, the sounds of battle raged. The castle walls shook with impact. Smoke scented the air. Laurence desperately sought to interpret the ebb and flow.

At true dark, the invisible bonds evaporated, and Laurence sprinted from the room. He burst through the entryway into the courtyard, the first vampire to arrive, and was greeted by a pack of prowling werewolves.

A large gray wolf glowered at Laurence, then stalked away. So they were guarding the entrance, good. He scanned the scene for Remy.

The sky played host to a crazed melee of movement. Witches flying, combatants locked in battle, spells and enchantments glimmering as they sparked to life only to be thwarted by another. A hazy cloud of smoke and magic hung over Bran Vigny, but Remy was nowhere to be seen.

Wolves lurked below the heavenly battlefield, waiting for witches to falter, ready to tear them to pieces when they did. The evidence of which lay strewn over the courtyard. The spicy scent of blood rose from the bodies. Laurence grimaced.

Overhead, his gaze climbed the soaring castle to the battlements. The fight raged on at the castle's pinnacle, with loyal witches fiercely defending the entryways. It dawned on Laurence that every vampire inside the castle owed their life to these brave wolves and witches who'd kept Emmeline and her army at bay until nightfall.

Vampires began to file out behind Laurence, taking in the situation for themselves, then joining the fray.

But where was Remy?

Hands seized his shoulders. Laurence whirled around, prepared to strike, but was met with Livia, her golden eyes intensely focused.

"Come, he needs you," she said, and raced back into the castle.

Laurence didn't waste time asking how she knew; he followed at her heels. Together they sprinted up flights of endless stairs to the battlements and out amidst the melee.

A line of loyal witches protected the doors against the enemy. In front of them and nearer to the edge, sparks flew and stones crumbled under the onslaught. Laurence had never witnessed a battle of this magnitude.

And finally, there stood Remy, arms outstretched, his chest covered in blood.

Laurence lunged ahead, determined to reach his side, but Livia's nails dug into his bicep, holding him back.

"What are you doing?" Laurence hissed. "I must go to him!"

"Wait, it's not safe. We'll need to act together."

Laurence seethed, but did as he was bid, taking in the details.

Remy struggled to stay upright, hunched and frail. With his feet braced widely apart and his body angled forward, it seemed for all the world like he fought to withstand a typhoon. His face twisted in effort, his hair whipping wildly in wind Laurence couldn't feel. Behind him huddled an older woman with one hand on his shoulder and the other held in front of her as if to block an oncoming attack. Which she very well may be doing for all that Laurence could decipher it.

Their opponents, a group of six women, stood in a V-shape formation not ten yards away. An aura of power radiated from the cluster, giving Laurence a foreboding sense that he should not approach.

No one should approach.

The energy pulsed around them, thick with menace, and aimed at nothing in particular; a shield to keep others back.

The woman front and center had a wild expression on her face, crazed and bordering on triumphant. She did not hunch like Remy; she stood tall, shoulders square, auburn hair torn from its partial knot and blowing in a wild halo about her head. Everyone involved in the standoff appeared trapped in a torrential wind.

The winning side was obvious, and it wasn't Remy's.

Liv leaned in to speak against his ear. "You must touch him. He can draw from you. I'll distract the others while you get into position."

Laurence glanced at the auburn-haired woman. Her focus remained on Remy, but the others in her group were poised to strike at anyone who interfered.

"Be careful," said Laurence, his body tense as he prepared to race forward.

"And you." Livia leapt into action, heading bravely toward the enemy witches.

A blast of power crackled her direction. She yelped, but Laurence had to ignore it. He made for Remy, swallowing the distance between them at a mad sprint and nearly colliding with him as a result.

Next to the old woman, Laurence grabbed Remy's free shoulder. An acute tugging sensation pulled him tight to Remy's back. He plastered himself against the witch, free hand wrapping round his waist. Remy sagged back against him.

"Laurence dear," said the old woman, "How good of you to join us. We've been waiting." Her voice was painfully strained but somehow still friendly, as if he were late for tea.

Hot blood welled under his palm where he held Remy. "What happened?"

"Stabbed," Remy rasped.

Laurence held his trembling lover upright. "What can I do?"

"Allow yourself to be used," she said simply, then turned to Remy. "Remigius, take what he offers. End this."

Remy took shallow, gasping breaths. "Might kill him."

"Do it," said Laurence and the old woman at once. They glanced at each other, her eyes the spitting image of Remy's but wizened with age. She continued, "Now, dear, before it's too late."

Remy straightened with a cry of anguish. Blood dripped from the wound across his chest—too much blood. The scent made Laurence's fangs drop unbidden.

"Hold on," said Remy.

The tugging sensation intensified tenfold. Laurence felt as if his innards were clawing their way outward. He repressed a sound of distress. He didn't want Remy to second guess using him, though fear crept along Laurence's every nerve. How was Remy still standing after so much blood loss?

The air changed.

A great gale swirled in mighty circles around them, collecting—What was that? Debris, dust...Laurence didn't know, but the churning mass thickened and became opaque. The vortex blocked his view of anything outside their triumvirate.

"That's it, Remigius," said Evanora, for who else could this woman be but Remy's dear grandmother? "You've got it."

Remy's body quaked against Laurence's chest. A charred scent arose, as if the air itself had burnt. Laurence held Remy firmly, keeping them standing even as the sucking sensation spiked.

With a violent motion, Remy heaved the swirling mass forward with such velocity that the void it created felt like a black hole of nothingness. A sudden terror seized Laurence. Would they be trapped in this gaping, empty maw? But no...the world came crashing back.

The rushing tide of Remy's power surged through the combatants, not just Emmeline's accomplices.

All.

At first it was impossible to make sense of the pandemonium. The chaos of bodies tumbling through the air seemed random, but then, as Laurence watched, he understood.

Remy directed this madness.

His arms weren't flailing wildly; they were conducting strategically. Enemies he hurled, sometimes one by one, sometimes in groups, through the massive portal back to wherever they'd come from. Bran Vigny's witches he isolated in prisons much the same as he'd done to Laurence and presumably for the same reason—to keep them safe. Werewolves he scattered to one edge of the castle wall; vampires were shoved to the other.

As for the rest of the souls on the battlements, he saved them for last. Vampires trapped as if frozen; castle witches behind a shimmering opal barricade. Emmeline's witches not presently engaged in her cluster were forced off the ledge and sent flying through the air and back through the portal.

Remy cleared the chessboard.

All of this done in the span of a minute, no more, leaving only Emmeline's group against Remy, Evanora, and Laurence. The little witch trembled in Laurence's embrace, his whole body shuddering under the onslaught of his efforts. Evanora slumped against his shoulder, barely holding her own weight.

Laurence was drained, weak, and half-starved. The hunger held its own dangers, as he felt Remy's blood hot against his palm where he braced the witch upright. The urge to bite into the pulsing jugular within inches of his deadly incisors threatened to overwhelm. Laurence choked back the desire.

Was it over?

His gaze shifted forward. Emmeline snarled, baring her teeth, her expression enraged, but not defeated.

The witches at her back began to falter.

"Gran," muttered Remy through clenched teeth. "I need to re-group. Can you hold her off?"

"Yes." Evanora gasped a deep breath and rallied, standing taller. "Do it." The old woman grabbed Laurence's wrist and clenched, fingers digging into flesh. Her eyes met his. "Lend me your strength."

Laurence nodded and didn't resist. The tugging sensation from Remy had never ceased, but now another one took hold, new and different, from Evanora at his wrist. Not as strong, but just as jarring.

Dropping his hand, Remy sagged, and Evanora took over. At once the three were slammed by a wave of menace so ferocious they stumbled backward.

Emmeline advanced, howling like a banshee.

Evanora couldn't possibly hold her off. They lost ground at a staggering rate, the old woman quivering against the enemy's force.

Within Laurence's embrace, Remy panted, his chest heaving. Blood loss would soon overwhelm him. He couldn't possibly muster another attack.

Evanora fell to her knees with a pained whimper.

Laurence had to stall. With the arm around Remy he reached for the witch's belt and pulled Berhan's knife from its sheath. Palming the handle, he took aim and threw the weapon with a practiced flick of his wrist.

A satisfying *thwump* sounded as the blade lodged in Emmeline's chest. Her head snapped up, and her eyes found Laurence with a vengeful glower. She didn't bother to remove the knife.

Damn. Laurence was out of ideas…and knives.

Emmeline braced, shoulders squaring, ready to finish them off, but Remy's swirling vortex returned.

Power multiplied at Remy's command. The burnt smell wafted strong in the current.

Emmeline's crazed expression—eyes impossibly big, lips pulled back in a snarl—disappeared behind the churning wall of Remy's energy.

With a primal, guttural cry, Remy launched his swirling weapon at their enemy.

Emmeline's shriek of defeat echoed off Bran Vigny's stone towers.

Laurence gathered Evanora in one arm and Remy in the other, even though his own legs had grown shaky. The magic around them dissipated. The otherworldly tugging snapped away like a slingshot released.

When the cloud dispersed and Laurence could see, the scene before him unfolded straight out of a nightmare.

Emmeline and her cronies were frozen in place, pain etched deeply into their graying features. Like statues carved from stone they stood immovable. The natural pink flush of their skin darkened to an unholy charcoal; their lifeless bodies still as the grave.

The remaining witnesses on the battlements began to move, free from their protective prisons. Bran Vigny's residents appeared dazed, their movement sluggish.

Livia limped forward. "Laurence?" Her normally confident tone was absent; her voice held the same fear Laurence felt in his heart.

Remy's shuddering breath came irregularly.

"Help me with them," said Laurence.

Livia reached for Evanora. She laid the woman down gently against the stones, cradling her head in her lap.

Laurence did the same for Remy, easing him to the ground and protecting his head because the little witch could no longer hold it up on his own. Exhausted himself, Laurence fought the panic threatening to take hold.

Remy had won the war, but at what cost?

Corinne hovered over them, her ivory gown blowing in the gentle breeze.

A natural breeze, thought Laurence. The air smelled fresh again, all hints of magic evaporated.

"He is dying," said Corinne with a kind of finality that caused Laurence's chest to clench with pain.

"No, no...he's only tired," said Laurence, but he knew Corinne spoke truth.

Blood still trickled from Remy's chest, the flow hadn't ceased, just slowed, and his skin was so pale the blue veins beneath gleamed like stria in marble. Eyes shut, Remy lay very still. Shallow breaths only served to push out more blood.

"He was a brave soldier, and won't be forgotten," declared Corrine, heedless of shattering Laurence's heart into hundreds of shards. "Send him off with dignity."

Send him off?

No! He would not. He'd never accept a world without Remy. Not when there was another option.

"Remy?" Laurence palmed the witch's cheek in his hand. The

flesh already grew cold. "Remy, look at me. I need you to open your eyes."

"Do it," Evanora rasped from Livia's lap. "He'd want you to."

His conscience warred fiercer than the recent battle; desperate to believe her but reluctant to make this decision for his fallen lover without permission. "Are you sure?"

Evanora nodded. "He loves you. Do it."

Corinne leaned in. "You cannot! He's in no state to consent, and you are too weak to work the miracle. The transition will fail."

Laurence barely had the energy to stay conscious. If he attempted to turn Remy and failed, they could both die.

Better to die with the one you love than to live an eternity without them.

Laurence stared at the beautiful witch in his arms and knew he had to try. He lifted Remy to his chest, tilted his chin to expose his vulnerable neck, leaned down, and bit.

25

Drifting in a chilled, watery current, sinking lower and lower beneath the surface, Remy stopped fighting.

He'd done it. He'd ended the war once and for all.

Laurence, Evanora, Livia, Clara…they would all be safe. Remy could let go knowing he'd done his best, and his best had been good enough. The icy womb of death tugged him under, and he didn't resist its embrace.

Would Laurence grieve him terribly? Imagining the kind vampire shedding tears over his grave brought profound sadness. He'd never meant to cause Laurence pain. Livia would be there to console him. She'd take care of Clara too. And who would guide the witches back to the light? Could Evanora take on such a task at her age? Remy hoped so. She'd make an excellent leader, wise and caring.

Life would go on without him. Remy sank further into the gray emptiness that beckoned, until—

Death's bony tendrils seized and retreated.

Agony came crashing back. A gasping, sucking breath rattled painfully in his chest. He wheezed but could not fight whatever preternatural force dragged him up to the surface.

Copper fire exploded on his tongue, splashing down his throat in a burning trail to his stomach. No choice but to swallow.

The ache in his chest faded and was replaced by a steady throb at his neck.

His heart thumped wildly, as if trying to escape its prison of ribs, then stopped altogether. His body let go, but his mind clung to life with a tenacity he hadn't known himself capable of.

"More. Remy. Take more." Desperation tinted the staccato words.

Laurence? he tried to call to his lover but couldn't form the name. His mouth was otherwise occupied. What was that? Blood? With sudden terror, he realized his teeth were clamped through flesh, piercing skin and muscle as he guzzled the fiery nectar straight from a vein.

His mind fuzzy, he remembered a conversation from their journey.

How does one become a vampire? Remy once asked.

Vampires are turned through a blood exchange. Laurence had answered.

A blood exchange. His mind caught up with his throat, which busily swallowed as much as it could get.

What? No!

He couldn't be made a vampire…he'd lose everything. All his power. Gone, as if a lifetime of study meant nothing!

Remy struggled. He desperately needed to stop drinking but couldn't tear himself from the ambrosia at his lips. Dawning realization brought clarity that wouldn't be refuted.

It was too late.

He'd died.

His heart had stopped. The eerie stillness in his chest would last forever. His lids fluttered open to reveal Laurence's slate-gray eyes, darkened with resolve.

"Remy! That's it. Keep drinking. You're doing so well."

He couldn't stop drinking if he wanted to.

Another vampire hovered next to Laurence, looming over his shoulder like a sentinel. His eyes glowed garnet, ringed in silver, and his presence radiated the timeless calm of centuries. Tension slipped from Remy's shoulders at the mere sight of him.

Awareness came in stages. His fingers grasped Laurence's wrist, holding it in place over his mouth. A mighty thirst still unquenched drove Remy to gulp after gulp as the world took shape around him.

Laurence's other arm propped him up. He rested against the vampire's chest, both on the stony ground of Bran Vigny's battlements. Stars glimmered overhead. A crowd stood farther back. People he didn't know. The air smoldered with the burnt embers of battle.

Remy focused on Laurence, who met his gaze with watery eyes.

"I thought I'd lost you." Laurence's hand flexed where it gripped his arm.

Remy could do nothing but drink.

"More, Laurence. He will need more," said the looming vampire with a gentle baritone tremor in his voice. "Here."

Without glancing away from Remy's stare, Laurence bit into the flesh of the offered wrist as it came around. His throat bobbed as he swallowed. Almost immediately Remy sensed the change, the power in this blood that now flowed through them both. Laurence's gaze was alit with it, silver over charcoal. When the stare became too intense and sensation overwhelming, Remy shut his eyes, taking comfort in the darkness of his lids.

Then it was done.

His breath returned, but his heartbeat did not, the dead lump in his chest nothing but a heavy anchor reminding him of mortality that was no more.

Remy was a vampire now.

His new fangs receded from Laurence's wrist. He licked his lips for the traces of blood that remained. Thirst still nagged at his senses, a vast hunger lingering in his gut. Would he always feel thus?

Laurence palmed his cheek. "Remy? Are you all right?"

Was he? Remy took a breath. Exhaled. Opened his eyes.

The world glittered in a spectrum of color he'd never seen before, a level of depth he hadn't known existed. Laurence, handsome as ever, his face etched with worry, hovered over him, blocking the others.

"You were dying. I had to," Laurence whispered, and his voice took on a musical quality Remy hadn't noticed before. "Please, talk to me."

Blinking, Remy stretched in Laurence's arms. The aches and pains from battle had vanished, the gash across his chest gone. His body felt strong and light. The urge to run, jump, and fuck hit at once. He gritted his teeth against the onslaught and sat up under his own power. Laurence retreated only enough to make room.

Reaching out, Remy trailed a finger over Laurence's crooked nose to his bloodstained lips. "Kiss me."

Their mouths met, Laurence's gentle and loving, Remy's harsh and biting. He wanted to mix their blood again, eliminate the differences between them, merge into one person. Laurence allowed it for a luxurious stretch of time, his hands cupping Remy's face, but then he gentled the kiss and pulled away to look him in the eye.

"You did it," said Laurence with pride. "You saved us all."

"And you saved me." Remy smiled his new wicked smile, pointed teeth catching his lower lip. "Again."

Gasping, Remy remembered their last moments, and panic slammed back with such force he feared he'd swoon. "Evanora!"

Had he killed her? She'd collapsed at his feet as he rallied for the final attack. Remy would never forgive himself.

"I'm here, doll baby. I'm fine." Evanora's thready voice came soft and sweet like an answer to Remy's prayers. He clambered up with Laurence's help, though he didn't need it, and went to where she lay sprawled against Livia.

Evanora didn't look fine, frail and leaning on Liv for support, but she was alive and that was enough for Remy.

"Oh, Gran!" Remy dropped to his knees in front of them. "I'm so relieved. I thought—"

"Come, Remigius. I'm all right. Let me see you." Evanora lifted a hand to his cheek. "Why look at that. Your eyes. They're glowing."

Remy covered her hand with his. Her warm hand. Blood pulsed beneath her skin. He could *smell* it. He dropped his hand back to his side.

"Did you know about this?" he asked, but he already knew the answer.

"Yes," she said with a twinkle in her eyes. "Much of this was in my vision."

"You knew, and you didn't warn me?"

Her brows lifted. "You know that I could not."

Remy sniffed. "You could have trusted me. I'd have let it happen."

She shook her head, her silver curls bouncing with the movement. "You don't know that, and nor could I have known it. Everything had to be this way. You will thrive with him." Evanora glanced at Laurence, her gaze fond. "Excellent choice, by the way. Quite handsome. Beautiful hair."

Laurence was at his side, smiling at his gran.

The mysterious vampire lingered close. The rooftop was full of observers Remy noticed now that he began paying more attention to his surroundings. Bran Vigny's remaining witches, their red-haired leader, half The Dozen, Corinne and Ash.

They'd all witnessed his transformation, leaving Remy feeling an uncomfortable sense of exposure. And irritation at being on display. He turned to the crowd.

"Go," he ordered. "I would be alone with them."

To Remy's surprise, people he had no authority over respected his wishes and began to clear out. When the garnet-eyed vampire made to leave with them, Remy held up a hand. "No. You stay."

The tall man made a slight gesture that gave the impression of a shrug without the actual movement. "As you wish."

"Who are you?" asked Remy, somewhat lost in the ancient creature's two-toned eyes. His presence gave off a thrumming power like no other Remy had sensed—primal.

He bowed his ebony head, haloed with a mane of onyx-black hair. "Mahu."

"You gave us your blood."

"I did."

"Why?"

"You needed it," said Mahu with an odd, archaic lilt to his words.

Laurence slipped his hand in Remy's. "I was too weak to change you alone. Without Mahu's help, the transformation would have failed."

Remy squeezed the hand in his while watching Mahu closely. "Thank you."

"You're welcome." His head twitched. A look of embarrassment swept over his expression. "If you'll excuse me, I must go."

"Of course. And really, thank you. I'm very glad not to be dead."

Mahu flashed a grin and took his leave.

"Who is that?" asked Remy.

Livia answered, "Mahu is the eldest among vampires. He is well respected, and well liked. Rumor has it, the sickness has begun to take him from us."

"He is the one your rulers want me to help. Valeri's mission —it's to save Mahu." A determined urge swelled in his gut. Remy would help this vampire who'd just given his blood to save him and Laurence. "Of course I'll do it."

Laurence stroked the back of Remy's hand with his thumb, a sad expression on his face. "That was before."

Before what? Oh. His powers. Remy would be useless now. "I didn't think about that."

Evanora straightened. "Help me up, my dear," she asked of Livia. The two women stood. "Come, Remigius. Hold out your hand."

Remy did as he was told, reaching forward with his free hand, still clinging to Laurence with the other.

Evanora backed up a step, putting another arm's length between them. In her palm she held an orange and brown striped stone—tiger's eye. She carried it with her always. As a child, Remy had loved to hold the precious rock.

"Take it," she instructed. A twinkle in her eyes accompanied the gentle smile on her face.

Remy stepped forward to do as she said.

"Ah, ah, not like that. Use your magic."

Remy felt his brow crumple with longing. "But—"

"Try," Evanora insisted.

Everything was different now. The tingling that had always lingered around his hands and fingers to do his bidding had vanished. With nothing to draw from, he didn't know how to do as she asked.

"Laurence," Evanora whispered. "Help him."

Laurence looked as lost and confused as Remy. The vampire shuffled closer, slid his hand under Remy's tunic to the small of his back, skin on skin, just like Remy had asked for their very first night together.

An inkling of the tingling sensation Remy yearned for sprang from the touch. Faint, but definitely present. He drew from the shallow well of power and concentrated on the tiger's eye.

Uncurling his fingers, he willed the stone into his palm.

And it obeyed, jumping from Evanora's hand to his.

Remy gasped in delight. "I did it!"

Evanora smiled. "So you did."

On his back, Laurence's fingers spread and trailed up his spine. Remy sought comfort in his lover's warm expression. "We did it together," he corrected.

"I didn't do anything," said Laurence.

Evanora's tawny eyes sparkled with mischief. "You will."

26

The nights that followed were crammed full of lessons, meetings, and plans for their future mission. Remy had very little time alone with Laurence or to grow accustomed to being a vampire. The gnawing thirst troubled him constantly —a nuisance everyone assured him would pass in time, but presently made it difficult to think. He was stronger than most fledglings as a result of Mahu's participation. Mahu's ancient blood had passed from Laurence's veins to Remy's, causing both to be transformed as a result.

Laurence's gray eyes had taken on a metallic silver ring around the edges, lending him an otherworldly appearance. His muscles were hard as marble beneath Remy's questing fingers. Even his fingernails gained a milky-opal sheen.

Remy had spent some of his time in the company of other young vampires and couldn't help but note the differences between them. He was faster, stronger, and also more independent from Laurence than these fledglings were from their makers. He rose earlier in the evenings and could stay alert later in the mornings, like an elder vampire. The advantages of Mahu's gift would be a boon in this new life.

But perhaps the most shocking discovery thus far had been that despite all odds, Remy retained his powers. Or rather, a version of them. Magic no longer danced at his fingertips waiting to do his bidding, he had to work harder for it. Had to summon the energy, tug the particles from the ether and sweet talk them into bending to his will. Laurence had to be touching him for this to work, but it did work, and they grew stronger with each session.

Evanora, who would be leaving tonight, believed Remy would regain his full strength with practice. Remy wished he had her confidence.

They stood together in the forest outside Bran Vigny's walls, Remy, Laurence, and Evanora, working on improving Remy's stamina one last time before she left.

The red-haired amazon witch watched from a distance, her green eyes sharply intelligent and increasingly disapproving. She'd be taking over their lessons when Evanora left. Her name, Remy had learned, was Aella, and she'd been born at Bran Vigny to a line of witches that had allied with vampires for centuries. Her presence made him uneasy, as if he were being judged and found unworthy.

"That's it," said Evanora. "Steady."

Remy concentrated, using his magic to lift himself and Laurence from the ground, a task that had once been easy but now felt like a battle against the earth's mighty suction. Their feet hovered only inches from the forest floor, when once Remy could have had them soaring in the clouds.

He faltered, and they dropped to the ground. "Ugh. I can't."

"You can," said Evanora, her voice firm. "The power comes from both of you now. You must rely on Laurence. Again."

Squaring his shoulders, Remy shook off the failure. "All right."

Aella crossed her muscled arms over her chest, narrowing her gaze. She looked down her nose at their efforts.

Remy ignored her and focused on the welcome weight of Laurence's hand on his shoulder. Channeling the energy came easier when their skin touched, but since that may not always be convenient or possible, Evanora insisted they learn through a layer of clothing. The barrier between Laurence's palm and Remy's flesh muddled the flow and demanded more of his effort.

Struggling to pull through the muck, Remy tried again. Laurence's solid presence behind him was both a comfort and a source of power. He used the added strength to convince the ether to do his bidding.

They rose from the ground. One foot, two, three…until swooping pine branches got in the way.

From below, Evanora cheered. "Good, that's very good. Now hold."

Laurence gave Remy's shoulder an affectionate squeeze. "Soon the birds will be jealous of us."

Remy grinned and kept them floating until Evanora directed them to come down. He even managed a soft landing. His grandmother appeared thrilled, but Aella remained unimpressed and silent.

Evanora approached, smiling. "The next step must be to accomplish the same feat but without touching at all. Don't be discouraged if it proves difficult, I know you can do it." Her gaze shifted to Laurence. "Now you."

Possibly more surprising than Remy retaining his magic was that Laurence had gained his own version of the power.

They switched roles. Remy laid his hand against Laurence's back, and Laurence drew energy from the ether.

His style differed, and a swoosh of air strong enough to ruffle their clothes blew beneath their feet as they lifted from the ground then dropped back down with a thud. Laurence wasn't yet adept enough to keep them airborne, but that he could lift them at all was unheard of. Who knew what they could accomplish, given time?

And soon they would have that time. Not much, only a few months, but each night would be precious as the weeks ticked away before their inevitable departure overseas.

Remy didn't want to think about that, not when they'd had such success in this session. He grinned at Laurence. "Well done."

"Not as good as you," said Laurence, "but thank you."

Evanora gave a loud sigh. "And now, I must be going. They need me back home, and you have Aella to guide you."

Remy wasn't sure how he felt about Aella as their instructor, but Gran leaving brought tears to his eyes. He didn't want to say goodbye, though he knew Evanora must depart. The elder village needed her, and she'd agreed to govern what was left of their tribe of witches until a new order could be established—one in which everyone had an equal voice. Important work, but the responsibility would take her from Remy. He dug into his pocket for the tiger's eye stone. Its smooth texture and lovely striped pattern were as familiar to him as the back of his own hands.

Remy passed the stone to her. "You should have this back; it's yours."

Evanora reached forward, took his hand in both of hers, and folded it closed over the tiger's eye. "No, doll baby, it's yours now. For good luck."

"Thank you." Remy put the stone back into his pocket. "I have something for you too. Clara helped me pick it out."

Laurence handed over the satchel they'd brought, and Remy pulled out the book and presented it to Evanora. "Poems, in the Latin. I thought you might like it."

She took the gift with great reverence. Her eyes soon grew as watery as Remy's. "I love it. I shall think of you whenever I read it. And please thank Miss Clara for me as well."

"Of course." Remy blinked back tears.

Evanora held the book in one hand and reached to Laurence with the other. "Take good care of him for me." They shared an embrace.

"I will," Laurence promised and dropped a kiss to her cheek.

"I know." Her smile broadened, and her gaze returned to Remy.

They stared at each other through misty eyes, amber gazes mirrored from grandmother to grandson. Remy's heart sank. This would be goodbye. He had no idea when he'd see her again.

Evanora opened her arms, and Remy sank into them with a sigh. "Thanks for everything."

Her voice came gentle, whispered in his ear. "I love you, Remigius."

"I love you too, Gran." Remy sniffled.

She pulled away because Remy could not and turned to Aella. "I'm ready, if you wouldn't mind."

Aella gave a stoic nod and lifted her arm. Magic burst forth from her fingers in a massive wave of orange light, the same shade as her flaming hair. The air crackled and sizzled around them as the wind picked up, and a glimmering portal took shape.

When the glowing rip in space had grown large enough to allow passage, Evanora gave a final charming grin, and without further ado, slipped through the portal to return home.

Laurence's arms came around Remy's shoulders. Leaning his back against his lover's chest, Remy let the tears fall. He wasn't comfortable with Aella seeing him cry, but he couldn't hold back.

"You're lucky to have each other," whispered Laurence.

"I know," said Remy as the portal snapped shut and the three of them were left alone. He wiped his eyes with the back of his hand. "I am also lucky to have you."

Laurence kissed the crown of his head and released him

from the embrace. They had to head back to the castle for yet another round of goodbyes.

"Thank you, Aella," said Laurence. "We're looking forward to learning from you."

The witch tipped her head. "And I you."

Remy suppressed a shiver.

27

Livia and Clara lounged comfortably in Laurence's sitting room. Clara leaned into Livia's space like a long-term lover might. In the span of only a few nights, the two women had become inseparable. Laurence was happy for them. Livia loved companions, the more the merrier, and Clara would be a welcome addition to her cottage nestled in the mountains.

"That's wonderful," said Remy, learning of their plans to head to Livia's home, "but what of your bookshop? What will happen to it?"

Clara's gaze flit from Remy to Livia, and a grin spread across her face. "Livia's taking care of that, too."

Livia twirled a lock of Clara's nut-brown hair between her fingers. "Bran Vigny has plenty of human servants. Two will be dispatched to run the bookshop in Clara's absence. Below the sales floor lies a cellar that will be converted into a safe spot for traveling messengers. The shop will remain Clara's to go back to anytime she wants."

"Isn't that wonderful?" Clara's cheerful tone made Laurence smile.

"Indeed, it's great news," said Remy. "Who knows, perhaps I shall sleep in your cellar someday."

"Yes, well, you and Laurence will always be welcome at my shop, but do come visit at Liv's please."

"You really must," said Livia. "When you've returned from your mission, we'll want to know every detail."

Laurence, though still reluctant to mix with Valeri, had agreed to accompany Remy in his effort to save Mahu. Actually, he'd insisted on it, but he needn't have. Remy wanted him along, and so, to his great annoyance, did Valeri.

Though Remy had sacrificed more to protect The Dozen than they had to protect him, the vampire-witch couldn't be dissuaded from following through on his commitment.

Laurence should have known as much, but he'd still hoped they could slip away and leave all this behind, but Remy wasn't one for quiet exits or shirked duty. He'd told Laurence he felt they owed their lives, in part, to Mahu, and the least he could do in return was help the ancient vampire evade the aging sickness. Laurence wondered if such a thing were possible. Valeri insisted the cure lay hidden overseas in the Northern land of the Lapps. So in five months' time, after the cold season, they would make the dangerous voyage. Until then, they would practice their magic under Aella's guidance in a private house not far from Bran Vigny, and Remy would learn to control the thirst.

"We will look forward to that visit," said Laurence with a glance to his lover. "I'll be glad to see the end of that task."

Remy caught his gaze with amber eyes that sparkled like jewels. They carried a faint glow all the time now and grew brighter when he worked magic. Laurence found it difficult to look away.

"I've spoken with Valeri," said Livia.

Laurence clenched his jaw. "Have you?"

"He's ashamed of how he treated you, or so—"

"Horse shit," interrupted Laurence.

"—he says. You know, of course, that I wouldn't take his word at face value." Livia chided Laurence's outburst with a raised brow. "Rather, I couldn't fail to notice how taken he is with his new fledgling, Elias, who he either truly dotes on, or simply made a show of doting on for my benefit. Either way, Valeri is otherwise occupied, and you're no longer under his thrall."

"Of that, I'm thankful, but let's not discuss the bastard now, not just before we must say our goodbyes."

"Agreed," said Remy, who sat at his side valiantly paying attention to the conversation when he must have been preoccupied with hunger. "Besides, I wanted to thank you for the part you played on my behalf with The Dozen. I owe you a favor; please call on me if ever I can be of service. I won't forget."

"Nonsense," said Livia with a wave of her hand. "I did that for Laurence, and he already owes me. I'll put it on his tab." Her luscious laughter filled the sitting room with its warm rolling tones.

Remy grinned. "Call on Laurence, then. I volunteer his services. I once saw him take out an entire pack of werewolves single-handedly should you ever find yourself at the mercy of an angry horde."

The four friends smiled, and the light atmosphere in the room drifted toward melancholy as a comfortable silence stretched between them. Laurence took in his old friend Liv and her obvious joy at having the delightful young Clara at her side. The pair looked happy together. He wrapped an arm over Remy's slight shoulders and sighed. Remy needed to feed, and the time for them to part ways had arrived; they all sensed it.

Clara was the first to rise, and as if on some silent cue, Remy met her halfway. The two of them fell into each other's arms.

"Oh, Remy! I shall miss you." Her eyes watered over. "Thank you for the kindness you've shown me."

Remy held her tight. "I will miss you too. I'm sorry for disrupting your world so thoroughly."

"Never say that! I was miserable in Wyckshire. The town was never a good fit for me. I won't even look back."

"Of course you won't, brave Lady Clara. Not when there is so much for you to look forward to. You'll have to write me a new story." They pulled apart and both glanced at Livia as she elegantly rose to her feet.

One corner of her lip curled in a mocking half smile. Livia said to Laurence, "Shall we have ourselves a tearful goodbye as well?"

"Let's not," said Laurence as he stepped in to kiss her cheek. "Safe travels."

"Until next time," said Livia, who took Clara under one arm with an expression of pure indulgence.

Laurence opened the door for them, and the two women left. They'd depart Bran Vigny immediately and should arrive at Livia's cottage within a few days. It was a relief to know Clara would be safe and happy. One less thing for his lover to worry about.

Shutting the door, Laurence turned and found Remy watching him with a gleam in his tawny brown eyes.

"You're hungry," said Laurence.

Remy's chin dipped. "Yes."

"Come, feed from me." Laurence offered his neck. Remy had expressed remorse that they could not exclusively feed from each other but was generally happy to accept when Laurence offered.

This time he shook his head. "I'm tired of these castle walls. I miss our nights under the stars. Take me into the forest. Teach me to hunt."

Laurence couldn't think of an idea he liked more. "Lead the way."

———

Remy lay on his back under the moonlight in a lush meadow far enough from Bran Vigny they could not see the castle spires. For this moment, at least, his raging thirst had been quenched. He was near to bursting at the seams with cow's blood and grateful for the respite. Fighting hunger all the time left him exhausted.

"You know," said Remy to Laurence who lay next to him, both of them gazing up at the sky, "when I asked you to teach me to hunt, I'd imagined a more agile target."

Laurence chuckled. "You had not the patience for tracking, I saw it in your eyes."

Remy turned his head to admire his lover's profile. "Why are you right all the time?"

"Rest up," said Laurence, wisely ignoring the question, "and when your body has burned through the cow's blood, I'll teach you to stalk deer."

"Will a deer taste any better?"

"No. Animal blood will always be inferior, but it's useful in a pinch. I'm surprised you asked for it when you could take your pick from the donor pool."

Remy had been rather surprised to learn there were plenty of humans perfectly eager to offer their blood to a vampire. Still not over the disappointment that he and Laurence could not simply sustain each other, he tired of the willing donors.

"I think I'd prefer to live independent of such relationships. Growing accustomed to animal blood seems wise under the circumstances."

"I've grown accustomed to it," said Laurence.

"Then I'm sure I shall too."

Coming to terms with being a vampire presented constant challenges. Already, Remy mourned daylight, and he feared his intense longing for the sun's warm rays on his shoulders would only grow stronger. But this new life was infinitely better than being dead, which would have been the alternative had Laurence and Mahu not come to his rescue, so he would not complain.

Remy sighed as he listened to the rise and fall of cicada calls accompanied by the sound of a swiftly flowing creek nearby. If he couldn't have sunlight, at least the majesty of night would always be beautiful. And there was so much to admire with his new senses. Everything heightened to a level of near overload: colors brighter and more crisp, sounds clear and easily heard from a vast distance, and taste… Taste was a whole new world entirely. He'd never known blood came in such a variety of flavors—sweet, tangy, bitter, spicy—no two sources alike.

Laurence tasted best of all, like an aged wine, savory and smooth, and Remy could never get enough. He'd drain the vampire dry if he didn't know better.

Aside from his magic, everything he'd experienced before his transition, he experienced tenfold afterward. The intense sensations, though welcome, were exhausting. One particularly enjoyable experience remained untested, and he planned to remedy that immediately.

Remy stretched, sat up, and got to his knees. He climbed

over Laurence, who watched with a sly grin, and sat astride his hips. Without a word, he began to undo the fastenings of his own tunic, parting the fabric down his chest.

Laurence shifted beneath him and cupped his ass in both hands. "Stop."

Remy's eyes widened. He paused. "Why? Is something wrong?"

"Everything's perfect." Laurence's answering smile revealed a row of white teeth, two of them razor sharp. "You're gorgeous, and I want you naked. But don't use your hands, use your magic."

Anything could become a test lately. At least this one would be fun.

"Challenge accepted," said Remy.

He dropped his hands to his sides, set his weight back against Laurence's groin, and opened his shirt with his mind. The disrobing was slow going this way, but the worshipful expression on Laurence's face made up for the delay.

As he worked, Remy rocked slowly until Laurence's shaft hardened beneath his bottom. Energy tingled between them. The magic came with an ease he hadn't felt since before the change.

Remy pushed the tunic off his shoulders with nothing but the ether, then set to work on undressing Laurence. First the belt. Heavy black leather, worn by time and use, obeyed Remy's command. The latch popped, and the tail came through the buckle and flopped to the side.

"Well done," Laurence murmured, his hips thrusting enough to jostle Remy and break his concentration.

"Settle down," he ordered. "I'm not finished."

"Beg your pardon." Laurence's hips didn't quite still beneath him, but their motion no longer threatened to topple Remy as he focused.

Grinning, Remy rucked up Laurence's shirt with invisible

hands so he could feast his eyes on the hairy chest beneath the fabric. He loved those soft curls.

Reaching down, he ran his fingers over Laurence's abdomen. The muscles were hard as stone after drinking so much of Mahu's blood. That change in Laurence would take some getting used to, but with his own body now similarly statuesque, they made a matching set. He wished to discover all the things these bodies could do for each other.

Fingering both nipples until Laurence arched into his touch, Remy sent the magic beneath Laurence's pants to swirl around his swollen cock. The trick pulled a shocked gasp from Laurence that Remy would never forget.

"You like that?" he asked with a smirk.

"Oh my god. Yes." Laurence's hands clenched Remy's hips, holding him in place to rock against. "I didn't know you could do that."

"Neither did I. Let's see what else I can do, shall we?"

"I'm yours to play with as you please."

Remy leaned in for a kiss. "Careful. I could get used to that." He stretched his legs next to Laurence's and lay on his chest. "Let's see about getting the rest of our clothes off."

"Yes." Laurence pulled Remy in for more kisses.

It wasn't easy with the two of them squirming on the ground, but Remy used his powers to rid them of boots, pants, socks, until there was only the delicious feel of skin on skin. Then he sent magic everywhere, enveloping Laurence in a bubble of sensation from head to toe. Remy massaged his shoulders and down the long curve of his spine. He paid special attention to the round globes of Laurence's ass, gently kneaded hamstrings and calves, and kept a warm swirling vortex focused on his twitching, hard length.

"Remy," Laurence huffed, breaking their kiss. "Can you do this, what you're doing to me, to yourself as well?"

Until that moment, Remy had been delightfully pleased to be

pleasuring Laurence. Now he paused to consider this new temptation. "I don't know. Let's find out."

He used the energy that had been building between them to enhance the spell, surprised to find there was nothing to it. The strength of the current they shared rivaled the power he'd wielded before his transformation. Making the ether do his bidding came with ease.

Remy moaned against Laurence's throat. "Yes. Yes, I can. In fact, it would be reasonable to assume I could single-handedly conduct an orgy for dozens with this kind of power."

Heat rose in every place they touched, intensifying between their rutting shafts as they writhed together. Laurence's hands gripped Remy's back, the sensation of his fingernails along Remy's flesh standing out in sharp contrast from the rolling caresses of magic.

"You try," said Remy, releasing control.

Laurence took over with shocking force. Their combined power coiled over them with shuddering strokes, filling Remy with a maddening urge for release.

"I'm close," he sighed out, quaking in Laurence's arms and under his power.

"Not yet," ordered Laurence, and in a show of strength and speed, he swept Remy up and laid him on his back, reversing their positions. His weight settled against Remy's chest, between his spread legs. The energy returned to work magic on their cocks trapped together between them.

Laurence kissed him, and Remy parted his lips to welcome him in. He sucked Laurence's tongue into his mouth, tasting the lingering coppery tang of blood. Wrapping his arms around Laurence's shoulders, his whole body on fire, Remy held off his own climax with the sheer force of his will.

Pressure at his entrance drew a gasp from Remy's throat.

Oh!

He hadn't thought to try that; Laurence was a genius. Energy swirled between his cheeks, warm and insistent.

His legs opened wider for the magical caress, welcoming whatever Laurence wished to give him. A tugging sensation teased his rim, pulling another long moan from Remy as he submitted to the tantalizing touch.

Above him, Laurence's hips rocked in rhythm with the magic working their cocks. Remy did his best to match the motion, so overcome with pleasure he bit his cheek to prolong the thrill.

"Laurence," he whined. "I can't hold back any longer. Please."

Laurence's arms around him tightened. "Yes, now. Come with me."

The pressure intensified until they shook with release, climaxing together in a frenzy of escalating spasms. Their seed mixed between them, slicking the way for slower, sensual strokes as neither could stop their rhythm yet, both basking in every tingling aftershock.

Laurence's lips pressed against the delicate skin of Remy's ear, his breath humid as he whispered, "I love you, my feisty witch."

Beneath him, Remy melted, his heart warm, spirit light. "I love you too."

They settled on their sides, facing one another, their legs tangled. Remy ran fingertips over Laurence's fine cheekbones, down the bridge of his crooked nose.

"This is going to work, isn't it? Us?" asked Remy.

Laurence gave a slow nod and pressed a kiss to his lips. "Yes. We'll get through the mission, and then we'll have our forever."

Remy grinned. "Forever." He savored the sound of the word. "I'll take that."

Available now! Join Remy and Laurence as they cultivate their new powers with the dubious instruction of The Dozen's head witch, Aella. Get a glimpse of Remy as he gets used to being a vampire. This steamy bonus content is free with a newsletter sign up https://mailchi.mp/d04e03b10ccf/leecolgin . The journey will continue in book two as our heroes struggle to save Mahu, and Valeri struggles to deserve Elias! Thank you for reading.

~A jaded vampire too damaged for love

~A lovesick shifter who refuses to give up

Will destiny unite them—or will old enemies reign?

<u>A Bridge to Love</u> (coming Dec. 2020)

~A sweet messenger werewolf

~A lonely troll stuck guarding his bridge

Can love blossom across a massive cultural divide,

or will Arlo and Toby always be alone for the holidays?

Visit Lee at <u>www.LeeColgin.com</u> for more!

ABOUT THE AUTHOR

Lee Colgin has loved vampires since she read *Dracula* on a hot sunny beach at 13 years old. She lives in North Carolina with lots of dogs and her husband. No, he's not a vampire, but she loves him anyway. Lee likes to work out so she can eat the maximum amount of cookies with her pizza. Ask her how much she can bench press.

Connect with Lee
Email: LeeColgin@gmail.com
Facebook: www.facebook.com/groups/leecolgin
Twitter: www.twitter.com/leecolgin
Website: www.leecolgin.com
Newsletter: http://eepurl.com/gJEu35

BENEATH THE OPAL ARC
(BOOK TWO)
SYNOPSIS

Valeri Kostin has secrets. He holds information promising a lost cure for the aging sickness that brings down elder vampires without mercy. The Dozen would pay dearly to have the cure for themselves. Enough that they'll risk the most powerful witch ever known and their own messenger to track it down.

Laurence must tolerate the grating presence of his petty sire while keeping Remy out of his clutches. Meanwhile, Valeri's new fledgling, Elias, is up to something and Remy plans to find out what.

Join our four adventurers on their dangerous quest for hidden treasure where the line between enemies and lovers may as well be drawn in sand. Can they find the cure in time to save the ancient vampire Mahu, or will they die trying?

www.ingramcontent.com/pod-product-compliance
Lightning Source LLC
Chambersburg PA
CBHW060542190726
48283CB00003B/833